Chris would be picking her up in ten minutes

Anna would never be ready on time. Trying to wipe the steam off the mirror with one hand, she tried to continue applying her eyeliner with the other—and then froze.

Jim's face was staring out at her from the mirror, his eyes boring into hers. Her mouth formed his name but no sound emerged. "Why?" she breathed at last. "Why are you here, Jim?"

But he remained silent, and the mirror began to steam up again, shrouding his features. Anna could still make out his mouth, but just barely. His lips were pale, bloodless and twisted in a sardonic smile he'd never worn in life. Then he was gone.

Anna gasped and sagged against the sink, her knees trembling in terror. "Why can't you leave me in peace?" she muttered. "What do you want?"

Suddenly Anna knew the answer. This time Jim had come because he knew what had happened that afternoon. He'd seen how she'd fallen into another man's arms...on the very hillside where he'd crashed his plane and lost his life.

ABOUT THE AUTHOR

"Neither of us knows if we believe in ghosts," says Carla Peltonen, who writes as Lynn Erickson with longtime friend Molly Swanton. "But there have been well-documented cases where survivors of airplane crashes have been visited by the dead pilot, which is what happens to our heroine in *A Wing and a Prayer*. Maybe all those people just imagined seeing the pilot's ghost...but I wouldn't bet on it."

Carla and Molly make their homes in Aspen, Colorado, and have been writing as a team for over fourteen years.

Books by Lynn Erickson

HARLEQUIN SUPERROMANCE

Lynn
Erickson

A WING
AND A
PRAYER

Harlequin Books

TORONTO • NEW YORK • LONDON
AMSTERDAM • PARIS • SYDNEY • HAMBURG
STOCKHOLM • ATHENS • TOKYO • MILAN
MADRID • WARSAW • BUDAPEST • AUCKLAND

Published October 1992

ISBN 0-373-70520-4

A WING AND A PRAYER

Rest, rest, perturbed spirit! . . .
The time is out of joint. O cursed spite
That ever I was born to set it right!

Hamlet, William Shakespeare
Act I, scene V

This book is dedicated to Ed Sypniewski,
a pilot for one of the "big guys," who answered a
thousand questions, even though he doesn't
believe in ghosts.

PROLOGUE

THE SPRING SNOWSTORM swooped down out of the Cascade Mountains suddenly, blotting out the sun and swirling snow around the fat black tires of the Convair 580 that sat on the runway. But in the cockpit it was warm. The pilot, Jim Fleisher, was switching off contact with the tower, where he'd been checking on the weather. The sound of the turbine engines roared throatily, and the aircraft rocked back and forth a bit, warming up.

"I don't know, Jim," his copilot said. "Maybe we should wait on this one. It's getting bad out."

"I've seen worse," the pilot said, eyes on his dials and gauges.

"Think, uh, think we need to get deiced again?" his copilot ventured.

Fleisher keyed the mike. "WestAir 629," the tower said into his earphones, "taxi into position and hold. Be ready for immediate."

"WestAir 629, position and hold," Jim said. Then he turned to his copilot. "Relax, Len, we'll be above this mess in a few minutes. Tower says it's fine in Seattle."

"Yeah, sure. I'm always amazed at how that runway appears there right where it's supposed to be." The copilot gave a short laugh. "Uh, Jim, how long's it been since they deiced us?"

"Quarter hour or so."

"Hmm, I thought it was longer. Think we should ask—"

But Jim was revving the engines. "Hell, Len, we're on immediate. You know what kind of paperwork we'd have to fill out if we pull out now, especially after that delay with the luggage. Miller would cancel my vacation time. Relax."

Cabin attendant Anna Parish stuck her head into the cockpit doorway. "We're on our way, guys?" she asked cheerily.

"Yeah, better go sit down, Anna," Jim said.

She bent over and peered out the cockpit window. "Lousy weather."

"Sure is. But it's fine in Seattle."

"Want some coffee?" she asked.

"A little later, okay?" Jim was busy with the rudders; the plane was rolling forward into the snow, its two turboprop engines vibrating, the deicing fluid blowing off the left wing in a pink spray as Anna looked out. Around the Winthrop, Washington, airport the Cascade Mountains were rapidly being obscured by veils of snow.

"Springtime in the mountains," she said lightly.

"March isn't spring around here," Jim replied.

"Not today, anyway," the copilot concurred.

"All right, you two, I'll go buckle up now. Coffee later."

"Thanks, Anna."

The stewardess turned and walked back into the main cabin, trim in her maroon suit and white blouse. Her smile was genuine as she nodded at the passengers in the nearly filled aircraft. Madeline, the other stewardess, was already buckled into one of the jump seats as Anna pulled the other down and fastened her own seat belt.

"Nasty out," Madeline remarked.

"Tower says it's clear in Seattle."

"It makes me nervous, though."

"Jim's careful. Don't you worry now. He's flown out of here a thousand times. If it wasn't safe, he wouldn't go," Anna said firmly.

"I know," Madeline sighed. "I get nervous, that's all. I'm getting too old for this."

"Come on! You love flying."

Madeline smiled wryly. "That's right. I forgot."

The plane was rolling forward faster now, the engines whining, sucking at the cold air. The wing flaps were set in takeoff position. Anna sat in her jump seat, securely buckled in, relaxed, feeling the bump of the tires as they raced faster and faster down the wet runway. She leaned her head back, closed her eyes and waited for the familiar lift as the plane became airborne. Yes, there it was, a little late, but that was because of the slush. She pictured Jim in the cockpit, pushing on the throttles, hands on the control wheel, pitching the nose up for takeoff. She trusted Jim Fleisher implicitly, having flown with him dozens of times. Jim was chief pilot of WestAir, one of the best, most experienced men around. He was also her best friend, her lover, her fiancé.

They kept their relationship absolutely professional at work. Jim had insisted on it. But they planned to get married in the fall, and Anna was just about as happy as a woman could be. She'd waited a long time for a man like Jim Fleisher to come along—a strong man, self-confident, really sure of himself. Jim had charisma. Everyone said so, and Anna had noticed it right off, the minute she'd started working at WestAir three years ago.

She relaxed, closed her eyes and thought back to when she first met Jim. A smile played around her mouth. Outside, the storm raged and battered the metal body of the plane. Passengers idly turned magazine pages or talked or tried to doze.

Later, much later, Anna would recall that no more than thirty seconds had lapsed after the last thump of the tires on the runway when she noticed the plane beginning to quiver. Her whole body tensed even as her mind recoiled from the notion that all was not right.

"Anna?" Madeline sat bolt upright. "What—?"

Then the shaking. A rapid, shuddering, terrifying rhythm: whomp, whomp, whomp. Everything lurched and bounced. The dishes in the galley rattled wildly.

"My God," Madeline whispered harshly.

The seconds slowed to a crawl, yet Anna had no time to do anything. *The passengers . . .* "Brace position!" she cried loudly, hoping, praying they'd hear and understand. "Everyone forward into brace position!"

Outside the window the mountains tilted as the plane banked crookedly, yanked by unseen forces. Anna could see the ground, hundreds of feet below, race by sickeningly, and still the awful banging and shuddering shook her down to her bones.

"Fly! Get this thing up! Fly, damn you," Anna said to herself. She dragged Madeline's head down and bent over, hugging her knees, her heart bursting with terror and adrenaline, beating in time to the wham-wham-wham of the plane as it struggled to pull itself through the air, to rise, to fly, to be free.

Abruptly there were trees outside the small window, tall, black, snow-covered firs, spiraling dizzily at Anna as she twisted her head sideways to see. Then a terrible, grinding noise. Screams beat at her ears and a horrible spinning took hold of her, as if she were on a roller coaster.

Then the impact. Horrendous, bone-cracking, unbearable. Her body stopped with immeasurable G forces, a shock beyond the capacity of the brain to comprehend. She felt herself unable to breathe, slipping toward unconsciousness. In that last split second she thought with pain and regret and love of Jim. *Jim. Oh, my God, I can't breathe. Jim ... Jim ...*

ANNA KNEW SOMEWHERE in her consciousness that she'd been fighting for a long time to open her eyes. It was so hard, so very hard, but she had to; she knew that, too. She concentrated, willed it to happen. Glaring, dazzling white made her blink. It was white all around her. White walls, white cabinets, white sink, white sheets covering her. A hospital.

It all came rushing back in horrible clarity. The crash! Her body jerked uncontrollably, and then she felt the pain. She hurt everywhere, her entire being a pool of soreness with spots of real agony here and there—her ribs, her wrist, her head. The crash ... Madeline ... the passengers ... Jim.

She shut her eyes, filled with a terrible feeling of powerlessness and plagued by questions—awful, tearing questions, a bottomless morass of questions. Every breath hurt, and she was so frightened, but so tired at the same time, so filled with pain and fear. Was she drugged? Was she going to die? She shut her eyes and tried to think. Why wasn't a nurse there to answer her questions?

But when she opened her eyes again Jim was there, his maroon uniform a stark contrast to all the white. He stood over her, a serious expression on his face, his hand reaching out to touch her.

"Oh, God, Jim," she whispered, filled with the most exquisite torrent of relief.

He said nothing, just stood there, looking at her, his eyebrows drawn together, his mouth severe. He was worried about her, but she'd be all right. Now that she knew he was all right. She tried to tell him that, tried so hard, but she was dreadfully tired—drugs, proba- bly—and she just couldn't. She tried to smile at him, thought she succeeded, then she was slipping away down a smooth, dark corridor. But it was okay now, and she let herself slide down into the warm, welcome darkness.

SHE WOKE UP LATER—much later she thought, but she couldn't tell. Her head was clear now. It still hurt, but she was lucid. The hospital room was dark except for a dim light over her bed. It was night then, or maybe early morning. The crash had occurred the morning before. She must be in Seattle, because Winthrop had no hospital like this one. How many had been hurt or killed in the crash? Maybe no one had died. Maybe Jim had steered them in and saved everyone.

Madeline? Anna twisted her neck to see the other bed in the room. It was empty.

Oh, God, she hurt all over. Slowly, carefully, Anna wiggled her toes, bent her knees, flexed her fingers. They all worked. They hurt, but they worked. She tried to lift her left arm, but there was something heavy on it. A cast. Oh, no, she'd broken her arm. She could feel the pain there, a sharp, nagging ache. But it would heal. Sure, it would be as good as new.

She lay there, coming back into her body as if after a long absence, tensing muscles, testing her limbs. Then she relaxed and lay still, thinking that she'd better ring for a nurse to find out exactly what was wrong with her and how many others had been hurt and if Jim had left word when he'd be back to visit. She hoped he'd been checked out by a doctor, because he was so darn macho that he'd probably walk around even if he was hurt and never say a word about it. She'd make sure he was checked out if he hadn't been.

She felt around for the buzzer clipped to her sheet and pressed it. Even that hurt. Maybe she'd ask for a pain pill, just one, just to get through the night. She hated pills, but maybe this once . . .

A nurse bustled in, a quick, professional smile on her face. Anna recognized it and tried to smile back.

"Well, Miss Parish, you're awake, I see. How are you feeling?"

"Okay. Sore all over. Can you tell me—?"

The nurse cut her off. "You have a broken wrist, cracked ribs, a cut on your forehead. Nothing serious. I'll bet that's what you wanted to know."

Anna felt with her right hand. Yes, there was a bandage on her forehead. She winced as her fingers touched it.

"Yes, it'll be sore for a while." The nurse picked up Anna's wrist and kept her eyes on her watch, checking Anna's pulse. "Nice and strong. Good."

"Will I have to stay here long?" Anna asked.

"Dr. Masters will talk to you in the morning. But probably not. Nothing too serious wrong with you."

"Uh," Anna began, "the others . . . were there—?"

The nurse's expression remained carefully bland. "Perhaps you better ask Dr. Masters in the morning."

Anna's heart seized with fear. "No, tell me. I have to know. It was my job, my flight. Please." She started struggling to sit up.

The nurse pressed her back. "All right. I'll tell you. I'm not supposed to, though."

"God, tell me. Madeline? The passengers? How many?"

"There were some fatalities."

Anna closed her eyes. "My roommate...the other stewardess, Madeline Vernon?"

"I believe she's being kept overnight for observation."

"Oh, thank heavens." That sweet flood of relief again.

"You two were very lucky. The rear of the plane where you were was in pretty good shape. Eight passengers were saved."

"Oh, no." Then so many had died, so many.

"As I said, there were fatalities. Now, Miss Parish, you'd better get some rest. Would you like a sedative? Something for pain?"

"Wait, no, wait." Eight passengers alive. That meant more than forty dead. The rear of the plane, but that meant... Oh, God, Jim was lucky. But the copilot. What about Len? "Wait. Do you know if the copilot made it, Nurse?"

"No, I'm sorry. He was killed on impact."

She lay there, hurting for Jim. He must be suffering such an agony of guilt. Poor Jim. She'd have to be so careful with him. He'd need her desperately now, need her love and support. Poor Jim...

"Now, Miss Parish, I've told you more than I should have. You need rest. You need to forget."

"Is Jim Fleisher still in the hospital?" Anna asked.

"Jim Fleisher?"

"The pilot. He came to see me when I woke up earlier. He didn't seem to be hurt, but I wondered if he was still here. I'd like to—"

"The pilot came to see you earlier?" the nurse asked in a curiously flat tone.

"Well, yes, we're . . . actually we're engaged, and I guess he was worried about me. He just stopped in, but I was still pretty fuzzy. Anyway, I wondered if he were still here in the hospital or if he left."

"Miss Parish, Jim Fleisher was killed instantly upon impact. I'm so terribly sorry to have to tell you this, but—"

Anna shook her head. "No, you're mistaken. I woke up and he was here, standing right where you are. I . . . I spoke to him."

"I am sorry, but you must have been dreaming, Miss Parish. No one in the front of the plane survived."

"You're confused. It was the *copilot* who was killed. Jim is fine. I *saw* him. He was right here." A swelling dread lodged in Anna's breast. The nurse was confused, that was all. Jim was alive. He was fine. He wasn't killed. She knew that, she knew . . .

"Miss Parish, I'm sorry. I didn't realize you were engaged to the pilot. You have my greatest sympathy but, really, you're going to have to calm down now. I'll get you a shot in just a moment," the nurse said.

"No, Jim was here. I saw him. No."

"I'm sorry," the nurse said, pressing the buzzer, one hand on Anna's arm, holding her still, "but the pilot of the aircraft was definitely one of the fatalities."

Something inside of Anna swelled and shifted and burst.

CHAPTER ONE

GETTING RIGHT BACK UP on the horse again, Anna thought as she pulled into WestAir's parking lot at the Winthrop airport. She'd been getting back on that proverbial horse for weeks now, but each time still felt like the first. She wouldn't give in to the occasional urge to quit her job and quit flying, though; she needed to work it out in her head, and she sure as heck needed the job.

The morning was warm, springtime warm, and the fragile green of May touched the trees that gathered along the banks of the Methow River. Anna climbed the metal steps to the waiting plane and drew the soft air into her lungs. Maybe this would be the flight that signaled the turning point, the point where she'd begin to smile again, to feel alive.

"Morning, Larry," she said to the pilot, who was already pouring himself a cup of coffee.

"Well, hello, Anna." He turned and eyed her. "Beautiful day, huh?"

"Perfect." Anna hung up her jacket and straightened her skirt. "Who's working this run with me, do you know?"

"Madeline, isn't it?"

Anna shook her head. "She's home sleeping like a baby at our house."

"Then it's Norma, I guess." He kept staring at her, then cleared his throat finally. "Ah, Anna," he began, leaning a shoulder casually against the door to the lavatory, "how are things?"

"Things are fine," she replied, going about her business of setting up the galley for juice and coffee and sweet rolls. "How many passengers this morning?" she asked, ignoring his perusal.

"Fourteen."

"Um. Off-season in tourist land."

"It'll pick up in June. Always does." He cleared his throat a second time. "So you're comfortable back in the saddle?"

Oh, God, Anna thought, every employee she ran into at WestAir phrased it the same way. Couldn't they come up with a new way of asking her if she was okay? "Sure, I'm easy in the ol' saddle again, Larry," she replied matter-of-factly.

"Um. Good, good. That was a rough time. Well," he said, straightening, "guess I'll step on out and check this bird's big belly."

Anna gave him a smile.

Maybe she *should* quit, at least quit flying. She could work the counter in the airport, anything, really, except climb aboard three times a week and make the Winthrop-Seattle run. She could. But Anna knew she had to overcome the obstacles keeping her prisoner.

She'd worked with WestAir's psychologist in Seattle. Eight sessions, in fact. And she'd come to understand the guilt commonly experienced by survivors of disasters, learned to cope with the question, "Why did *I* survive when so many others died?" Yes, she understood that life often dealt out random winners and losers. On that March day she'd been dealt a winner.

So had her co-worker and roommate, Madeline, and some others. Still, forty-two had lost their lives....

Anna honestly believed she'd overcome her initial fear of flying when, in mid-April, she returned to work. It had been hell. To make matters worse a sudden spring storm had massed over the Cascade Mountains, and the plane had climbed, descended and climbed again until they'd reached Seattle safely. She'd deplaned with her white blouse clinging wetly to her back.

Okay, Anna thought as she brewed another pot of coffee, she'd glued herself together and overcome a load of troubles. All but one, that is.

"Hi, Anna, sorry I'm a few minutes late." It was Norma, one of the alternate stews on the Winthrop-Seattle route. "My son called from Seattle this morning. He couldn't find his history book or his baseball jacket. God, you'd think his father could lift a finger."

Oh, you bet, Anna was still thinking as Norma rattled on, she'd gotten through the terrible ordeal of the crash better than she'd have dreamed. Except for Jim.

The fourteen passengers boarded on schedule, and the Convair 580 taxied out to the single runway. Larry and Ed, his copilot, asked for coffee and rolls for later, after they reached altitude and the passengers were made comfortable. On takeoff Anna closed her eyes as she always did and let the throaty roar of the jet engines settle around her.

Norma talked. "God, you'd think they'd let it alone."

"What?" Anna shifted, eyes still closed as the plane lifted above the narrow mountain valley.

"Let that crash alone. The National Transportation Safety Board is sending some big hotshot investigator in to question everyone all over again. The Human Factors Group Chairman, he's called."

"I know."

"I think it's disgusting. It's like raising the dead or something. God, things just happen sometimes. You might think—"

"Norma," Anna said, "there *are* reasons why planes go down."

"Well, sure there are. And they say more often than not it's pilot error—"

Norma had clammed up even before Anna said, "*Human factors.* That's what it's called now. Modern terminology."

"I'm sorry, Anna. I forgot about you and Jim Fleisher. Besides," she added hastily, "they'll probably call it icing on the wings, anyway."

Anna undid the safety strap that crossed her breasts. "I don't know what this investigator hopes to learn, because the NTSB has already gotten depositions from all of us. I guess it's routine."

"Sure it is."

What Anna didn't tell her fellow stewardess was that she herself was scheduled for an interview with the so-called hotshot from the NTSB that very morning in Seattle.

She served coffee and rolls and a few beers to the passengers. She got down pillows and blankets from the overhead compartments and chatted for a while with a neighbor of hers in Winthrop who was headed to Seattle for a conference.

The flight was routine, the passengers a relaxed group now that the long ski season was over and summer just around the corner. There were times when the flights were overbooked—for President's Weekend or some such winter holiday—and nerves were ragged among the passengers. Inevitably there would be a storm, delaying everything further. Lost luggage, missing skis, babies wailing—the pressure on the airline crews was terrible. But spring was coming, beckoning. The warm May sunshine was turning the mountainsides green, muddying the rivers with melting snow cascading into the deep valleys.

Anna got the pilot and copilot more coffee, checked on the lavatory and collected the passengers' empty cups.

Summer, she thought, a mellower time of year. Surely by the end of summer her life would be back in order. This crazy business with Jim would end.

Together and down-to-earth. That was what she'd always been called—easygoing. Anna had never let the ups and downs in life get to her. She was like her dad in that respect—on an even keel. Nowadays he and her mom played golf in their retirement community in Palm Springs, California. He'd retired from his job in the aerospace industry in Seattle two years ago, and they'd taken off for sunny California. Simple folks, like Anna. Or as Anna had been, that is. And it wasn't the crash that had changed her, either. She was dealing with that the best way she could. No, it was this baffling business with Jim.

Damn, Anna thought while she cleaned up the galley for landing. This interview with the NTSB was the last thing on earth she needed. She'd talked and talked about the crash. She'd given her deposition to an NTSB investigator once already and talked to the psychologist the airline had provided for the survivors. She'd talked to him, all right, probably too much.

"Oh, my Lord," Anna whispered. Could that shrink, Morty Heller, have spoken to someone from the NTSB about her? Would he have said anything about Jim? That was all supposed to be confidential. Oh, no, what if this...this...what was his name? Galloway, that was it, from Washington, D.C., the special investigator who was flying in to conduct the final inquiries into this airline disaster—what if he knew about Jim from the doctor? Was *that* why he'd asked for this interview?

What had Anna told that doctor? Yes, too much, but exactly what?

Pieces came back to her. "Okay, Anna," he'd said, "I know you saw Jim in the room with you at the hospital, but hasn't it occurred to you that he'll always be with you in some way? You loved him."

Anna had shifted uncomfortably in the soft chair. "I know you're going to tell me I'm projecting my guilt. That it's all a part of mourning."

"Those are *your* words, Anna. What I did say earlier is that you have every right to keep Jim alive in your memories."

"It's a lot more than that," she'd whispered, her hands folded in her lap.

"He seems real to you."

"Oh, yes. You could say that."

"Anna," Morty Heller had said, "is there something you're not telling me?"

Anna had avoided his question that session. Instead, they'd shifted the conversation to her sudden lack of companionship after the crash. Namely her single and very much available status. At thirty-four

years old Anna had been more than willing and ready
to settle down with Jim. She'd played the singles routine, although not very well, and found it to be shal-
low and unfulfilling. She was still a very lovely woman,
Morty Heller had pointed out. And Anna guessed if
you called kind of old-fashioned and homey-looking
"lovely," that was okay. She did have good skin, a
pale, sort of translucent complexion that suited her
hazel eyes and small-boned features. Her hair was thick
and naturally curly, and she kept it medium length,
blunt-cut, and it stood out from her head like a
springing dark halo.

But being known as lovely wasn't what she wanted.
Jim was what Anna craved. A good, strong man, children someday, a home together.

Morty Heller had gotten it out of her the next week.
"So Jim is still very real to you," he'd said.

"It's not just in my head." Then she'd fallen silent.

"Anna, do you see Jim? I don't mean in your mind's
eye. Do you think you *see* Jim Fleisher?"

She'd swallowed hard. "Yes."

"How often?"

"Once, twice a week."

"Where?"

"Usually at night. After a dream. I wake up
and...and he's...he's..."

"Okay," Morty had steepled his fingers under his
clean-shaven chin. "Anna, is it possible you're referring to particularly vivid dreams?"

"No."

"I see. Okay. So you said *usually* you see him at
night. Where else, then?"

"Once in the galley of the plane."

"In the galley."

"Yes."

"Just standing there."

"Sort of."

"Did he speak to you?"

"No. Never." Then she'd added, "But he does communicate."

"I see. His love?"

"No, not really. Well, I suppose. But it's more like he wants something."

"What?"

"It feels like, well, vindication."

"Vindication? You mean...?"

"I don't know what I mean, Doctor. I'm sorry I started this. I—"

"You're sorry you told me?"

"Yes. You think I'm suffering from guilt."

After a very long moment, Morty Heller had said, "Anna, I want you to answer this very carefully. Anna," he'd repeated, holding her attention, "do you believe in ghosts?"

She had told him no. Firmly. But then, of course, he'd asked her how Jim could possibly appear to her, and she'd had no answer. All Anna knew was that too often, in the dark and cold shadows of her room, Jim had come to her in a strange sort of intangible light, his figure solidifying, collecting in that eerie half glow until he stood there in the surrounding blackness clad in his uniform, his eyes sunken, pleading, tormented...

"Anna?"

She spun around in the galley, dropping a tray. Tears sprang into her eyes abruptly.

"It's all right," Norma said, bending to retrieve the tray. "Go and buckle up. We'll be landing in a few minutes."

ANNA TOOK a taxi to downtown Seattle and her interview at the NTSB office. Where was that "together" person she'd always been, whose goals and needs were clear-cut? She was beginning to wonder. As the cab sped along the freeway past the immense Boeing Industry complex, Anna was besieged by doubts.

She didn't believe in otherworldly spirits. Someone whose feet were firmly planted on the ground couldn't possibly believe in such nonsense. Often over the past weeks Anna had told herself it was the deep loss she'd suffered that was playing havoc with her psyche. The awful cold misery crouched and hunted her like a predator, waiting to take her in its sharp teeth anytime she was alone. It was just wishful thinking that conjured Jim up, the inability to accept his loss. Sure, Morty had explained it all to her. And yet...

"National Transportation Safety Board," the cabby said, glancing at her in the mirror. "You work for that outfit?"

"No, I'm just going to their office."

"That was something, that crash a couple of months ago. Lotta folks killed, huh?"

"Yes, there were."

"Wouldn't catch *me* on no WestAir plane. No way."

Anna looked out the window. The sky was gray and grainy—dreary. Fog lay in patches on the distant hillsides across the wide sound. Boats, heading in and out of the city's long harbor, were partially obscured by the mist. On the eastern slopes of the Cascade Mountains where Winthrop lay the sun would still be out, shining brightly. But not here where water dominated the landscape.

She sighed. What if this Mr. Galloway really did know about her sessions with Heller? About Jim? Oh, he couldn't really *do* anything to her—that wasn't the function of the NTSB. But this morning's question-and-answer session might be the beginning of yet another long line of interviews—to see if Anna Parish, as one of the only two surviving crew members, could give credible testimony about the crash.

"Probably clear up this afternoon," the driver said, switching on his wipers. "Usually does."

"Yes, it does."

Of course, the worst part of this interview would be having to relive the accident all over again. The federal agencies just wouldn't leave it alone. Whereas the NTSB was responsible for passenger safety on all modes of transportation, the FAA was charged with overseeing the airline industry alone. When an accident occurred, it was the NTSB that instantly sent in a Go Team to begin the long and tedious investigation. But there was always someone from the FAA questioning crew members, air traffic controllers, passengers, looking for possible violations of the federal air regulations, the FARs.

Oh, you bet. Anna had first been interviewed by the NTSB and then, only a few days later, the FAA representative. Both parties had asked dozens of questions about Jim. Had Anna flown with him before? Was he prone to take risks? Did he intimidate his copilot or the flight crew?

Norma, of course, was dead wrong about the future outcome of this investigation. The disaster wasn't going to be blamed on ice on the wings, although that was a contributing cause of the crash. No. Anna was certain the fault was going to be laid squarely on Jim Fleisher. Human factors. They'd say Jim should never have taken off that morning, that the weather had been too bad, the wind too strong, the deicing not current enough, or that he'd made a mistake with the controls. They'd say his judgment was at fault. But the truth wasn't so tangible. The truth was that Lee Miller, the owner of WestAir Express, was truly to blame.

Over the eight months Anna had been dating Jim she'd gotten a real earful about good old Lee Miller and his less-than-perfect procedures.

"Cutting corners" was what Jim used to call it. And evidently cutting corners was a common ailment among the owners of small commuter airlines, a result of the small outfits having to compete with the big boys. The bottom line, according to Jim, was that Miller pressured his employees, trying to squeeze out more profit from his airline, pressured them in many subtle and unsubtle ways.

"Hell, Anna," Jim had once said, "the mechanics even complain that he falsifies their maintenance records when they turn them in."

And Anna knew that pilots were pressured to run their flights on time despite touch-and-go weather. Planes were overloaded with luggage and skis so the tourists heading to the ski area of Early Winters wouldn't be inconvenienced.

"He plays head games," Jim had said. "He's got this way of implying that we're less than macho if we play it conservative. Miller seems to get a kick out of pitting us against one another. It's sick."

Of course, Anna knew Jim hadn't played those games. He was too strong, too self-assured to buy into Miller's pressure. Maybe other pilots played along, but not Jim.

"I'm keeping a log," he'd told her. "I've got it all documented. Every last demand Miller has put on us pilots. The times, dates, places. Some of it's subtle stuff, but I've got it all recorded.'' He'd patted the breast pocket of his uniform jacket.

Anna had wondered why he hadn't simply turned his notebook over to the FAA, but Jim had explained that it wasn't quite so easy. Both the NTSB and the FAA dealt in concrete facts, and as Jim had said, ''Miller never directly tells us to take off in lousy weather or with our plane overloaded. He's too smart for that. He just plays these head games with us, comparing his pilots to guys working for other airlines. He implies we're wimps.''

But Jim was no wimp. And that horrible morning he'd followed procedures, crossing all the t's and dotting all the i's. Anna didn't know exactly why the plane had crashed. Maybe the mechanics had made some mistake no one had discovered yet. But she did know Jim had done his job flawlessly. And she was certain that somehow Miller was ultimately to blame.

The taxi turned off the freeway and headed up a ramp and into the heart of Seattle. It was a hilly city, compact, its tall buildings marching up steep inclines from the harbor. The city bustled with businessmen and tourists snapping pictures of quaint fish markets, the Space Needle, the elevated monorail. Anna usually enjoyed the sights and aroma of her childhood home, but not today. It was too dreary out.

Maybe she should tell this investigator about Jim's log. It hadn't been found in the wreckage, which was strange because Jim had always kept that record with him on flights.

Vindication. Anna had told Morty Heller that was what Jim was seeking. Yet she had no real way of knowing, since Jim—or his spirit—had never actually spoken to her.

Anna could just see herself sitting in front of this stern investigator from Washington, D.C., telling him that this apparition from another dimension was tormenting her, pleading with her to find his log, to prove his innocence.

She had tried to find the notebook. She'd called Jim's family, spoken to the medical examiner in Seattle, talked to the NTSB who'd overseen the recovery of the wreckage. She'd even called the police in Winthrop.

Nothing.

The Seattle NTSB branch office was located off Madison Street in the heart of the waterfront district. Anna paid the cabby and stepped out into the clinging drizzle. For a moment she stood and gazed up at the unprepossessing gray stone building. Damn, she thought, this was going to be brutal.

A secretary greeted her in an outer office that was cheaply furnished. There was an odor of stale cigarette smoke and the carpet was threadbare. Anna guessed these NTSB officials weren't concerned with appearances; instead, they fixed their efforts on public safety. But they followed so many rules and procedures—too many, and that made them miss the real issues, issues such as airline owners looking for higher profits. Everything accomplished in this bureaucratic jungle of paperwork was based on fact, hard evidence. How could she tell this investigator about Jim's notebook and then be unable to produce it? And if she did too much talking about Jim, she might just do more harm to Jim's reputation than good.

"Take a seat," the secretary told her, nodding. "Mr. Galloway will be with you shortly."

Anna sat in a chair near the single window. There were no magazines on the table next to her, only an unemptied ashtray and a too-big lamp. It was still raining outside, the small cold drops dripping slowly and raggedly down the dirty glass. Her heart sank as she thought of the sunny morning in Winthrop on the other side of those tall, whitecapped barrier mountains to the northeast. Madeline would be up by now, probably bicycling with Flip, her boyfriend. Flip was a copilot at WestAir who'd recently switched runs from Yakima-Seattle to the Winthrop route because he and Madeline were getting married soon.

They'd be having fun this morning, laughing, playing, stopping on their exercise route up the North Cascade Highway to touch and kiss. Anna had seen them do it a dozen times. Once, she and Jim had behaved like first-time lovers. Once.

Anna could hear a voice coming from the other side of the door to Galloway's temporary office. He must have been on the telephone. She crossed and recrossed her legs, willing the minutes to hurry by. Why on earth had she been called in for this interview? Couldn't Mr. Chris Galloway get all he needed from her previous statements? Really, what a waste of her time. But if this session was going to be about Jim, then she didn't know how she was going to handle it. Morty Heller wouldn't really have spoken to this investigator, would he?

Anna sat and sat. Twenty minutes ticked by in slow agony. She took a deep breath and closed her eyes momentarily, conjuring up an image of a warm hearth on this dreary spring day, and a man by her side, snuggling up to her. Jim. God, how she missed him, how deeply she longed for him. Oh, yes, Anna knew she was still in love. But somehow, insanely, she was in love with a ghost.

CHAPTER TWO

"YOU CAN GO IN NOW," the receptionist said after a thirty-minute wait.

Anna stood, took a deep breath and slung her black leather carryall over her shoulder. She looked competent in her regulation suit and raincoat, neat and tidy and efficient, and that was the impression she wanted to give this Galloway person.

She opened the door and went into the room, closing it with a snick behind her. The office was small and cluttered, piles of papers and manila folders on the desk, a still-damp raincoat hanging crookedly on a coat tree, a briefcase open on a chair, papers sticking out of it haphazardly.

A man stood at the rain-streaked window, his back to her. He was tall and slim and had dark blond disheveled hair. All she could see was his hair, the back of his rumpled tweed sport coat and the worn leather patches on his elbows.

He must have heard her come in, although he gave no sign of it, just stood there looking out at the rain, his elbows crooked casually, hands in his back pockets. Anna didn't quite know what to do. Stand there and wait? Cough? Shuffle her feet? She cleared her throat a little.

"Oh, ah, sit down. Have a seat," he said.

"Thanks," she said, moving to the chair in front of the desk.

After what seemed at least another minute, he finally squared his shoulders and turned away from the window to face her. He looked younger than Anna had first thought, in his late thirties. Then, with more deliberation than she'd expected, he leaned over his desk to brace himself on both arms and just stared at her for a few seconds. Anna met his eyes unflinchingly; she wouldn't let this man intimidate her. After all, he was just doing a job.

He had strongly molded cheekbones with hollows under them, deep-set light blue eyes, a pugnacious thrust to his jaw and an ironic quirk to his mouth. There was an interesting, gravelly quality to his voice. She kept staring back at him.

"Anna Parish," he said in that low, resonant voice. "Thirty-four, unmarried, WestAir employee for three years. Two years at the University of Washington studying sociology."

"Yes." Carefully she didn't add "sir."

"Injuries from air accident March 8, 1992, broken ribs and wrist, facial laceration. Satisfactorily healed."

"Yes," she repeated.

He straightened from the leaning position. "Also, I understand you were engaged to Captain Jim Fleisher, pilot of flight 629."

"Yes."

"You have my sympathy, Miss Parish."

"Thank you."

He sat down then, leaning back in the chair with a kind of careless grace, and put his hands behind his head, fingers locked. His blue shirt pulled across his chest. "You've been deposed before about this accident."

"Twice."

"Yes, I reviewed the depositions. Did you know they were taped?"

"Yes, I did." Anna shifted her position, feeling her heartbeat speed up despite herself. Galloway was direct, too direct. His light blue eyes were disconcerting, piercing. She had the sudden impression that he wasn't just doing a job, that he was on a crusade.

He stared at her unblinkingly for a moment, his eyes searching for and finding the fading red scar that parted her hair on the right side and extended down an inch onto her forehead. Her curling hair neatly covered it, but she still had to fight an instinctive urge to put her hand up to touch the scar.

After an uncomfortable moment, he moved his hands from behind his head and opened the top file on the cluttered desk. Still looking at the file, he said, "Excuse any repeat questions, Miss Parish. I'm sure you've already answered them. I ask your indulgence. Please just answer them again. This interview will be taped. I'm switching the tape recorder on now. This is Special Investigator Chris Galloway deposing Anna Parish, May 25, 1992—" he glanced at his wrist "—11:14 a.m."

She hated recorders, hated the sound of her own voice on tape. The whole thing made her tense.

"All right, Miss Parish, please describe your duties on the morning of March 8, WestAir Express flight 629."

She told him. God, she'd repeated it over and over again.

"So you were in the cockpit for a time that morning before takeoff?"

"Yes, two or three minutes maybe. Everything seemed routine."

"Describe the weather."

"It was starting to snow. You could see it coming down out of the mountains, just starting to stick to the ground."

"Do you recall when the plane was deiced?"

"No, really. I was busy in the galley. I only remember seeing the deicing fluid spraying off the wings of the plane when I looked out the cockpit window."

"When was that?"

"I don't know the exact time. Right before departure."

"You looked out the cockpit window and had a clear and unobscured view of both wings and saw that they had been sprayed with deicing fluid. Is that correct?"

She thought back. She'd bent down to see. She'd been behind Jim on the pilot's side. She saw in her mind's eye the silver wing, the pink spray, felt the vibrating of the plane, smelled Jim's after-shave... She snapped her eyes back to Chris Galloway. "I saw the left wing. I didn't see the right wing. I assume—"

"Assumptions don't count for much, Miss Parish." He flipped some papers. "Were you aware the plane wasn't deiced again after a twenty-minute delay?"

She shook her head. "I really never paid any attention. It wasn't one of my duties." Anna frowned then. "But it didn't seem like twenty minutes."

Galloway regarded her without expression. Slowly he tapped a pencil on the desktop. "How about fifteen minutes? Would you say it was no longer than fifteen minutes?"

Anna shook her head. "I don't really know. Like I said, it wasn't one of my duties."

He stopped tapping the pencil. The room was suddenly too silent, too close. Anna crossed and recrossed her legs, her fingers smoothing her maroon skirt.

"All right," he finally said, "when the plane took off, did it seem to gain altitude at a normal rate of ascent?"

"Mr. Galloway, I'm not a pilot. I have no training—"

"I want your opinion, Miss Parish, that's all."

She thought back again: sitting in the jump seat, the plane thumping along the runway. "I thought it lifted off a little late, probably because of the slush. Then a few seconds later—"

"How many seconds?"

"Oh, maybe thirty or forty. It began shaking."

"How long did it shake?"

"Oh, I don't know. It happened so fast. A minute, no, more like two or three. It shook as if it was going to come apart. I yelled for everyone to assume crash position. I saw trees—" She stopped short, aware that her voice was shaking. Her hands were damp and trembling slightly.

His eyes were on her vigorously, waiting, not helping. He had no intention of helping her out; he was a sadist. She took a deep, quavering breath. "And then we hit. I guess we hit the trees first. There was a terrible noise, people were screaming. Then I must have passed out."

Silence settled between them once more. Only the thin hum of the tape deck could be heard. Then Chris Galloway leaned back in his seat again. "Answer me this, Miss Parish, just your opinion. Do you think Jim Fleisher should have taken off that March morning?''

She sat there, stunned and angry. ''I have no opinion on that. I'm not qualified,'' she said stiffly.

He regarded her for a while, his face expressionless. She looked back, determined not to give way. High cheekbones, thick, tousled hair, with an errant curl over his forehead, a strong neck, loosened collar and striped tie askew. Deep-set eyes with fingerprints of gray under them. Tired ... He looked tired.

''I realize you'd protect the pilot under any circumstances, especially since he was your fiancé, Miss Parish, but you owe it to the flying public to express any doubts about flight 629. Any doubts at all,'' he said.

''I'm not protecting Jim,'' she retorted angrily. ''His record stands. He was a careful, skilled pilot.''

''They all are, Miss Parish,'' Galloway said, and she detected a hint of weariness in his voice. ''It's just that some are more careful and skilled than others. Or maybe just plain luckier.'' He rubbed his temples with a hand and flipped some more papers in her file. ''And the copilot, Len Whittaker, what did he think about flying that day?''

''I don't know. He said nothing in my hearing. You have the cockpit recording. You tell me,'' she shot back.

A faint smile tugged at the corner of his mouth. ''You're right. I probably do know more than you.''

''Can I go now?'' she asked.

''Not yet, Miss Parish. I have a few more questions.''

She was damp under her arms, her nerves scraping against one another. She kept seeing those dark trees through the window, remembering the noises, the screams.

Galloway stood and stretched a little, and Anna had the impression of lean muscles. He was tall, over six feet, anyway, but overlying the grace with which he moved was weariness again. He sat back down, tossed two files onto the already cluttered chair next to the desk and opened another one. The tape continued to whir quietly while Galloway flipped pages, scanning them until he obviously found what he was looking for.

He glanced up at her abruptly. "I'm aware that some of WestAir's employees aren't happy with Lee Miller's management. You're one of them."

"That's right, but I don't see—"

"I have here a copy of a complaint filed with the local FAA office six months ago. Your name is on the complaint, along with several other employees. Jim Fleisher's isn't there."

She stared down at her hands. "Jim wanted to wait until he had concrete evidence. He said the complaint wouldn't do any good, and he was right. Nothing happened."

"I'm also aware that the WestAir employees have set up an acquisition corporation to buy the airline."

"It's a matter of record." She shrugged.

"Listen, Miss Parish, don't you realize how this looks to everyone?"

She glanced up at him, and his eyes bored into hers. "How does it look?"

"It looks like a pilot made a mistake and the employees are grabbing at straws, trying to find a convenient scapegoat, proof that Lee Miller was actually to blame for the accident."

"No," she said.

"No what, Miss Parish?"

"It's not like that. I'm not trying to protect Jim, but Lee Miller is a bad manager. There have been lots of small mishaps at WestAir—flat tires, close calls, engines failing. Miller doesn't even bother to report them. It was only a matter of time until there was a serious accident, I guess. Jim had the bad luck to be the pilot on it. If you investigate, if you really try, you'll find out that it wasn't Jim's fault. There was probably some maintenance problem, some shortcut with deicing. Something like that."

"It's being looked into."

"I'm aware of that." She leaned forward. "Lee Miller is a dangerous man. No matter what your blue book report finally says, the fault for that crash is Miller's. Maybe indirectly, but it's his nevertheless. I know you have no control over the owner, but you shouldn't blame a pilot when the owner has created an unsafe airline."

"Please, Miss Parish, you're talking nonsense. The pilot has the final judgment call about whether to fly or not. Miller can't force anyone to fly when it's not safe."

"You don't understand. It's the constant pressure. Pressure on the baggage men to overload, on the mechanics to leave in old parts, on the pilots to fly in marginal weather."

Galloway studied her again. She thought for a moment she'd made an impression, dented the bureaucratic mind-set that looked for concrete proof, not psychological pressures, but then he shook his head. "Facts are facts. Jim Fleisher took off in bad weather. Preliminary evidence leans toward blaming ice on the leading edges of the wings. The behavior of the plane that you yourself report supports this conclusion.''

Anna felt frustration grip her stomach. Nobody would listen. And now Jim would have to bear the brunt for Miller's bad habits. It was almost better Jim was gone; he couldn't have borne the blame and the guilt. It would have destroyed him.

''Perhaps you'd care to listen to some testimony you gave earlier. You were still in the hospital. March 11, I believe it was.'' Galloway switched cassettes in the recorder, pushed a lever and fast-forwarded the tape.

She heard a man's voice, the FAA man, asking a question, then another voice she recognized as her own. ''It was snowing, yes, but the visibility wasn't bad yet. Jim knows, knew, when to abort a flight. It wasn't that bad.''

''Miss Parish,'' the FAA man said, ''I have in your own words on the cockpit voice recorder that the weather was nasty.''

''It was, yes, but we'd taken off before, lots of times, in that kind of weather.''

Listening to the recording now in Galloway's office, Anna could hear desperation in her voice. She sat there watching the rain slide down the window and couldn't believe the person talking was her. She could barely remember what she'd said.

The tape went on. ''The copilot expressed some doubts, Miss Parish. Are you aware of that?''

''I didn't hear him say anything like that. But Len was new. He hadn't flown in mountain weather very much. Jim said he was a little uncertain.''

''Was Jim Fleisher in the habit of listening to his copilots?''

"I...I don't know...I..." And then her voice broke and there were muffled sobs on the recording, the FAA man said something and then her own voice, quivering, full of anguish, cried, "Oh, God, why did he take off? Why?"

Anna put her face in her hands. She couldn't bear hearing any more. Why was Galloway forcing her to listen? Why was he torturing her like this?

He stopped the tape. "Would you like some coffee?" he asked abruptly.

She took a shuddering breath and lowered her hands. She wouldn't cry; she was done with that. She'd shed all her tears.

"Coffee?" he asked again.

"All right, sure."

"Cream, sugar?"

"Just sugar."

He rose, went to a coffeepot set on a shelf behind his desk and poured two foam cups. He was pretending to be sympathetic, but she hated him, detested him and the destructive bureaucracy he represented that rode roughshod over people.

He handed her a cup with a plastic spoon in it. She took it, stirred absently and waited.

"Rains a lot here, doesn't it?" he observed.

"In Seattle it does."

"And Winthrop?"

Anna sighed and shrugged faintly. "Not as much, I guess."

"Do you ski?"

She looked up at him. "Yes."

"I've never tried it, myself. Too busy."

He was trying to settle her down, Anna knew, taking another tack. And then he'd start in all over again, grilling her, pushing her. She was surprised he didn't have a bright light glaring in her eyes.

"Are we through?" she asked again.

"Not quite." Then he added, "Sorry."

Anna watched him carefully, like a mouse cornered and waiting for a cat to spring. He sipped on his coffee, closed the file in front of him and took up another one. She found herself wondering if he ever smiled or laughed. He'd be a nice-looking man if he weren't so stern. She switched her eyes back down to her coffee and stared at the twisting plume of steam rising from it.

"You're still flying," he finally said.

"Yeah, I'm back in the ol' saddle," Anna replied dryly.

"Lots of people don't...can't."

"I had to."

"Um." He sipped his coffee.

Anna looked at him, her head cocked. "Mr. Galloway," she said, "why *are* you here? I mean, why this special investigation when you seem to have all the facts already?"

"I don't have *all* the facts, as you put it. The final determination as to the cause of the crash hasn't been made yet."

"I don't—"

"The employee buy-out bid complicates things," he said abruptly.

"Why?"

"In part because of the complaints against Lee Miller, if you must know."

"Really?" She was truly surprised, and pleased.

"Understand, Miss Parish," he said, "that just because an airline owner is accused of cutting corners doesn't necessarily add up to a disaster. You yourself in that taped interview asked why Fleisher took off that morning. Unless you're much harder and cleverer than I think, trying to purposely discredit Miller—"

"That's not true. I was asking a rhetorical question on the tape, that's all. Not blaming Jim. I was still in the hospital then. I was...devastated. I hurt. My fiancé was dead."

He blew on his coffee and sipped it. He had long fingers, slim, with a few golden hairs on the back of his hand. A plain stainless-steel watch encircled a strong wrist. Anna noticed, almost against her will, that he wore no wedding band. Outside, the rain fell unceasingly and slid in molten sheets down the window behind Chris Galloway.

"Miss Parish," he finally said, looking up from his coffee, "I'm not here to nail you or to search out a scapegoat. I'm an investigator for a government agency, a civil servant. My job is to find the truth, to figure out how airline accidents happen so they can be prevented in the future. Believe me, I've seen too many of them, and I'm well aware of the devastation they cause. There's seldom an easy answer to why an accident happens. It tends to be complicated. I'm looking for all the angles, everything. I'm not your enemy. I'm trying to prevent what happened to you from happening to anyone else. So if you can help me—in any way whatsoever—you'd be doing us all a service."

So that's his line, Anna thought. *Let's all work together on this. Sure.* She kept her head down, sipping the coffee, thinking for a minute. When she glanced up, he was regarding her steadily, his light blue eyes unwavering. "I *am* trying to help you," she said, "but you won't listen. Look at Lee Miller, look at the way he runs the company. Ask other pilots."

"Oh, don't worry, I plan to. The problem is, it's to the benefit of all WestAir employees to point the finger at Miller, so I've got to take that into consideration."

"Do you really think we'd all lie? Do you think we'd let other accidents happen just to get Lee Miller? What kind of people do you think we are?" she asked heatedly.

He held up a hand. "Take it easy. I'm not accusing anyone, understand? I have to be objective, take everything under advisement. It's my job."

She stayed silent, stubbornly silent.

He finished his coffee, crumpled the cup and tossed it into the wastebasket. "Okay, let's go on. I do have a few more questions."

Great, Anna thought, frowning.

He switched cassettes again and pressed a lever. "I just want you to listen for a minute. Try to be objective. Try not to have preconceived notions."

"What is it?" she asked.

He held up his hand again just as a man started speaking. With a shock of recognition Anna realized it was Lee Miller, the owner of WestAir, talking.

"Listen," Miller was saying, "I got back here in '71, straight outta those damn jungles in Nam. I'd flown over there, flew reconnaissance, sweated out my time and earned my medals. I was good, too. So I get back to Washington State and this little smoke jumper base was up for grabs. I got it and bought one lousy, beat-up flying crate. I worked my butt off for years, barely survived running charters to smoke-jump sites during forest fires, hiring out for a few people in a hurry, stuff like that. Then they built the ski area, Early Winters. Let me tell you, my life changed. I had to sink a lotta dough into buying aircraft, convince the county to enlarge the airport terminal, but it went. Went big.

"I built WestAir from nothing with my own sweat. I own it, and I can run it as I like as long as I follow the rules. And I follow 'em, damn it. You just check out my records. They're in order, every last form filled out. I've been checked and rechecked by the FAA, and no one ever found anything wrong. Now my employees have the gall to try to buy me out, undermine me at every turn. Resist everything I tell 'em, lie, try to get me into trouble. If a plane crashes, the pilot did something wrong, and I won't take responsibility for that!"

Galloway stopped the tape, and Miller's angry voice was shut off. Neither of them said anything for a time, but Anna knew he was watching her, gauging her reaction. He remained leaning over the tape player, weight on his elbows, eyes on her. The quiet stretched out into an uncomfortable hiatus.

"What do you want me to say?" she finally asked.

"I don't *want* you to say anything. I want your objective reaction to Miller's statements."

"My objective reaction? He's a tough guy. He worked hard, that's true. But he's tight-fisted with money and has a way about him of dealing with people—abusive, loud. He makes enemies of his employees instead of trusting them. He's a bad manager. I told you that. Everything he said on that tape is true, but it's all *his* side of things."

"He has adhered to all the rules, all the paperwork. The FAA regional head found nothing wrong with his records."

Anna sighed. It was impossible. "That's not my area. I don't know about that. I only know what the pilots think, what Jim—"

"What Jim Fleisher thinks?"

She swallowed. "Yes, what Jim *thought.*"

"What did Jim think, Miss Parish?"

She looked away, shifted in her seat. "I've been trying to tell you. Look, why don't you ask the other WestAir pilots these things? They know the facts."

"They're reluctant to go on record with facts. You understand, if a pilot does something unsafe, whether or not he feels he was coerced into doing it, he's in violation of federal air regulations, so he's not likely to come forward with it."

She knew that already. Hadn't Jim told her that often enough? That was why he was keeping his notebook—for evidence.

"So you can see why I'm asking you and other employees of WestAir. For the whole picture. If you or someone else could provide me with actual concrete evidence against Miller, that would be a different story. As it is . . ." He spread his hands and shrugged.

Evidence. It all hinged on evidence. Jim's record, his notebook, which had conveniently disappeared.

Anna cleared her throat. She had to tell him about the notebook. Maybe with his power as an NTSB investigator Galloway could find it. "I . . . uh . . . know of some evidence like that."

He looked at her sharply, his sandy eyebrows rising.

"Jim Fleisher had a notebook. He was keeping a record of everything Lee Miller did, the kind of pressure he exerted, things like that. Names, dates. Other things, too, like bad parts Miller wouldn't replace, falsified records, lack of training. He wrote everything down. When he had enough, he was going to the FAA with it.''

"Terrific. Where's his notebook?"

She gripped the foam cup tightly and kept her eyes down. "I don't know."

"You don't know."

"He always carried it with him when he flew. Always. But it wasn't there."

Galloway said nothing for a moment, then asked, "You mean it wasn't in his effects?"

"I called his parents. I felt terrible, but I had to do it. They never received a notebook. I asked at the hospital. I checked everywhere. Nobody ever found it."

"You *saw* this notebook?" he asked.

"Many times. It was just a plain blue spiral notebook, a small one, an assignment-sized one. He used to read me what he'd written in it once in a while." As she said the words, Anna could hear Jim's voice in her head, could smell the slightly smoky odor from the wood stove, could feel his hand resting on her arm. "The chief mechanic, Harry Logan, told me on January 22, 1991, that the boss made him reuse a tire that had landed hard, bending a motor mount and a flap, even though this was against regulations," Jim had read to her. "I can't believe this guy, Annie. He's gonna kill somebody one of these days. Just a little longer and I'll have enough on him."

"Miss Parish?" Galloway asked, regarding her with a questioning look, eyebrows raised.

"Sorry." She straightened and shook herself a little.

"So this notebook . . . ?"

"It's gone. I looked everywhere. Maybe . . . well, maybe you could ask around. Maybe somebody has it and doesn't know what to do with it, doesn't even realize what it is."

"If anyone had found a notebook like that, it would have been turned in."

"I know, but—"

"You're sure he had that record? You're sure he had it on him?"

"He always carried it."

Chris Galloway looked at her for a moment, drumming his fingers on the desk, his brows drawn together. "You're sure this blue spiral notebook actually existed?"

"Well, of course I am! What do you think...I mean, why would I be telling you about it if—?" She stopped short, unable to fathom this man's obtuseness. "Look, I didn't make this up. What good would it do to tell you about it if it doesn't exist?"

"You didn't make it up, you say. Yet there's no record of any such notebook. I can only assume you're engaging in wishful thinking or your imagination is working overtime." His voice had an edge to it, as if he were insinuating something.

"What are you getting at?"

"Maybe this record Fleisher kept is a figment of your imagination."

"I resent that."

"I understand." He paused, then said, "There's been some question about your credibility, Miss Parish."

He glanced down at the papers in her file, almost inadvertently, but her own gaze followed his, and she saw a neat manila folder with a name typed on the white tab. Her name. There was some printing on the cover, too. Upside down she read a familiar name:

Morton Heller, Clinical Psychologist. She drew in a quick breath, then felt anger surge through her.

"You got my file from Dr. Heller," she breathed. "It's confidential. I thought—"

"I'm sorry, Miss Parish, but the doctor was hired by WestAir. I'm afraid you misunderstood."

She just sat there, feeling the anger splotch her cheeks with red. This man, this utter stranger, knew everything she'd said to Morty Heller in the strictest confidence. She felt stripped naked, defiled, betrayed.

"Your file *is* confidential. It will never be released to the public," Galloway said, as if to placate her.

"Thanks. That's very reassuring," she said bitingly.

"Look, and I ask you to be objective here, but you, as a surviving crew member, can provide vital testimony about those events of March—"

"Oh?" Anna snapped. "How can I if I'm not credible?"

"Listen," he said, "I didn't write the report. I can only base my questions on—"

"Morty Heller's evaluation. Great."

He tried again. "Okay, you tell me about a notebook . . . one that no one else but you has ever seen, and—"

"I can see where this is leading."

"Can you? Have I said I didn't believe you?"

Anna thought for a moment. "No, you haven't quite put it in those words."

"So what would you have me do, Miss Parish, ignore Heller's report entirely?"

"I don't know."

"You profess to have seen . . . Jim Fleisher since the accident." He paused. "If you'll forgive me, Miss Parish, I—"

"No, I don't forgive you. That's private. It's none of your business." She stood to leave, but the foam cup was still in her hand. She looked around, distracted, for a place to put it down. Tears stung her eyes, and she fought them with everything she could muster.

"Here," he said, moving around the desk swiftly and taking the cup from her hand. "Sorry. Are you all right?"

"Yes," she muttered, refusing to meet his eyes, humiliated. "Can I go now?"

"I'm not finished."

"I am," she replied. "I'm through. You have my file. Read it."

But he was shaking his head slowly. "I'd like you to be back here at nine in the morning. We can be through the interview by—"

"I'm finished, I said. I have nothing more to tell you." She averted her eyes then, but he was too close, just in front of her, his strong neck at eye level, his pale blue glance probing, judging, cutting through her like a hot knife. She stepped backward, came up against her chair, then turned away from him.

"Be here in the morning, Miss Parish. It's in your own best interest," Galloway said to her back.

"No, it isn't. It's in yours," she retorted, heading for the door.

CHAPTER THREE

ANNA SPENT the night at a hotel by the airport, taking her dinner in her room, not even turning on the TV. She needed to think, to try to sort out in her mind the past couple of months and the radical changes in her life. She probed her heart, too, for her feelings about Jim. It was like twisting a knife into an open wound. But she lay on the bed until sleep took her and examined her most profound feelings. She missed Jim like mad, true, but Anna had to wonder if now her memories were based on reality. It wasn't just all the blame being tossed in Jim's direction. She knew better than to believe that. It was his appearances.

Anna was a no-nonsense sort of person, firmly grounded in practicality. She'd always been pragmatic and clearheaded. Philosophy eluded her; arithmetic made perfect sense. She balanced her checkbook to the penny every month, budgeted carefully, remembered details. An eminently reasonable, down-to-earth woman. People like Anna didn't believe in ghosts; it simply wasn't possible for them to accept the reality of anything they couldn't explain away scientifically.

Yet Anna had seen Jim, seen him as clearly as she saw anybody in the same room with her. And she accepted his presence by performing some peculiar balancing act inside her head. He couldn't exist, yet he did. That was the only way she could explain it. Dr.

Heller had listened to this explanation and tried to appear wise, but she knew what he thought. Heck, she thought the same thing.

So Jim, or the soul of Jim, appeared to her—that she accepted. The question that continued to pound at her was why? What did he want?

As she lay there in the dark, she had, once again, to ask herself if Jim's spirit was real. She'd tortured herself with this same question until she'd given up. She'd let it alone. Maybe she *was* crazy. But if she was, then so was Madeline Vernon.

Anna was scheduled to work the early flight back to Winthrop the following morning. She rose, showered and put on her uniform with every intention of calling in to her supervisor and explaining about her meeting with Chris Galloway. It wasn't as if it were her fault. Her supervisor would simply assign another flight attendant to the morning run, and Anna would work the early-afternoon one. But as she sat on the edge of the unmade bed she felt herself snap.

"No way," she whispered angrily. Chris Galloway wasn't going to put her through another second of torment. No rule said she had to give in to NTSB pressure. Anna wasn't going to submit to any more questioning. Let them think she was crazy, suffering from delusions due to her deep grief. She knew better. And she was past caring what NTSB Group Chairman Galloway thought, too.

MADELINE VERNON, Anna's roommate and fellow flight attendant, was still in her pajamas when Anna got home to Winthrop at noon the next day. And so was Flip Akers, Madeline's boyfriend, the "pilot of her dreams," although he was really a copilot.

The two were in the kitchen, frying eggs. Even before Anna had put down her bag and raincoat she could hear Madeline giggling and saying, "Ouch, stop that! I'll have a bruise on my fanny for a week! Ouch, Flip!"

Anna smiled and shook her head. "Hi, guys, I'm home from the wild blue yonder."

"Oh, hi, Anna," Madeline called back in a small voice.

Flip stuck his handsome head around the corner. "Why, if it isn't my roomie, Anna."

"Not your roomie, Flip," Anna replied. "You were going to rent a place for you and Madeline."

"This is cheaper."

"Yeah, and too crowded. Grow up, Flip," Anna chided, marching past him into the kitchen. "Take a stab at independence."

"Yeah, Flip," Madeline echoed, "grow up."

They were a great couple. Madeline with her blond Nordic good looks and those long legs that seemed to go on forever, and Flip—boyishly handsome with bright blue eyes and a dark mass of thick curling hair. He was head over heels in love. And so was Madeline.

"Coffee? Eggs?" Flip held up the frying pan.

Anna shook her head. "I ate on the plane."

"So," Flip said, sitting, shoveling in eggs, "how'd the interview go yesterday?"

"Bad."

"Oh, no," Madeline said, "what happened? God, I have one tomorrow."

Anna sat down across from them and rested her chin on her hands. "It was mostly about Jim," she said. "They're going to blame it on him. I know it. I tried my best to explain about Miller and his procedures, but this NTSB guy, this Galloway, is a hard-core 'facts' man. I didn't get anywhere."

Flip put down his fork. "He didn't even flinch when you told him about the pressure Miller puts on his people?"

"Not once. In fact, he brought up the employee buy-out bid and insinuated we'd say anything to discredit Miller."

"Swell."

"Exactly," Anna said. She knew Flip Akers was very active in the pilots' organization that was pushing hard to get their case to court. Buy-outs were a long and tedious process, involving federal agencies and courts, dozens of lawyers, a mountain of red tape. And WestAir's employees needed a strong case against Miller. It sure didn't look good that Chris Galloway was questioning the motives of employees such as Anna, wondering if she was using the March disaster to heap more blame onto Miller's lap.

"Look," Anna said, pushing some spilled grains of salt around the table with a finger, "I hope I didn't make a mistake talking about Lee Miller to that investigator."

But Flip shook his head. "It's better if you do it than if the pilots do. We've got a higher stake in this."

"Did you tell him about the missing notebook?" Madeline asked.

Anna nodded. "But it's that old bureaucratic line about 'concrete evidence.' The man wants facts."

"Poor Jim," Madeline whispered, and then she gave Anna a meaningful, frightened glance and the subject was dropped.

"So," Flip said, taking his plate to the sink, "I really do have a line on a rental house. But you're the expert, Anna, and I'd like you to take a look at it for me. The rental agent said you knew the place, the old Ledbetter cabin down the road."

"I know it."

"Is it rentable? I mean, does the place have decent heat? Water?"

"It's all right. How much are they asking?"

"Five hundred till December, then it jumps to seven-fifty."

Anna whistled through her teeth. "That's steep."

"Would you take a good look at it for us?" Flip asked sincerely.

"Okay."

"Today?"

She wasn't the pro Flip thought she was about rentals and leases in Winthrop, but she wasn't entirely ignorant, either. She'd moved to the small Cascade Mountain resort when the ski area was first being built and put a down payment on her little house on Bluff Avenue. She'd looked at several run-down old Victorians and cabins but found this place to be the best buy. Her folks had been worried, wondering if the ski area was going to be successful, or if Anna's house wasn't going to cost her an arm and leg to fix up. And she'd spent every dime of her savings—twelve thousand dollars—on that down payment. But since Early Winters had opened as the premier ski resort in the Pacific Northwest, Anna's gamble had paid off. If she sold out tomorrow, she'd double her investment.

"So you promise to stop by and check out that place for us?" Flip asked as he and Madeline headed out for their afternoon bike ride.

"I'll stop by and get the key from the agent," Anna said.

"Today?"

"Yes, today."

Flip patted Madeline's backside and called over his shoulder, "You're a treasure, Anna, thanks."

"My pleasure." Of course, it would be heaven to have the small two-bedroom house back to herself. She and Madeline had fitted in fine, but Flip was the straw that was breaking the camel's back.

Anna changed into khaki hiking shorts, an old University of Washington sweatshirt and tennis shoes. She had a car, a 1987 Subaru wagon, perfect for the slippery winter roads. But today it was heavenly out, and she figured she'd walk over to the rental agent's and get the key. She fastened her hair back loosely in a barrette, pushed up her sleeves and headed out.

It *was* lovely. The late May sun warmed her shoulders as she walked down the hill toward the river and town. Everywhere spring flowers turned their colorful faces to the sun, and half the town seemed to be out gardening.

"Hello, Mrs. Simpson," Anna called, waving. "Great day, huh?"

Ida Simpson waved back with pruning shears in her gloved hand.

Anna loved her adopted home. She'd loved Winthrop since she was a girl of ten when her folks first started driving over to enjoy the dry, hot summers on the eastern mountain slopes. They had gone horseback riding and fishing. Camped out beneath the dazzling stars and tall Douglas fir trees. And when the old, little-known lumber town had been refurbished, its streets and buildings given a true facelift by a generous local benefactor, Winthrop had slowly found a place on the tourist map of Washington State.

It was charming. Old-fashioned boardwalks replaced concrete sidewalks. The three downtown blocks of shops, restaurants and hotels now had false fronts, turning them into Old West-style buildings that drew in thousands of tourists year-round to snap pictures. And up the valley, along the North Cascade Highway that connected the eastern and western Cascade slopes, was the ski area of Early Winters—ultramodern and convenient, with perfect, wide Alpine ski slopes surrounded by glorious primeval forests.

Yes, Anna had come to love both the old town and the new resort, seeing them as dependent upon each other, complementary. She'd always wanted to live in the mountains, away from the city. But when she first made the move from Seattle, she'd wondered if she truly would like it year-round. Well, that fear had been allayed a long time ago. And now, well, now she felt a part of the friendly community, a "local."

Her life would be complete, Anna thought as she walked and nodded to people, but for one thing…Jim.

Bill Murray at the rental agency insisted on driving Anna back up the hill to the Ledbetter place. Although Anna liked Bill and his wife, Alice, he was getting so old Anna wondered if he remembered one day from the next.

He asked her four times before they got to the house, "Now you're flying for that outfit that Miller owns, aren't you?"

"Yes," Anna said four times.

At other moments old Bill was as sharp as a tack. "It's a damn shame about your friend Jim Fleisher. Damn shame. Only met him that one time at the Firemen's Ball. Lived in Seattle, didn't he?"

"That's right," Anna said, "but he was considering moving here this coming fall. He loved to ski."

"Nice fella. Damn shame. It's a downright pitiful thing to lose a loved one, I'll tell you."

And Anna's heart gave a sick thump, remembering with stark clarity the last time the specter had appeared in her bedroom, that horrible, unearthly light, the torment on his bloodless face...

"Damn shame."

The Ledbetter cabin was in need of repair, a lot of repair. The toilet in the bathroom was half sunken into the floor, the tiles in the old shower were peeling off, the sink minus half its enamel. The kitchen was equally as bad. And for heat there was a potbellied stove in the living room. The cabin had been built back in the lumbering days, a vintage 1900s shack. And Flip and Madeline would be fools to pay such outrageously high rent.

"Darn," she said, poking her head into a bedroom, "I'd hoped the family had fixed it up a little."

"Now I can talk to them about lowering the rent, Anna, if you want. Might get it for two-fifty in the summer."

"But Flip and Madeline would freeze here in the winter, Bill, under any circumstances. It's not going to work."

"Lolly Ledbetter had hoped to get it rented. She'll be real disappointed."

"Tell Lolly," Anna said, "she better put a few bucks into this place. It's highway robbery."

"I'll tell her, but she won't do it. You know there's a housing shortage here, what with that blamed ski area right up the valley now."

"I know. But ripping people off isn't going to solve a thing."

Anna drove down the hillside with Bill and back into the town's tiny core. Disappointment settled over her. Flip was going to be an added roommate for some time longer, at least until he and Madeline got married this summer. Poor Madeline was too timid to put her foot down and tell him he had to find his own place. Anna couldn't really do it, either. Flip was in Madeline's room, for one thing, and she was paying for that room. But mostly it was because Madeline had been so undone lately, so upset by everything. It was Jim, Anna knew. Madeline had weathered the plane crash like a true champ, pulling herself together, going on with her life.

And then Jim had come back.

Anna walked through town and up the hill to her house with a frown creasing her brow. The apparition had first appeared to Madeline in early April, only a few nights after Anna had seen it. Maybe it would have been easier on Madeline if Anna had confessed her own incident. But she hadn't. And when Madeline came screaming and crying out of her room at four in the morning, Anna had been unable to calm her. Flip was still living in Yakima then, and Madeline had begged Anna to call him, to have him drive up immediately. But at nine, when Flip came tearing in, Madeline was quiet, withdrawn and had refused ever to speak of the incident again. Around Madeline the subject was taboo. Even Flip disliked speaking about it. Once, when Madeline went to the grocery, Anna had asked him what Jim could possibly want of them.

Flip had said, "Hell, Anna, I don't know. Maybe he was never here at all."

"Flip," she'd begun, "Jim did keep this notebook on him and—"

"I don't want to talk about it, Anna. Madeline's going to be back in a minute, and she goes nuts when I even say Jim's name."

So that had ended it. And now Anna suffered Jim's "visits" alone. She was afraid to go to another psychologist or psychiatrist and seldom mentioned Jim around her own house.

Yet the disembodied soul of her lover still came. And came.

Anna walked faster, trying to shake off her mounting discomfort. It was no wonder at all she'd avoided this morning's meeting with Chris Galloway. As long as the NTSB man had that report in his hands from Morty Heller, he'd want to question her further, try to judge her credibility, as he'd said. And she just couldn't talk about Jim without breaking apart inside. And even in her own home she couldn't mention Jim around Madeline. It was hell, an isolation Anna wondered if she could bear much longer.

As she came up her walk, she heard the phone ring. It turned out to be a jam-the-key-in-the-lock, stumble-over-the-doormat telephone call where you grabbed the receiver only to hear a buzzing sound. The caller had hung up.

"Figures," Anna grumbled as she put the receiver down. On the other hand, it could have been Chris Galloway in Seattle. She couldn't imagine him just letting her not show up. Not that crusader.

Maybe if the phone rang again she wouldn't answer it. Sure. But what if it was her folks? They weren't so young anymore.

The phone rang. Anna stared at it for a moment, then shrugged. If Galloway wanted to find her, he would, regardless of how hard she tried to avoid him.

"Chris Galloway here, Miss Parish," he began, and she slumped onto her couch, shooing the cat aside.

"Mr. Galloway," Anna started to say.

"That was quite a stunt you pulled this morning. I even gave you the benefit of the doubt and checked with your supervisor to see if you tried to switch your run to Winthrop today."

"You called my supervisor?" Anna put a hand on her forehead.

"Of course I called her. Do you think this is some sort of a game we're playing here?"

"What did you tell her?" Anna insisted.

There was a pause, then he said, "I merely asked if you'd switched shifts today. But this lack of cooperation, Miss Parish, isn't going to cut it."

"I'm not some sort of puppet, Mr. Galloway. I can't be manipulated. If I don't want to talk to you, I don't have to. You don't believe anything I say, anyway."

Again there was a long pause. "Look," he said, his tone less harsh, "I'm going to be in Winthrop this afternoon. I have to get depositions from the tower personnel, the mechanics and your roommate, Miss Vernon—"

"How about Lee Miller?" Anna was quick to interrupt. "Aren't you going to talk with him?"

"Mr. Miller is on my agenda, if it's any of your business."

"Good."

"That's beside the point. I want to talk to you again."

"I won't go over the same issues another time. I just won't be subjected to it. I mean that."

"I have other issues, as you put it, that need clarification."

"And I'm the *only* one who can do that?"

"Yesterday," he said, "you made certain accusations that need addressing."

"You mean like Miller and his half-baked procedures?"

"I didn't say that. There's only your word on that. But if you can point me in any helpful direction, perhaps we can be of benefit to each other."

"You mean that?"

"Miss Parish," he said, "I'm trying to put the cause of this crash together. It's often like a puzzle. Sometimes the pieces fit. Sometimes they don't. I'm only asking for a few minutes of your time to clarify a couple of points you yourself brought up. Now where and when can we meet?"

Anna let out a long breath. She didn't believe him, not really. She knew these bureaucrats—they single-mindedly dug for the facts, not real answers. Still, it would be impossible to avoid this relentless man, especially in Winthrop.

"Miss Parish, I'm waiting."

"What flight are you on?"

"The three o'clock."

"Well, I guess I'll be at home."

"And your correct address is in the file?"

"Yes. It's my house. Anyone can tell you where it is."

"Small town." It wasn't a question. "I'll be there at, say, four."

"Fine."

"And listen—" she could hear a softening in his tone, just a tad "—I'm not the ogre you seem to think."

"You don't know what I think, Mr. Galloway," Anna said, then hung up.

Three o'clock came and went. Three-thirty. By the time Madeline and Flip arrived home, Anna's nerves were raw.

"I should have told him no," she said, pacing. "He just wants me to go over and over those last few minutes before the takeoff that day. He wants me to tell him Jim was a tyrant in the cockpit and Len was scared to death of him and that the plane should have been deiced again..." She put her face in her hands. "Oh, God, it wasn't Jim's fault! He was always so careful! He was keeping that log. Why would Jim have kept a record and then fallen prey to Miller's tactics! He never would have!"

"Anna," Madeline began, nervous, putting her arms around her.

But Flip nodded her away. "Jim was the best, Anna, we all know that. He followed all the rules. Len was young, real wet behind the ears. The NTSB knows that, too."

"So what does Galloway want from me?" she breathed.

"Who knows?" Flip said, smiling, fluffing her hair.

"He doesn't believe anything I say, anyway. He suspects my credibility," she said, looking from one to the other. "He had Morty Heller's report right there in front of him. He knows...he knows I've been seeing Jim."

Madeline turned the color of ashes.

"He, ah, he can't do a thing to you, Anna. Don't worry," Flip said, but Madeline had already fled the room. Flip sighed heavily. "Listen," he said, "you didn't mention anything about that night Madeline thought she saw...well, you know...Jim?"

"No, I didn't say a thing."

Flip released a breath. "Good. She can't take that kind of an interview with Galloway. It would kill her. It's been bad enough getting over the crash as it is. You know."

"Yeah, I know."

"And you won't say anything, will you?"

Anna shook her head. "No, I won't. But it would sure help if Madeline would corroborate my story."

"She won't."

"I'm afraid you're right."

Flip studied her for a moment. Then he asked, "Anna, do you, ah, do you still see Jim?"

"Yes."

"Are you okay, though? I mean—"

"I *know* what you mean, Flip. And the answer is no, I'm not okay. I don't know what Jim wants, and I don't know if I can stand another—"

But Madeline was back, her face frozen into a smile. "Well," she said too brightly, "I'm starved. Let's go get a burger and a few beers. Anna, you want to come along? We'll all go to Sam's Place. How about it?"

"I can't," Anna said, "I've got that meeting."

"Oh, that's right. Oh, well, come on, Flip. Let's go. I'm famished."

Flip started to follow her out, but then hesitated. He turned back to Anna. "Sure you'll be all right? I can stay—"

"I'm fine. But thanks. Oh, and by the way," Anna said, a lopsided smile coming to her lips, "skip the Ledbetter mansion. It's a dump."

"Really? Damn. Guess I'll just have to stay here a while longer." He shot her a devilishly handsome smile.

"Guess so," Anna replied, and pushed him out the door. But it wasn't five minutes later that she suddenly felt her nerves begin to crawl again. Galloway. He'd be along in another twenty minutes. Maybe she should have asked Flip to stay while Galloway was there. If Flip could hear the conversation, the insinuating questions the man was going to put to her about the employee buy-out, then maybe Flip would speak up. All the cockpit crews were aware of the pressure Miller put on them but, of course, none of them wanted to admit it officially. It could cost them their jobs.

No, she couldn't expect Flip to stick his neck in the noose for her or for Jim. Darn.

She fed the cat, stuffed some laundry into the dryer and straightened the tiny living room. She should have gone for a beer with them. Two beers. Never before in her life had Anna thought she needed a drink to get through something, not even Jim's funeral service. But this NTSB official made her nerves leap and quiver. There was just something about him, his brusqueness, the sharp, penetrating gaze. And his probing. He was like a hound dog on the scent, or maybe a pit bull hanging on.

"Oh, hell," she said, and strode purposefully to the kitchen counter and the notepad there. She scratched out a few words, found a thumbtack in her junk drawer and marched to the front door. She pinned up the note, locked the door and headed off down the hill, her hands jammed into her pockets. Five minutes later she was seated at a table alone in Three-Fingered Jack's Saloon, a nice tall cold beer sitting before her. *Here's to you, Galloway,* she thought, lifting the heavy mug.

CHAPTER FOUR

CHRIS GALLOWAY WAS no longer fond of flying. His attitude had nothing to do with safety; rather, as an NTSB investigator it was difficult to step aboard an airplane anywhere in the United States and remain anonymous.

He wasn't a liked individual. It was the circumstances that demanded his presence on airlines that created this response from airline employees. When Chris or other NTSB investigators came rushing in after a disaster had struck, they were greeted like the Grim Reaper. It didn't truly bother Chris, this misplaced resentment; instead, he viewed it as human reaction. And besides, he was often too exhausted to pay it much attention. What he usually did aboard flights was sleep.

"Mr. Galloway?" the flight attendant on WestAir's three o'clock to Winthrop asked.

"Yes, I'm Chris Galloway." He stepped inside the half-empty plane.

"Our pilot, John Henderson wanted to know when you boarded. Would you like to speak to him in the cockpit?"

"Sure, of course, that would be fine." What Chris really wanted to do was sit in the back and close his eyes for an hour.

"John Henderson," the pilot said, rising from his cramped seat and taking Chris's offered hand. "Welcome aboard, sir."

"Thanks," Chris said, smiling, trying to be friendly.

"On your way to Winthrop, huh?"

"That's right."

"Well, I wish you luck, sir. All of us at WestAir Express want to make our passengers as safe as possible."

"I'm sure you do." There was an awkward moment. "Well, I imagine you want to get runway clearance. I better take my seat."

"You're welcome to sit up front with us," the captain offered.

But Chris declined. They'd hate it.

It was a smooth takeoff. The Convair 580 lifted easily into the afternoon sky, then banked to the northeast, heading toward the tall barrier mountains. Their route would take them close to Canadian airspace, since Winthrop was practically on the border. Chris imagined it was going to be a pleasant flight; there was no one within four rows of him to disturb his thoughts, and there were only clear skies ahead. Minutes after the plane reached altitude he closed his eyes. He was out cold in seconds.

"Coffee, Mr. Galloway?"

Chris snapped awake. He rubbed his eyes with a hand, remembering he hadn't told the flight attendant he planned to sleep. Darn it. "Ah, sure, coffee would be fine."

"Cream, sugar?"

"Black, please."

The plane was passing over the foothills of the western Cascades. Ahead Chris could see the spiraling peaks, glistening white in the late spring sun. They were a different form of mountains than, say, the Rockies. The Cascades, though lower in altitude because they rose from sea level, had a massive, craggy look to them—deep narrow valleys, water twisting and rushing violently down jagged rock walls, rumbling to black depths below. And the trees. Magnificent green forests. Big trees that had never been touched by the hand of man.

The Pacific Northwest wilderness lay spread below him. It was raw. Wild. Pure. There had been a time in his life when he dreamed of living in this kind of pristine environment, but the years had slipped away. As a boy in upstate New York, he and his dad and big brother had camped in the mountains almost every summer weekend. They'd only given up when the snows fell in late October or early November. God, those had been the days. Where had the time gone?

"Your coffee, Mr. Galloway. Would you like a pillow, a blanket?"

"This is fine. Thanks." He gave her a weary smile and watched her make her way back up the narrow aisle. She was pretty and seemed genuinely friendly, although she wasn't as pretty as Anna Parish, he found himself thinking.

Anna Parish. Despite a gut feeling that she wasn't entirely fabricating Jim Fleisher's notebook, Chris's logical thought pattern was that Anna, like many of WestAir's employees, would gladly and willingly draw the blame for that crash away from the pilot and dump it squarely onto Miller's shoulders.

And Chris wasn't about to forget, either, that Anna Parish had been Fleisher's lover.

He shook off the notion and dwelled instead on the employee buy-out bid for the airline. Surely it had created hard feelings between the employees and the owner, Miller. And Miller seemed a hard case as it was, if the tape Chris had listened to was an example.

It was a messy investigation at best, with the employees pitted against their owner, and Miller resentfully blaming his workers for every last hitch in the system. But that was why he'd been called in after the initial investigation. Chris always got assigned the tough ones.

Anna Parish, he thought again. Was she blinded by her loyalty to fellow employees? Was that why she'd dwelled so intently on this purported notebook of Fleisher's? Could very well be. And as for her stability and credibility as a witness...

A ghost. How could such a poised woman sit in his office and insist she'd seen a ghost? Chris had been working at the NTSB for nearly ten years, and that was a new one on him.

Crazy. It was crazy for him to entertain the impossible images darting around his brain: shadowy phantoms, moans, white sheets. It was crazier still for Anna Parish to claim she'd seen her dead lover.

But Chris couldn't quite believe Miss Parish was insane. She appeared completely normal, except for that one thing, and he'd been out of line to bring it up. Her psychologist's file was for his eyes only, inadmissible in a hearing or in court. It had no relevance to his investigation, so he should have read it, then put it aside. The trouble was it had made him curious, fascinated—a stewardess who believed in a ghost.

Morty Heller had explained the situation away by saying that Anna Parish was suffering from survivor's guilt. She'd lived; her lover had died. She wouldn't, or couldn't let go, and Chris guessed that was what it was. Even if Anna Parish didn't agree.

The stewardess made another round, and Chris took a second cup of coffee and a bag of peanuts. He hadn't eaten since... well, last night. No, he'd had a doughnut at the NTSB office that morning, hadn't he? He raked a hand through his hair and let out a tired breath. Some life he'd been leading.

Below, the mountains seemed to stretch away in all directions. If a pilot did get into trouble, he'd be hard-pressed to find a spot to set down. The earth below was rocky and scored by deep, narrow cuts, with not a high meadow in sight. And yet if a plane did run into trouble, Chris would be called to delve into that pilot's reactions, the instant, stressful decisions he'd make when, in reality, anything short of a fatal crash would be a miracle. Still, Chris would probe and dig. Were there any choices the pilot could have made? Was there a town twenty miles to the south or west, an airstrip? Had the pilot made the correct moves, decisions, described his plane's condition properly to the control tower?

In the case of the March disaster near Winthrop all evidence Chris had seen pointed to pilot error, now carefully dubbed "human factors." And the pilot was, after all, ultimately responsible for any and all decisions made in his cockpit. Like the captain of a ship, the pilot's judgment was law. In Chris's estimation, thus far, Jim Fleisher had made a mistake.

He settled back in his seat, the warm coffee cup in his hands, and closed his eyes. The notebook. It was bothering Chris, an itch in his mind. It was a loose end. Perhaps it existed, perhaps not. Perhaps it contained nothing of interest at all even if it did exist. Regardless, Chris was hesitant to close the files on this case until he was damn good and sure that there was no pressure put on WestAir's pilots by the owner. He owed that much to the flying public. It was his job, and Anna Parish's depositions to the FAA and NTSB had turned out to be a snag in the case.

Chris opened his eyes and stared out the window. He rubbed his jaw and finished his second cup of coffee. God, he *was* tired. He was always tired, though. His job was like walking a high-tension wire. Seldom were there clear-cut answers to plane mishaps. And the icing on the cake was the constant battling between the FAA and the NTSB, all the bureaucratic hassles. The two agencies were often like two dogs sniffing each other, growling, establishing territories.

Many people thought the FAA's true function was muddled because not only was it charged with setting rules for the nation's air carriers but also with promoting the industry. The two tasks were often at odds. Naturally the FAA shied away from publicizing problems in the industry, but the truth was that since deregulation in the seventies, there were many problems, some unsolvable due to manpower shortage, lax federal laws and unscrupulous airline owners who took advantage of deregulation.

The NTSB, on the other hand, had plenty of clout, but was often stymied by the FAA. Great system. No wonder Chris's job was a real bitch.

There were other gripes, too, that Chris seldom had time to address. Not only was he overworked, but he was underpaid, as well. He'd been living for months out of hotels when he wasn't at his home base in Washington, D.C. And there he'd lived in a boarding house since his divorce when his wife left and moved back to Syracuse, New York. Chris hadn't had a day off in over eighteen months, and he was dragged out. It was no wonder at all that his wife had left him. And as for Todd, his teenage son, hell, Chris barely knew him anymore.

But he guessed he was about to get to know Todd better, because his son was going to spend the summer with him. In fact, Chris had called a house rental agency in Seattle to try to locate a suitable place for the two of them. Of course, Chris had no idea how long he and Todd would be in the northwest.... Anyway, the rental agent had found a few places but, typically, Chris hadn't had a chance to look at them yet. Hell, he never seemed to have time, much less a place to call home. No wonder he didn't know his own son. It hurt. Sometimes, alone at night, sitting in yet another hotel room, Chris felt like weeping for what he'd lost.

And yet...his job was vital. Chris believed in it. Without men like him the safety of every airline passenger across the nation would be at risk.

"We're about twenty minutes out of Winthrop," the stewardess said to him, breaking into his reverie. "Can I get you anything else?"

"No, thank you. Another cup of coffee and I won't need a plane to fly," he quipped.

"Oh, was it too strong? I—"

"No, no," Chris said, shaking his head. "I only meant I drink too darn much of the stuff."

Satisfied she'd done her job properly, the woman smiled and moved on.

Chris stared out the window again and reviewed his plans for the next twenty-four hours. He'd talk to Anna Parish, of course, and the tower personnel. He'd track down the mechanics. Then there was the other surviving flight attendant, Madeline Vernon. But it was Lee Miller he really wanted to interview. He'd heard too much about the entrepreneur—all bad—since flying into Seattle last week.

Clearly Miller could be one of those men running a small commuter airline who had myopic vision, chasing profits, forgoing safety. Nothing made Chris angrier than someone entrusted with the public safety who betrayed that trust.

Chris deplaned at the new Winthrop airport and took a short cab ride into town. The place took him by surprise. He'd expected chalets, cute little trinket shops, a mountain flavor to the ski resort. But Winthrop, whose welcome sign read population 805, was a replica of an Old West town right down to the wooden sidewalks and saloons. He tried to find a word for the place and came up with charming.

"So where do you want to get dropped, mister?" the driver asked.

"Bluff Avenue. I'm looking for Anna Parish."

"I know Anna. Nice lady. House is right up on the hillside."

The cabbie drove through town, all three blocks of it, and made a swinging curve to the right. The road rose, and there was Bluff. On the corner was a small yellow wood-frame house, vintage 1930s, and the painted mailbox read Parish.

He paid the driver and stepped out, toting his overnight bag. There was a tidy stone walk that led from the curb to the front porch. Lining the stones on both sides were spring flowers—daffodils and tulips of many colors. The lawn was trimmed and green, and to the side of the house was a huge cottonwood tree, its upper branches lying on the gravel roof.

Chris strode up to the front door. Inside, in a sunny, south-facing bay window, a gray cat lay napping on pastel cushions. Chris smiled inwardly until he saw the note pinned on the door: "Gone to Three-Fingered Jack's. Down the hill, two blocks. On the left. Anna."

Three-Fingered Jack's, Chris thought. It could only be a saloon. Anger simmered inside him. A saloon. He was tired and hungry and in no mood for this avoidance game Miss Parish seemed to be enjoying.

He glanced down the street. The cab was long gone, of course. His overnight bag was still in his hand, and he didn't have an inkling where the nearest hotel was. He'd been planning on asking Anna Parish.

Chris walked around to the back of the house, pulled open a screen door that led to a porch and deposited his suitcase inside, next to an old broken wicker chair.

His hands jammed into his trouser pockets, he walked down the hill and around the curve to town. After a block of checking signs and bars, he stopped a passerby and asked if he knew where Three-Fingered Jack's was.

The man pointed. "Right on this corner. Half a block. Say, you new to town?"

"Yes," Chris replied.

"It's a nice place, huh?"

"Seems very nice. I only just got in."

"Well, stay awhile. We're real friendly folk here."

Chris smiled. "Thanks. I can see that."

He strode on. It *was* a friendly place, a sort of laid-back mountain community. And despite his frustration over Anna Parish he had to admire someone who could make a go of small-town life. No stress, no rushing here and there, no traffic jams on the way to the airport where you knew you'd either missed your flight or it was delayed forty-five minutes. He glanced across the street toward the bank and corner grocery store. Locals stood out front, chatting in the afternoon sun. Dogs ran unleashed up and down the wooden sidewalks, tails wagging. Chris realized Winthrop was similar to the little town where he'd been raised. But that was a lifetime ago... before he'd gotten his job as an aeronautical engineer in Washington, D.C., before he'd signed up with the NTSB. Before the work overload and his divorce.

Fleetingly Chris thought of his son, Todd, and all those stolen years they should have been spending together—camping, hiking, fishing.

Suddenly a cold sweat seized him. The kid was due to arrive in Seattle tomorrow, and Chris hadn't taken the time to check out those rental houses. Damn. Well, he guessed they'd have to live out of a hotel for a while. For a few days, a week maybe, just until he had time to get a place lined up.

Chris's hand paused on the doorknob of Three-Fingered Jack's Saloon. What in the name of God was he going to do with a child in tow? His thoughts were so consumed with the problem that he had to stand in the entranceway and force himself to remember where he was and what he was doing there.

Anna Parish. Yes. He needed to talk to the woman. He'd think about his son later.

He spotted her then, sitting alone at a table near the back wall. The place was big. Lots of bar space in the center, dozens of tables and a few pool tables to the left of the bar. There were the ubiquitous neon beer signs, trophy heads of deer, postcards from the owner's friends on the walls. The tables were wooden, scarred. They'd seen a few good Saturday nights in this joint. Clearly it was a local hangout. Chris started toward Anna and passed a long "joiners" table where men sat studying blueprints over tall, frosty mugs of beer. A businessman's hangout, too, he surmised.

Anna Parish looked up at him and nodded toward the chair opposite hers. "Want a beer?" she asked as he pulled out the chair, scraping it on the worn hardwood floor.

But Chris declined. "Coffee."

"Black?"

"That'll be fine."

Anna signaled a cocktail waitress who was clad in jeans, checked shirt and a Stetson.

Anna eyed him. "Have you eaten? Are you hungry?"

"I'm fine." He folded his hands and stared at her. When the waitress was gone, he said, "I'm not sure I like your choice of spots to continue our interview, Miss Parish."

But she only shrugged. "Anna. Call me Anna. I'm uptight enough as it is."

He studied her for a moment, his cool blue eyes giving away nothing. "It's Anna and Chris, then. But it's not going to change anything."

"Oh, I'm sure of that," she said under her breath.

He looked at her attire—the old University of Washington sweatshirt, the shorts he'd noticed before sitting down. And her hair. It was hastily swept up and pinned somehow. Springing dark strands escaped to frame her face and the pale column of her neck. Her cheeks showed a hint of pink, and he noticed then what lovely skin she had. Translucent, flawless. She was very delicate-looking sitting there, pretty and fragile, her hazel eyes framed by long, spiky lashes looking sadly into her beer.

He wondered aloud, "How many have you had?" He nodded at her drink.

"This is still my first," she said. "But I feel like emptying the whole keg."

"I told you on the phone I'm not some kind of ogre, Miss . . . Anna."

"Aren't you?"

He let it drop. And he realized suddenly that he wasn't going to press this woman as hard as he'd intended. Surprise gripped him momentarily, and he became aware of an emptiness deep in his gut. He glanced up from his coffee cup to find her watching him, her head tilted slightly. He pulled himself together. This was business.

He heard her sigh and saw the rise and fall of her chest. "Look," she said, "I'm not in the habit of missing appointments. But I admit I deliberately blew you off this morning. I just couldn't . . . I couldn't go through another interview." She gave a strained smile. "Just doing your job, right? A simple government employee."

"My job," he said, "is to get at the facts."

Anna laughed. Again it was forced. "I don't suppose my . . . let's call it my *experiences* the past couple of months fit into that category, do they?"

Chris sat back in his chair and folded his arms across his chest. He held her gaze for a long time before saying, "You don't fit into any category I've ever come across, lady."

"I'm *not* crazy," she said ardently. "I'm a perfectly run-of-the-mill woman. But I'm not going to sit here and lie to you. I *have* seen Jim Fleisher."

Chris rubbed his jaw and felt a muscle working tightly in his cheek. She seemed normal. All of her reactions truly seemed as normal as the next person's. And if her story weren't so off-the-wall, he'd almost believe her. Almost.

He picked up his cup, took a long sip and set it down. He looked her straight in the eye. "Let me ask you this, Anna," he said, "and then I'll drop the subject."

"Shoot."

"Do you *want* to see Jim Fleisher?"

A curious look played across her delicate features, and Chris couldn't quite read it. There was fear, but also regret. And sadness. He wanted to withdraw his question suddenly.

"I," she began, "I don't know quite how to answer you. I miss Jim. I loved him. But . . . but he's not the same now. He's so . . . so tormented."

Very quietly Chris asked, "Why do you think he's tormented, Anna?"

She looked at him squarely. "Because he's being blamed for all those deaths and he wasn't at fault."

"I see." A moment of grave silence fell between them. "So who *is* to blame, Anna? You tell me. Exactly where does the responsibility lie?"

"Right on Lee Miller's shoulders," she replied without a second's hesitation.

He watched her carefully, his face utterly expressionless. "Go on."

"I told you."

"I want you to elaborate."

"I told you," she repeated. "I've told everyone. Miller runs a bottom-line operation. He does everything on the cheap. Maintenance, training, stuff like that."

"You know all this as fact?"

"I have no proof. But there's a lot of talk."

"And where there's smoke, there's fire. Is that it?"

"Yes."

"So you think there could have been a mechanical failure that morning on 629?"

"Maybe. I don't know."

"You realize the wreckage was gone over with a fine-tooth comb?"

"Well, yes, but—"

"But nothing. There was no mechanical failure. It would have been found. We have what's known as a Go Team that flies immediately to the scene of an accident and—"

"I know all that," she interrupted. "But they could have missed something."

"Highly unlikely."

"But not impossible," Anna put in.

Chris chose to ignore her inexperience. Instead he asked, "So what other unsafe practices does Lee Miller condone?"

"Okay," she said, leaning back toward him. "Miller plays mind games with his pilots."

"Go on."

"You know, he has subtle ways of making them feel inferior if they hold too long on a runway or maybe want to have a tire rechecked. You know."

"So you're saying Miller tells them their judgment is poor."

"He doesn't say it right straight out. He . . . he implies it. He once told Jim that Truscott Express pilots fly in any kind of weather. That those pilots are real aces who care about their passengers."

"Go on."

"Well, say a WestAir flight is late getting into Seattle and passengers miss their connections. Or maybe they make the connection, but their luggage doesn't."

"I see. But Miller has never come right out and actually *ordered* one of his pilots to fly. To your knowledge, that is."

"No. I told you. He implies things. He pits one pilot against another. He'll say stuff like, 'Well, John flew through that weather last week and didn't have a hitch.'"

"How can you know Jim Fleisher wasn't just as susceptible to that kind of mind game as the next pilot?"

Anna shook her head vehemently. "He kept a record. I told you. He absolutely refused to play those games with his passengers' safety at stake." He saw her eyes glistening then. "If only his notebook had been found. You'd see. You'd believe every word I'm telling you."

Chris said nothing. He merely watched her fight for control.

"Listen," she said, "I'm not a nut case. Jim . . . Jim's been . . . appearing to me, you know, because of his notebook."

"He *told* you that?"

"No," Anna shot back, "he's never spoken. But he . . . he has a way of conveying it. I mean, I can almost hear him in my head. It's . . . it's so awful."

"Anna," Chris said with more compassion than he'd known he possessed, "have you considered you might be hallucinating? Have you at least considered that possibility?"

She nodded slowly. "Of course I did at first. But not anymore."

"I see."

"You don't see at all. I *loved* Jim. We were going to be married. All that's true. And I do miss him terribly. But I'm positive I'm as sane as you are. Jim has come to me several times. He's *real.*"

Again Chris offered no words.

"Look," she said, "I can't give any explanation whatsoever. I can only take it on faith. Jim wants me to prove that he didn't cause that crash, and I don't know how to do it."

Her voice was so filled with conviction, with anguish, that Chris felt sorry for her and, frankly, he just couldn't believe she was crazy. She was so sure. . . .

If Chris had learned nothing else in his ten years with the NTSB, he'd learned that seldom were answers as simple as they first appeared. *Had* Lee Miller challenged his pilots to push the limits? Had some sort of competitiveness been awakened in Fleisher that he wasn't even aware of?

He needed a true "feel" for the crash. If Chris could get that special sense that sometimes came to him on an investigation . . .

Suddenly his head snapped up. "Listen," he said, unaware of her startled expression, "how far is the crash site from town?"

"A few miles."

"Is it reachable by car?"

"Well . . . yes."

"Do you have a car?"

"I—"

"*Do* you have a car?"

"Yes. A four-wheel-drive Subaru. But—"

"Can we drive there?" And abruptly Chris was aware of all the color draining from her face. She sat there looking stunned for a very long time, and he was almost ready to apologize, to say forget it.

"All right," she whispered.

"What?"

"I said I'll drive you there."

"You will?"

"I just said I would."

"Okay. All right," he replied, then pushed his chair out from the table, but not before he saw the dread in those soft hazel eyes.

CHAPTER FIVE

THEY WALKED BACK to her house in the fading sun of late afternoon. Side by side they strode up the flower-lined walk, and he stood silently while she unlocked her front door. Flip and Madeline weren't back yet, and somehow she was grateful not to have to deal with introductions, with Flip's lightheartedness, Madeline's anxiety.

"We better take along some jackets," she said. "It can get real chilly in the evening around here."

"I don't have one with me," Chris said.

"Oh, I'll grab one of Flip's. He won't mind."

She went into her room and pulled an anorak from her closet.

"It could turn cold," she started to say, returning to the living room. Chris Galloway stood, back to her, looking at photographs on her bookshelf. Photographs of her and Jim, she realized. Pictures of happier days that she left in place out of love and loyalty and the aching need to remember.

"Nice pictures," he said offhandedly.

"Thanks. That's Jim."

"Yes, I know."

"Of course, you've seen his file."

"Yes, I have."

An uncomfortable moment stretched out too long between them, the silence mounting like a bill that would come due.

"Well, as I was saying," Anna finally said, "you never know when a snowstorm might blow in. There were some clouds coming down the valley." She pulled one of Flip's jackets off the coatrack by the front door. "We better get going. You won't be able to see a thing once it gets dark."

"Exactly how far is it?" Chris asked.

"Well, not far from the airport. But by road a few miles, four or five. Over a ridge, you know, so we have to drive around the long way." She started toward the door, but his voice stopped her.

"Look, maybe you could just give me directions. I mean, you don't have to go. I could—"

"No, I'll go, really. I think...I think maybe it's a good idea."

"You're sure."

She nodded solemnly, her mind made up. Maybe there was something there, at the place Jim had died. Maybe his notebook was there, lying on the ground, uncovered now that the snow had melted. Maybe Jim wanted her to go. Or maybe she was being just plain morbid. Crazy and morbid, unable to let go. "We better head on out," she said firmly, "before it gets dark."

She turned north out of town, driving the familiar highway. Her hands trembled slightly on the steering wheel, and she hoped Chris didn't notice. Her mind fought itself, fear vying with hope. But this short trip had become a sort of odyssey for Anna, something she had to do no matter what. She couldn't think of anything to say to the man who sat next to her, and he didn't seem to be interested in making conversation, either. It was a bit awkward, but then Chris Galloway didn't seem the least bit concerned with appearances or courtesy or anything else. He was single-minded, dogged, on a crusade, just as she'd thought at first. But maybe she could use his stubborn pursuit of the truth so that Jim would be vindicated and he could rest.

"Nice country," Chris remarked.

"Um." She was looking for the turnoff, a dirt road that snaked through the hills behind the airport. It led close to the spot where flight 629 had skimmed a ridge, caught the trees with a wingtip and crashed into the ground nose first. She shut her eyes briefly, trying to chase the waking nightmares, the black trees, the screams. . . .

She wasn't sure she'd recognize the exact spot; she hadn't been back there before. "I hope I can find it. I mean, there won't be a sign or anything."

"We'll find it," he said with assurance.

He was right, of course. The spot was unmistakable. There were gouges in the earth, raw furrows as if a giant plow had turned the dirt up. Slivers of metal glinted in the fading sun, and the burned stumps of Douglas firs stood in a row, ghostly reminders of that terrible day. Anna stopped the car and turned the key off, sat there and stared through the windshield at the aftermath of devastation. "My God," she whispered.

For a long time they both just sat there, heads still, the quiet of the forest surrounding them. The sun was slipping behind the ridge and gusts of cold wind rattled the windows. Somewhere a squirrel scolded them from the brush, and the treetops soughed in the breeze, a strange, unrelenting moan. The back of Anna's neck prickled as a long shadow fell over the car.

Chris was as silent as she was, as if taking in the scene, absorbing it, living it. How many ghastly sites like this had he viewed? Too many, Anna thought, too, too many.

After what seemed an eternity, he finally moved his hand to the door latch. Still looking through the window, he asked, "Are you all right?"

Anna took a deep, ragged breath. "Sure," she said, "just give me another second. I haven't been back here. It's—"

"It would have looked entirely different," he offered. "Sure you don't want to stay in the car while I walk around?"

"No, no, I want to go, too."

He gave her an odd, piercing glance, light brows drawn down over his eyes. He set his jaw in that way he had, as if steeling himself, but his expression remained implacable. She wondered if he was affected at crash sites, if anything got to him anymore, and started to ask him, but he was already out of the car, standing in the dying rays of sun on the scarred hillside.

Anna stepped out on her side. The cold, wet wind blew down out of the Cascades as a final spear of light glared, then faded with the setting sun. She shivered and reached into the car for her anorak. "Want the jacket?" she called to Chris.

He came around the car, took Flip's jacket from her with a brief, muttered "Thanks" and shrugged it on. The squirrel chattered more angrily.

Chris was methodical in his examination of the area. He kept the ridge where the plane had come in to his back and began walking slowly to the northwest on an angle to where the aircraft had soared into its final resting place. He walked slowly, hands in the pockets of the jacket, collar up against the chilling wind. His head was down as he moved patiently along the track of the downed plane. Every so often he'd stop, pick something up and examine it for a long time, his brows drawn together. Then he'd move on, checking the angle of the ridge to his back until something else caught his eye.

Anna came up behind him, almost afraid to speak, to break his reverie. "Find anything?" she asked quietly, her face turned from the biting wind.

"No."

"Did you expect to?"

"No."

"Then why...?"

"I have to see the place, figure the plane's path, see how it hit. I need the feel, the taste of it, if you want to call it that. Sometimes it helps." He shrugged. "Sometimes it doesn't."

"Is it helping here?"

"I don't know yet."

He kept walking, looking, still stopping once in a while to glance toward the ridge in the direction of the airport, gauging the distance, the flight line. Anna left him and wandered aimlessly around the area, kicking at clods of dirt or stones. She picked up a ballpoint pen that lay in the dirt and held it, studying it as if it would tell her something.

She dropped the pen absently and kept walking, her shoulders hunched against the chill. What was she looking for? Jim's journal? Blue, it was blue, a blue spiral notebook. But there was nothing like that, nothing at all. She tried to feel Jim's presence, closed her eyes and pictured him. Sadness filled her, an awful, yawning emptiness. He'd been alive one moment, full of life and plans and love, and then…nothing. No, Jim wasn't here, not now. Wherever his spirit wandered so restlessly, it wasn't here on this ravaged hillside. Or was his spirit radiating that sadness, that guilt and sense of futility, or was it the collective sigh of all the dead souls on this lonely spot?

A shoe lay half-buried in the ground, a woman's pump lying there all by itself in the cold dirt.

She felt tears building up behind her eyes, burning. The shoe blurred in her vision. Who had worn that shoe? Did she miss it? Did she wonder what had happened to her shoe? Did she wonder anything at all? Was she alive?

Anna wandered on aimlessly, hands deep in the anorak pockets, hot tears pressing at her eyes. A scrap of cloth caught her attention, a piece of plastic. The detritus of a disaster.

Jim had died here. Jim and Len and so many others. Their lives had ended right here, right where she stood. What had Jim thought at the end? He would have known he was going to crash. *She'd* known it, sitting in the back of the plane, so Jim certainly had. *Oh, God, Jim,* she cried silently, *what happened? Why? What do you want me to do?*

The scolding of the squirrel was more distant now—he'd retreated from the unsettling location. But the wind still sighed in the tops of the tall fir trees as the light diminished. A soughing, moaning sound, the anguished cries of the dead.

Anna looked up at the darkening sky. So alone. They were all so very alone. Something broke inside her then, like a dam bursting. The tears spilled over, and she couldn't control them anymore. She turned and headed back to her car, stumbling blindly over the rough ground, almost running.

Later she wasn't sure how things had gotten so out of control. All she knew was that she was leaning against the car door, engulfed in abject misery, sobbing, and he was there mouthing soothing words.

How long she stood there so dismally alone Anna didn't know. She hugged herself, rocking, crying, swamped with misery. Chris must have been standing close, uncertain, out of his element. Somewhere in the far corners of her mind she was aware of him speaking to her hesitantly, helplessly.

"Oh, God, why?" Anna was sobbing. "Why did so many die? Why was I saved? Why did Jim have to die?" Hugging her belly, she rocked forward, the sobs racking every fiber of her being.

She was never sure, either, when Chris stepped closer and pulled her to him. She had no awareness at first of being held against his chest or his strong hands moving up and down her back. She was a wounded child, so desperately alone, so in need, and Chris was simply there. At first.

"It's all right," he whispered against her hair. "It'll be all right." He pressed her closer, gently, carefully, uncomfortably.

Eventually the straining sobs gave way to hiccups and a streaming nose, to Anna reaching up between them to wipe at her swollen eyes. Chris shifted slightly and produced a handkerchief. Silently he pressed it into her hand. She blew her nose and drew in a deep, quavering breath. The handkerchief was balled in her fist.

Awareness crawled slowly into her. Yet she didn't move; she couldn't. There was an emptiness, a huge hole deep inside her that craved human contact. It didn't even matter who. Anna simply allowed the closeness to go on and on, willing the hole to be filled.

"Better now?" she heard him ask.

His hand was still at her back, gliding up and down, warming. She began to move away, an inch at a time. And then she could see his face, his expression, and an unaccountable jolt ripped through her belly. There was something in that look, in those light eyes, something...

Suddenly she knew. Mingling with the weariness, the bleakness of a man who had spent his life's energy, was the very same aching need she'd just experienced.

He'd felt it, too, then, the gut-wrenching loneliness. Anna remained frozen, half in his embrace still, and searched his eyes, the windows to this man's soul. Oh, yes, so very alone... It was as if they were the last two survivors of a holocaust.

She moved away a little farther, fumbling with the hankie, unsure. "I didn't mean to... I'm sorry," she began, dropping her gaze, embarrassed.

"It's understandable," he said, knowing he sounded as awkward as she felt. "Listen, why don't I drive on back into town?"

"But are you through here?"

He nodded, studying her. "I didn't find anything concrete, but there's a feel to a site like this."

He took the car keys from her, and their fingers brushed for an instant, a mere fraction of a second, yet the contact sent an inexplicable tingling sensation up Anna's arm. She met his eyes in confusion. Yes, he'd felt it, too. Quickly she turned and went around to the passenger side, letting herself in, her cheeks stinging from the cold, raw wind.

The episode rested unspoken between them as Chris switched on the headlights and backed her car around. What had happened on that hillside? Anna was forced to wonder. But before she could search for an answer she was buffeted by an insane thought: what if Jim had been watching? What if his spirit had reached into her soul and felt that instant of contact between her and this stranger? Anna told herself she had nothing whatsoever to feel guilty about. But the horrible sensation persisted as she sat unmoving, staring out the passenger window, the damp handkerchief still crushed in her hand. Only once did she brave a glance at Chris Galloway on the ride home. He, too, was staring straight ahead, his expression set in granite.

They turned onto the main highway and drove into town. Anna fumbled for something to say, anything, but the words clogged in her throat.

It was Chris who finally broke the terrible silence. "I left my bag on your back porch," he said tonelessly.

Anna tried her voice. "Oh, you . . ." She cleared her throat. "You don't have a room yet?"

"No."

"Well . . . well, it shouldn't be a problem. It's off-season. There are lots of rooms."

"I thought you could recommend something," he said.

"Oh." Here they were, trading inanities, trying to obliterate what had happened between them. "You could try the Winthrop Lodge. It's a bed-and-breakfast place, very nice."

"That sounds fine."

He pulled up in front of her house, which was still dark. Good. Flip and Madeline weren't home yet. She couldn't face explanations right now. Chris got his bag from the back porch, and Anna moved over into the driver's seat.

God, she felt miserable. There was this *thing* between them now that couldn't be eradicated, something that shouldn't have happened. She realized suddenly, full of shame, that the "thing" made her terribly aware of Chris Galloway as a man, made her aware in a way she hadn't been since Jim.

Anna squeezed her eyes shut for a moment, willing these new thoughts to go away. But they persisted. Beneath the tears and sobs she'd allowed herself to enjoy the comfort of a man's embrace again. It was the truth. She knew it, and Chris surely knew it, too.

Chris climbed into the passenger side, tossing his bag into the back. She fought for control, for the down-to-earth person beneath the frayed nerves. She told herself it was her jumbled emotions; they were all mixed up. Fear, love, hate, desire. How was she supposed to separate one from the other? Perhaps Chris realized this. Perhaps he thought nothing of the episode at all. The best thing she could do was pretend it hadn't happened.

She drove him to the Winthrop Lodge and stopped the car in front of the charming old building.

"Well, thank you, it looks like a nice place," he said.

"It is. My parents always stay here when they visit," she managed to say.

He didn't get out of the car, though, just sat without speaking for a time. "Look," he finally said, "I shouldn't have made you go out there."

She looked straight ahead through the windshield, her hands on the steering wheel. "You didn't *make* me."

"You wouldn't have gone yourself."

"No, probably not."

"I owe you an apology."

"No, really, you don't. I could have refused." Oh, God.

He didn't reply, and the silence hung between them, full of unspoken words.

"Well, I better go—" Anna began.

"Look, I'd like to—" Chris said.

They both stopped short. Chris gave a brief laugh. "What I wanted to say is, I'd like to take you to dinner or something. On the NTSB. It's the least I can do."

"What's the 'or something'?" she couldn't help asking.

"A figure of speech. I guess dinner would taste better."

"You don't have to do that," she said, still staring ahead out the windshield.

"I know I don't have to. But it's one way to get a good meal, I've learned. Take a local to dinner," he said wryly.

She thought for a moment, weighing his offer. She didn't know how to behave; she was too out of practice. If she said no, he'd leave her alone. On the other hand, if she said yes, she could show him that she was a perfectly sane human being. And then perhaps he'd give credence to what she'd been trying to tell him about Miller and WestAir and Jim.

"Okay," Anna replied.

"You name the place."

"Well, there *is* this place. But it's the most expensive in town." She was amazed at the easiness in her tone. "Will that assuage your guilt?"

"It's a deal."

She turned her head to look at him, but it was dark in her car, and she could only see the shadows that molded his features and the light from the street glinting off his right cheekbone. "I'll pick you up in an hour. Is that all right?"

"Fine."

My God, what am I doing? she thought as she drove home. She had a date with an NTSB investigator. Well, not exactly a date. She should look on the practical side of it. Sure. If he wanted to make up for that awful trip this afternoon, fine, she'd let him. Why fight Chris Galloway? Why not help him in this investigation as much as she could? She had nothing to lose and a lot to gain. Just maybe she could convince him she was right about Miller and the accident. It sure wouldn't hurt to try.

The house was lit up now. Flip and Madeline were home, then. She pushed open the front door to find the house littered with biking shoes and helmets, the radio wailing country and western music. Madeline's bedroom door was closed, and giggling came from inside her room.

"I'm back!" Anna called out. She was uncomfortable when Flip and Madeline were so blatant about their lovemaking. It made her jealous and sad and hateful. She tried to cover it up, but it was so unfair that she had to live with a happy couple. It just pointed out her loneliness unbearably.

"Anna?" came Madeline's voice.

"Who else?"

"Where've you been?"

"Oh, for goodness' sake, Mad, come out here. I can't hear you!"

Madeline emerged from her room, carefully closing the door behind her. She had on a bathrobe, her hair was mussed, her mouth bruised from kisses. Anna studiously looked away.

"Where were you?" Madeline repeated.

"I was with Chris Galloway."

Madeline paled. "The . . . investigator?"

"He's not such a bad guy," Anna said, shrugging.

"Oh, sure, he's your newest best friend."

"He's taking me to dinner tonight," she said blandly.

Madeline stared. "Are you crazy?"

"No, why?" She felt spiteful, almost enjoying Madeline's discomfort. It wasn't fair that Madeline still had her man and her life while Anna's was gone.

"Anna, he'll pick your brain. He's using you. For God's sake, he's your enemy."

"What can he find out from me that would hurt Jim? If he really listens to me, he'll look more closely at Miller."

"Oh, so you're Mata Hari, vamp infiltrating the enemy's lair. Right, Anna."

"Why not? What have I got to lose?"

"Do you really think this Galloway is going to listen to you?" Madeline asked.

"I can try," Anna said. "He can't do anything to me."

"It's a waste of your time," Madeline said angrily.

"It's a free dinner," Anna said.

"Maddeee" came Flip's voice from her room.

"Just watch it, Anna. Be careful. Don't trust this guy. I'm certainly not going to. I dread that interview tomorrow."

"I'll tell him to go easy on you," Anna said facetiously.

"Oh, sure, that'll convince him."

"Listen, Madeline, don't worry. He's not out for blood. He's just trying to solve this case. If we can provide him with information, it's to our advantage, too."

"Madeline!" Flip called. "I can't find my clean socks!"

"Just a minute, honey!" she called back. "Anna, just watch out. Watch what you say."

"I will. You better go in to Flip. It sounds like he needs you."

Madeline rolled her eyes and went back into her room, but not before shooting Anna a last warning glance.

Anna showered quickly and went back to her room to dress. She put on a skirt, a striped blouse, a jacket over it, flat shoes. No-nonsense clothes, not so very different from her work uniform. No frills, no ruffles or wild colors.

Flip knocked on her door just then. "Anna? You decent?"

"As usual," she said. "Come on in."

Flip was upset about something. It took him a few false starts before he got it out. "Uh, you're going out with this NTSB character tonight?"

"In twenty minutes," she said, looking at her watch.

"Madeline's worried. You know how she's been about, well, about this whole thing. You won't . . . ?"

"Flip, I promise I won't tell Chris Galloway that Madeline's seen Jim, too. I promise. So he'll only think I'm nuts, not my roommate. But I sure wish she'd tell him about it and help me out. Maybe he'd listen to me then.'' While she talked Anna was putting pearl studs on.

"The man's not going to listen," Flip said. "And you'd be wise to button it up yourself."

Anna cocked her head. "You, too, Flip."

"Me, too, what?"

"Don't you have any loyalty to Jim, either?"

"That's not what I—"

"Oh, but it is," Anna countered. "You *could* go to the NTSB with what you know about Lee Miller. Any of you fly-boys could. But you won't. You're afraid of losing your jobs, of admitting you've fallen prey to Miller's tactics. If you really want my—" But she suddenly fell silent. "I'm sorry, Flip."

He shrugged. "You're just upset."

"I'm not upset."

"Come on, Anna, you've been a wreck since Jim first started..." He whistled. "Listen to me? Now you've got me talking that stuff."

"What stuff?"

"That business about Jim's ghost."

"You think it's bunk?"

"I don't know what to think."

"And do you think Madeline's crazy, too?"

"I think both of you could do with a good long rest."

Anna shook her head. It was no good. Flip had been humoring them.

"You'll be careful with this guy tonight?" Flip asked then. "That's all I'm asking."

Anna sighed. "Thanks for caring, Flip, but I've got to play this hand the way it was dealt."

She had to hurry putting on her makeup. The bathroom was still steamy, and she kept wiping off the mirror. Makeup base, a touch of blush. Mascara, pale pink lipstick. She took a hand towel and wiped the fogged up mirror again, squeaking the towel across the glass. Leaning forward, she wiped at some mascara that had blotted on her eyelid.

Darn that Flip, she thought. It was easy for him to say, "Get some rest, Anna." Really easy. He had nothing on the line. Only Madeline. And Flip was positioning her just the way he wanted to. Yeah, it was too easy for him.

Damn, the glass was steaming up again. She dabbed at her eyelid in a hurry. A shadow moved in the mirror, a face...Flip was bugging her in the bathroom now, she thought, exasperated. She swiped at the mirror again. "Damn it," she muttered to herself, ignoring him.

The face materialized in the now-clear glass, reflected from behind her shoulder. Anna peered closer at it, and the glimpse was like a blow, lethal and swift, buckling her knees, sucking away her breath.

Jim. Jim's face in the mirror, Jim's features reflected in the misted glass, staring at her, meeting her eyes. She stood stock-still, wide-eyed, her pulse thudding like a trip-hammer, gripping the edge of the sink with white knuckles.

Her mouth formed his name, but no sound emerged. It was Jim, his eyes riveted to hers. She stood, frozen in place, staring, staring into his dead eyes as the mirror slowly fogged up. She searched his waxen face, desperate for an answer. *Why?* she cried silently. *Why are you here, Jim? What do you want?*

Anna held her breath, the blood in her ears pounding as slowly, too slowly, the steam began to form on the glass again. Jim's features began to diffuse as the mist shrouded the reflection of his eyes, his nose, his chin. She could still make out his mouth, but just. His lips were pale, bloodless, twisted into an ironic smile she'd never seen. She sucked in a breath, held it, clinging to the sink with white fingers. Slowly his mouth began to dissipate until it faded completely, and she was staring in mute terror at the white fogged surface of the empty mirror.

Anna gasped and sagged, only her grip on the sink keeping her upright. Oh, God, why hadn't she whirled on him, demanded an answer to why he wouldn't leave her in peace? He was driving her crazy, utterly mad. What did he want?

She had it suddenly, the answer. This time Jim had come because he knew. He knew what had happened that afternoon on the lonely hillside where his life had ended.

CHAPTER SIX

ANNA'S HANDS STILL SHOOK as she drove to pick up Chris. Maybe she'd tell him that dinner was off. She'd go on home, fix herself some soup, climb into bed. Clearly she wasn't ready for dinner or anything else with a man no matter how innocent the occasion.

She pulled up in front of his lodge and let out a long, ragged breath. A thought brushed her then, suddenly and without forewarning: Jim had no right whatsoever to control her life any longer.

Just as quickly as the notion touched her, she forced it down guiltily. He did have a right—it had only been a few months since his death. And she'd broken down in front of a man, a stranger, and the man had held her, stroked her back as if she'd been a child. She cringed, shrinking from what she'd done that afternoon, what she'd let Chris Galloway do. How sad and lonely she must be to have let that happen, sadder and more desperately alone than she'd realized.

Jim—his wraith, his spirit, whatever she dared call it—was probably her guilt, personified in the man she was betraying.

But, God, how could she betray a dead man?

"Hello," a voice came through the passenger window. "I was in the bar and saw you pull up." He opened the car door. "Mind if I . . . ?"

"Oh, sure, climb on in." So much for canceling the meal.

Anna pulled onto the road and willed herself to relax. She'd put Jim out of her mind, banish any thought of him. She'd do nothing this evening to damage her credibility with Chris Galloway. So she'd obliterate that scene in the bathroom and act like a woman going to dinner. She'd do it even if it killed her.

"Dark road," Chris said. "You sure there's a lodge at the end of this thing?"

"Oh, it's up there," Anna replied. "Way up, though." She downshifted, taking a steep curve smoothly.

"Deer!" Chris suddenly called out, and she swerved, narrowly missing a doe and her fawn. "That was close," he said, sitting back again.

"They're all over these roads."

"People hit them often?"

"I'm afraid too often."

He wasn't pressing her, anyway, Anna realized. At least not yet. And she had to admit to herself it was pleasant having company in the car again. Male companionship. Somehow it seemed as if Jim had been gone a terribly long time. And she was so lonely, tired of being solitary, tired of seeing other couples, happy couples like Flip and Madeline. It must have been the desolation that had made her react as she had. Her body, starved for affection, for a man's comfort, had simply taken over. It was normal. She needn't feel so damn guilty just because she'd given in to her own needs for a moment.

The image of Jim in her bathroom mirror only an hour before crawled into her mind. But that wasn't Jim, not really. It was a shade of the man, a tormented soul. No, the spirit that came to her wasn't her lover. Jim was dead.

Anna glanced quickly at Chris and back to the road again. She'd work on him carefully tonight, feel him out about his thoughts on Jim's notebook. She'd make him believe her. And he would help in whatever way he could, because Mr. Chris Galloway was indeed a pro, an insistent, determined man who would doggedly track any lead to get at those vital facts of his.

"Sun Mountain Lodge is right up there." She pointed. Through the dark stands of fir trees lights could be seen now, stretching along a rim of the mountain, the stars bright in the black bowl of sky above. Anna's window was half rolled down, and a crisp pine scent filled the car.

"Looks beautiful."

"It's a great place," she said, "and it's expanded a lot recently."

"The ski area?"

"Yes," she said, pulling into a parking lot. "That and the influx of people to the Pacific Northwest. When they aren't out on the water in their boats, they flock to the mountains."

"And you, Anna? Is that what drove you out of the Seattle area—too many people?"

She dropped the car keys into her purse and cocked her head. "I guess so. But I've always liked the mountains. I like to hike and ski. You know. I fish sometimes, too."

Chris shook his head as they crossed the pavement to the imposing entrance. "God, I used to do those things. In the Adirondack Mountains with my dad and older brother. It was . . . I suppose I'd look back now and say a pretty good time in my life."

Anna paused at the door, allowing him to open it for her, and gave him an inquisitive glance. She wouldn't have guessed he'd done those things.

The Sun Mountain Lodge was a sweeping complex of massive beams and natural stone. The overall feel of the lodge was warm: earth tones and pastels, large hearths with glowing fires, lots of wood and stone and open spaces. The lodge was meant to soothe. No television sets. Classical music was piped into the background.

With his hand lightly on the small of her back they entered the bar area. Chris took care of everything, a man used to being in charge. He made a reservation for two in the dining room, then led Anna to a table near the huge stone hearth in the lower level of the bar. The room was enormous. Massive logs supported the walls and ceiling. Indian rugs graced the flagstone floors. The lighting was unobtrusive. In the corner of a wall of glass a young man softly strummed a guitar.

A stone terrace graced the rim of a cliff, and then the valley swept away below to arch majestically up the side of a distant mountain. The moon hung low in the night sky, turning the far-off forests of firs to silver in its glow.

Anna studied Chris while the cocktail waitress served their drinks. He was noticing the view, all right, even though he said nothing. He was noticing it and appreciating it. She was proud of her home, and she was glad he was impressed.

"Nice place, isn't it?" she observed.

"Not bad."

"Almost as nice as Washington, D.C., in August at rush hour?" she asked lightly.

"Almost." And he smiled just a little.

She watched him carefully as he stared out the window. She'd like to figure this man out. He'd been harsh and tender, easy and tense, a pack of contradictions, a man boxing with his own shadows. There were lines of stress on his face, lines that came from not enough sleep and too much frustration and responsibility. For a heartbeat of time Anna felt sorry for Chris Galloway, but she squelched it instantly. This man was doing exactly what he wanted to do.

"Well," she said, holding out her glass of wine, "cheers."

He clinked glasses, his light blue eyes holding hers. "Cheers."

"So," Anna began, "do you take all of your—what would you call me?—your clients out to dinner?"

He laughed ruefully. "Hardly. Dinner is usually a slice or two of pizza in an office."

"Sounds like you don't exactly eat right."

"When I do eat," he said dryly, "it's seldom got anything to do with nutrition." He leaned back in his chair and crossed one long leg over the other, his ankle resting on his knee.

"You know," she ventured "one minute you're all business, the next . . . well . . ."

"Go on."

"You're different."

"Human?"

"Yes, human."

Again he laughed, smile lines playing at the corners of his eyes. "No one likes government investigators. We're always the enemy."

"I can see that."

"This case for instance. You yourself. You see me as an adversary."

"I did at first," she admitted.

"But my goal is the same as yours—to make flying as safe as it can be for everyone. For the passengers as well as you. It's just that no one likes us meddling in their lives, and that's something we have to do."

"You take your job very seriously."

"Don't you?"

"Yes, but..."

"You're not as directly responsible for as many lives, I know."

"It must drive you crazy," she said, sipping her drink.

"It does. But you learn to cope."

Anna sighed, running her finger along the rim of the wineglass. "In that case you can't ignore any sort of evidence, can you?"

"You're referring to the notebook, the one you say is missing."

She nodded.

"I'll have to look into that," he said thoughtfully.

"Will you? Really? Can I depend on you to...?"

"Hey, I'll try."

Anna felt satisfaction warm her. *Okay, Jim, I've got this far,* she thought. All she said was "Thanks, I appreciate it."

He was looking at her steadily, as if he almost knew what she was thinking. He couldn't, though, and tonight she'd say nothing about Jim. Tonight she was a woman having dinner with a man, and she'd wipe her mind clean of everything else.

But her mind wouldn't erase like a blackboard. Jim's face kept slipping into her mind's eye. Then she'd feel Chris's hands on her back, feel his closeness, smell the male scent of him, cringe again at her own weakness.

How could she have done it? Why had she driven Chris to the crash site in the first place? He must be wondering, too, trying to figure out what kind of a weirdo she was, offering to take him there, treating him to a crying jag, then going out to dinner with him. She felt her cheeks flush and looked out the window, pretending to study the view.

Time ticked by endlessly.

She was on edge. This had been a bad idea. She could feel his gaze walk on her like the feet of a hundred tiny animals, and she continued studiously staring at the view, gripped by a kind of paralysis. What was she doing here, with this man?

Thankfully the impasse was broken by a voice. "Well, hello, isn't it Anna Parish?"

She turned in her seat to find Lee Miller and his wife, Teresa, standing behind her, holding cocktail glasses. Teresa was waving at an older couple sitting near the guitarist. Evidently the Millers were there to meet them.

"Hello, Mr. Miller," Anna said, "nice to see you." Then she said, "This is Chris Galloway." She stopped, uncertain whether or not to mention Chris's profession. The whole thing was awkward.

But Chris handled it with aplomb. He stood and said, "Chris Galloway, Mr. Miller, of the NTSB."

Lee Miller was clearly taken off guard. He said something like, "Oh, I see," then muttered they had best be joining their friends. He held up his cocktail glass in explanation, said good-night and showed his wife across the room.

"Oh," Anna said, turning back to Chris, "that was unfortunate."

"Why?"

"Well, he knew I was Jim's fiancée, and he has to know how outspoken Jim was in the buy-out bid for the company. He also has to know that *I've* spoken out against him in my depositions and—"

"What are you saying?"

"I'm saying that Miller must think it's really odd that we're having dinner and talking and—"

"Don't worry about it. It's his problem, not yours."

"What will you say if he ever asks you about it?" she pressed.

Chris shrugged. "I'll tell him it was business."

"Is it?" she asked quietly, finding the courage to meet his eyes.

Something passed between them, something Anna didn't want to happen but had no control over. Their gazes met and locked, and she was unable to tear hers away. A spark flashed between them, a current so strong that if she passed her hand through it, her flesh would sizzle.

Then she wrenched her eyes away and looked straight ahead, feeling the heat crawl up her neck.

"Not entirely," she heard him say, but she'd forgotten what it was they'd been talking about.

Chris ordered a bottle of fine wine with dinner. "It's to make up for my callous behavior this afternoon. It really was unthinking on my part."

"Dinner would have been enough."

"Well, then," he said, the light from the candle on their table reflecting in his eyes, "it's for me. I haven't dined like this in a very long time."

"You never eat out with anyone?" she asked.

"I'm not married," he said, "not anymore. And as for anyone else . . . there isn't time in my life."

"That's . . . too bad," she allowed.

But he only shrugged. "Maybe to some. But my life is too disorganized. I'm never home. This way it's easier."

"Is it?"

"Yes, and I learned that the hard way."

Dinner came and after that they shared a piece of carrot cake. There was an inch of wine left in the bottle. It was late, the dining room was emptying, but Chris ordered coffee, and she wondered why he seemed reluctant to leave.

Things had become a little easier between them. If Anna carefully controlled her thoughts and reactions, considered every word and pushed from her mind what had happened that afternoon, she could manage. She had the strangest feeling, though, that this man wanted something from her. But he wasn't pushing her, wasn't asking questions. Indeed, he was a laconic sort, and she had to carry a lot of the conversation. He seemed content just to be there with her, which made her even more on edge. She kept wondering why, asking herself unanswerable questions. She didn't like letting the conversation fall off, because then they just sat there, and she was much too aware of him. And always there was this tension between them, a disturbing tension, even worse when words died on the air. So Anna asked questions, trying to overcome his natural reticence.

"So you were married," Anna said. "Do you have any children?"

His reaction was curious. He grimaced and ran a hand through his hair.

"I'm sorry, I—"

"No, it's okay. You just reminded me that Todd, that's my son, is coming tomorrow to spend the summer with me."

She cocked her head. "That isn't good?"

"Yes, sure, it's great. I just . . . well, I'm still trying to figure out where we're going to live, what Todd's going to do while I'm working all day. It's a problem."

"How old is Todd?"

"He's sixteen now." Chris shook his head and whistled between his teeth. "Sixteen. I don't even know him."

"Haven't you had visiting rights?"

"Yeah, I do. Helen was smart enough to know I'd never have time to see Todd, anyway."

"So you haven't had him before?"

He raked a hand through his hair again. "I did have him come and visit me in the summers. Once, anyway. But I was living in a one-bedroom in Miami, and it was a bad scene. I was out in the Everglades for hours on end and back in the NTSB office half the night. Todd was really lost."

"Why don't you rent a place for the summer?"

"I'm trying to. I was supposed to go and look at a couple of places but . . ."

"Something else came up," Anna finished for him, thinking out loud. "I guess we all have our priorities."

Chris raised a brow.

"Sorry," she put in, "it's none of my business."

"Look," Chris said, "I never know where I'll be sent next, or when it will be or for how long."

"That's awful."

"It's my job."

"Take a vacation. Take a real break. Surely they owe you that much."

"I can't until this investigation is well under way."

"Well, you're going to have to make some adjustments. What do you think Todd would like to do?"

He laughed scornfully. "Helen tells me what he'd like to do is shoplift and drink beer. That's why she's sending him here for the entire summer. She says she can't cope with him, that he needs a father."

"Well?"

"Do I look like a father to you?"

"You look like a man who's . . . who's afraid."

"Yes, I'm scared. What if I can't handle him?"

Anna fixed him with a sober look. "Of all the people I've ever met," she said, "you're probably the one person who could handle *any* teenager."

"Glad you think so," he said doubtfully.

They left soon after that. When they got back into town, it was past eleven, but Chris asked her if she'd have a nightcap at his hotel.

"The bar's probably closed," she said, parking.

"Another spot?"

She never stopped to wonder how dinner had lasted so long, or why Chris was still seeking her company. She only knew that she wasn't ready to go home, either. "There's Sam's Place. It's probably dead as a doornail at this hour, but—"

"Sounds fine."

"It's only two blocks."

"The whole town's only two blocks," he said, and again his hand was at the small of her back, warm, feather-light, tentative. For a second Anna closed her eyes and allowed herself to feel that touch at her back, to recall with painful clarity Jim's many touches, his holding her hands, the way he'd draped an arm over her shoulders.

It hurt. God, how it hurt.

She opened her eyes and found Chris studying her as they walked. She wondered suddenly if he could read her mind. A hot flush crawled up her neck once more, and she looked away from his ice-blue eyes.

Sam's Place *was* dead. But Milly, the sixty-eight-year-old bartender, was still there and glad to pour a couple of snifters of brandy.

"I never drink like this," Anna said from her bar stool.

"I never drink. Period," Chris told her. "Coffee. I *do* drink that."

"I know," Anna replied, and again they clinked glasses. "Here's to a good summer with Todd."

"And here's to your little mountain town," Chris replied. "I like it here."

She took a sip of the sweet, fiery liquid and patted her throat. "Wow."

"It's good stuff," he agreed.

She leaned her elbow on the bar, supporting her chin in her hand, and ventured a look at Chris. "How did you ever get into your line of work? It seems such a...well, an unpopular job."

He thrust his chin forward in that way he had, as if to say to the world, "Sock me. Go ahead. I dare you." A muscle worked in his jaw. "You don't want to hear it. It's boring."

"No, really, go ahead. Tell me."

He shrugged. "I was an aeronautical engineer working in Washington. There was an air crash. I was asked to join the investigating team as an expert in the field, and the rest, as they say, is history."

"You were an engineer?"

"Yes, for a few years. I found this job more...let's say challenging."

"I can imagine."

"Don't get the wrong idea. I like what I do. It's important. I save people's lives."

"You don't have to justify yourself to me . . . or to anyone, for that matter."

He was quiet for a moment, staring off across the room, his brows drawn in a familiar frown. "No, I don't, but I feel this hostility from people. I guess it just gets to be automatic, defending myself." He shook his head. "You know, I was in Orange County, Los Angeles, last winter on this case. I was called in because there were questions about the flap position on a particular aircraft. Anyhow, it took three months of digging to prove that the flaps were perfectly safe. It turned out to be pilot error, after all. A stupid—" He checked himself abruptly and searched her face.

"It's all right," she said gently.

"I found the error, though. It was easily preventable. The airline now has its pilots check the—"

But Anna put up a hand. "I get the picture. You're indispensable, Chris Galloway."

"I didn't say that."

"But in your heart you believe it."

"No one's indispensable, Anna," he said somberly.

They drank their brandies and steered the conversation to other, less unsettling subjects. Anna told him about the winter cross-country skiing trails throughout the area and the summer bike path system. She bragged shamelessly about her life in Winthrop, knowing deep down inside she was trying to make this man envious of her simple, peaceful existence. She never mentioned the crash or his job or Jim. She especially never mentioned Jim Fleisher. Chris was viewing her now as a stable human being, as a woman with her life in order. The last thing she wanted him to remember was the other side of her, the part that was visited by a spirit from another world.

It was nearly midnight when she glanced at her watch. "Good Lord, it's late. I have to work tomorrow."

"Early flight?"

Anna nodded. "First one in the morning. We rotate a lot." She finished her brandy and looked up at him. "I better be getting home."

"It's been a pleasant evening," Chris said, and she had the impression that the words were hard for him to get out, as if he were making a confession.

They walked together back to her car, but this time his hands were in his pockets, not at her back.

"It's cool out," Chris observed as they crossed the empty street.

"Freezing is more like it."

"Um" is all he said, and she realized a veil of awkwardness was slipping back over them. She felt a moment of regret; the night had been interesting, different, worthwhile. She remembered sitting in her car hours ago and thinking about calling it off.

"You'll be all right driving home?" Chris asked as he opened her car door for her.

"In this town?" Anna smiled faintly. "You couldn't find trouble if you were looking for it."

"Sure?"

"I'm positive." Another moment of uncomfortable silence enfolded them. "Well," she said after the pause, "I enjoyed the evening, Chris. Thank you."

"I did, too."

Silence. Anna got into her car and started the engine. "You're leaving tomorrow after the depositions?"

"That's right. Todd's due in Seattle."

"Oh, of course, you said that. Well..."

"Good night, Anna."

She gave him another hesitant smile and backed out onto the road. He stood and watched her drive off, his hands still in his pockets, a lone figure on the street. Anna drove around the corner toward her house and glanced one last time in the rearview mirror. He was still on the road, a diminishing dark shadow now.

Anna parked in her driveway and opened the front door silently. She flipped off lights as she made her way across the living room. It occurred to her how wrong Flip had been earlier when he said that Chris was the enemy. Well, he didn't feel like the enemy, at least not to her. And he'd said he'd look into the matter of Jim's notebook. Or would he have said that just to pacify her?

She pulled her nightgown over her head, washed her face and combed her hair. The mirror was clear now—no diffused images in front of her. God, she hoped Jim would allow her a full night's rest. She felt so strongly that he wasn't a projection of her mind, that he existed outside of her. She hadn't made him up, not tonight, not when he came to her before. But crazy people didn't know they were crazy, and maybe she wasn't able to recognize her aberration. But if Jim *was* a separate entity, then why, *why* did he come to her?

Anna fell into bed and snuggled under her quilt. She whispered a silent prayer. *Don't come tonight, Jim.*

Her thoughts were darting as she closed her eyes. It was the brandy, but there was more. She'd had a date tonight. A real date with a man. She didn't know just how to fit that reality into her life. But, of course, it didn't really matter, because tomorrow Chris would be gone, and that would be that. She rolled over, her brain still a little fuzzy from the alcohol and weariness, and that was when she felt it, the spot where Chris had touched her on the small of her back. Guilt swept her. It should be Jim's touch she recalled, not another man's. It was too soon. It was too wrong.

CHAPTER SEVEN

CHRIS KNEW it had been a mistake to take Anna to dinner. He'd known it at the time, and he knew it now. He stood in front of the bathroom mirror, a towel wrapped around his waist, and flailed himself mentally for making that error. Running his razor under the hot water tap, he shook his head slowly. What a damn fool he was. Never before had he socialized with someone he was investigating. It was downright unethical. And if it wasn't, it should be.

Tilting his head back and to the side, he ran the blade up his neck and across his left cheek. He rinsed the shaving cream off the blade again and took a hard look at himself. Dark circles showed under his eyes, and his coloring was paler than usual. He twisted his head from right to left, his blue eyes still fixed forward, studying his reflection.

"You're getting old, buster," he said, and he wondered how time had crept up on him so stealthily. He looked over forty, even though he was still thirty-nine. Gone was his youth, the hopes and dreams. Now it was work and more work. Child support. Middle age.

Chris finished shaving, tossed the towel onto a hook and pulled on his briefs and trousers. At least he wasn't fat. And he had his hair, most of it. But he *felt* old. Hell, he felt eighty.

Why had Anna gone out with him, anyway? It was hard to believe she'd done it to help him assuage his guilt, or even for a free meal. And she'd seemed interested in him. She'd drawn him out, made him open up more than he could recall doing in years.

Why had she bothered?

He knotted his tie in the mirror, slipped it up and shrugged on his jacket. Anna was a funny combination of straightforward honesty and melting vulnerability. A very beautiful woman in many ways. In fact, Chris couldn't think of a single failing. Well, maybe that wacky business about her dead lover, Fleisher. That was as strange as you got. But if she'd just realize it was a form of grieving, she'd probably stop having those waking visions, or whatever they were. It was pretty weird dwelling on a dead man no matter what her relationship with him had been. Pretty sick.

And yet... yet it bothered Chris a lot. He had to admit it. It had irked him last night, too, when he sat across from her and knew she was wishing for the company of another man. Talk about nuts, he mused. He himself was exhibiting signs of jealousy.

Downstairs he grabbed a quick cup of coffee and a sweet roll and forced his mind back on track. Anna Parish had been a pleasant diversion for a day. But that was it. Not only did he have several depositions to complete today, but Todd was due in Seattle at four-thirty that afternoon.

He gulped his coffee and tried to imagine what his sixteen-year-old boy looked like now. His son. For the first time since Chris had been divorced, his boy would be spending the entire summer with him. It was something he looked forward to with both fear and delight. How would they get along? Where would they live?

What did Todd prefer to eat, to do? What was his son really like?

Chris thought about the last time he'd spoken to Helen on the phone, about a week and a half ago. She'd tracked him down at the NTSB office in Seattle shortly after he'd been sent out from D.C. She'd given him Todd's flight number and said, "He's yours for the summer, Chris. And I mean the *whole* summer. If he gets into trouble, don't go shipping him back to me. I've had it."

The entire summer. And just where *were* they going to live? A night or two in the hotel, fine. But not for the whole three months that he'd most likely be spending in Seattle on this damn case. Maybe the rental agent could find them a place outside of the city. Maybe with a stream or river nearby. They could do some hiking, camping, fishing. God, that would be great. With his son. He could juggle his responsibilities, couldn't he? The NTSB didn't have to own his entire life.

Chris checked the time and had a second cup of coffee, and while he downed it he reviewed Harry Logan's file. Logan was the maintenance supervisor at WestAir Express, Chris's first appointment of the day. He scanned the typed sheets of Logan's employment record right down to the man's initial job application. He was fifty-nine years old and had been with Lee Miller ever since Miller had started WestAir. They'd known each other in the air force in Vietnam.

Seemed pretty clear-cut. Logan wasn't likely to be helpful; he'd cover up his own mistakes and Miller's, too. Interviewing Logan was probably going to be a waste of time. Still, you never knew when you were going to learn something, some obscure, neglected fact that made the pieces of the puzzle fall into place.

Maybe he'd even ask Logan if he'd ever seen Jim Fleisher scribbling in a blue notebook. He'd told Anna he'd check into it further. And he'd keep that promise.

He started to take a sip of coffee, then stopped with the mug poised in midair as a scene suddenly filled his head. It was Anna's bookshelf. Lots of paperbacks, a few dictionaries, a flower arrangement, photos. His mind's eye focused in on them, like the lens of a camera. He could see a particular photograph as clearly as if it sat before him: Anna and Fleisher in hiking shorts and boots, arms around each other, grinning broadly, apparently on top of a mountain somewhere. He'd never seen her smile like that, and he could hardly imagine her in such an elated mood. Whenever he'd seen her she'd been much more reserved, quiet, thoughtful. It was the accident, naturally. A shame. But then all accidents were crying shames.

He recalled Jim Fleisher in the picture, too—a big-boned man, dark-haired, dark-eyed, the epitome of the stalwart airline pilot. Good-looking in a Gregory Peck sort of way. What in hell had Fleisher done that day in the plane? What had happened in that cockpit? What had gone on in the man's head? Abruptly Chris felt anger flare in him, irrational, hot anger at Jim Fleisher. Fleisher had made some kind of misjudgment and killed a lot of innocent people, himself included. Chris suddenly shook himself, surprised at his reaction. He usually felt pity for a dead pilot, not anger. Boy, he needed a vacation.

He picked up the keys for the blue Ford Taurus he'd rented at the front desk. The highway to the airport was beginning to look familiar, as it was the same one he'd driven with Anna yesterday. But now bright morning sun spread over the river valley, and the tall mountains receded back on either side, row upon row, like dark ranks of soldiers. The river danced along, glinting in the sunlight, and a sign announced Winthrop Airport, two miles. Yes, it was all starting to look very familiar.

He found Harry Logan in a hangar. The man had a potbelly and the thick fingers of someone who'd worked with his hands all his life. He was grizzled, florid and had bright blue eyes and a bald head that made him look like Santa Claus minus the beard. The wrench in his hand seemed as if it belonged there.

"Mr. Logan?" Chris began.

Harry shook his hand. Up close the twinkling blue eyes were shrewd.

"Let's go into my office, Galloway," he said gesturing toward an alcove in the giant metal hangar that contained a desk piled high with papers and greasy machine parts.

He sat on a cracked plastic kitchen chair and motioned for Chris to pull up another. "So, any new questions?" Logan asked. "I answered all the old ones."

"Probably nothing new. I just want to get straight in my head exactly what went on that morning from the maintenance point of view."

"I already told everyone. The weather was turning bad. It was around eleven in the morning. My crew, Bob Johnson and Ron Berensen, deiced the plane once. Then there was a little bit of a wait, something about the luggage, the usual stuff, and we had to recheck the fuel level. Jim took off. That's all."

"You said previously that you warned Captain Fleisher to come back in for another deicing if the plane sat for more than twenty minutes on the runway.''

Logan nodded. ''Routine procedure.''

''How long did flight 629 sit before Fleisher took off?''

''Oh, heck, I don't know. We were busy. Between a quarter and a half an hour.''

''Whose responsibility is it to note the time between deicings, Mr. Logan, the maintenance crew's or the pilot's?''

Logan shot him a look. ''Well, now, we got a small operation here. It's kinda casual, see. We all cooperate and work together. No hard and fast rules. I'd say it's the pilot's job, though. It's his plane and his call.''

''So you think Jim Fleisher should have called for another deicing before he took off?''

''I'm not saying that. No one's proved that ice caused that crash.''

''Then you believe the crash was caused by something else, engine failure, for instance, or a down draft?''

''No,'' Logan said diffidently.

''Then what, in your opinion, caused Jim Fleisher, a skilled pilot, to fly a planeload of people into a hillside that morning?''

Logan squinted an eye, cocked his head and said, ''I'll be goldanged if I know. Ain't it your job to find out?''

''I'm trying, Mr. Logan, I'm trying.'' Chris sighed. He'd better take another tack. ''Okay, how about maintenance records? We've had a complaint that they haven't been kept properly.''

"I follow FAA rules. Never had a complaint in my life. Everything's all up-to-date. The FAA's never complained to me."

"Is it possible someone could be filing false records or changing them after they're filed?"

Logan thrust his face forward. "You think I have time to check my records after I've done them once? Hell, I haven't got time to do them the first time! I never have enough time. Paperwork! I need to be out there working on aircraft, not wasting time on paperwork. Can't find a decent mechanic anymore, seems. If somebody's fooling with my reports, they're doing it after I'm through with them. There's no rule that says I gotta check them over again, is there?"

"No, Mr. Logan." Chris figured he had nothing to lose, so he threw out the next question. "Does Lee Miller pay much attention to maintenance records? I mean, does he ever look at them after you file them?"

"Now how in eastbejesus should I know that?"

Okay, he'd try *another* route. "I've seen the maintenance log for the Convair that crashed. But I wonder if there's anything you could tell me, anything at all, about that particular plane that isn't in the log. Eccentricities of that aircraft, pitch-up characteristics, unusual vibrations, complaints by pilots, anything at all. Off the record," he added.

Harry Logan pretended to ponder this question. "Nope," he finally replied, "not a thing. No complaints. Ran like a clock. Engine'd been overhauled two months before."

"Right," Chris said. "Well, thanks, Mr. Logan. I appreciate your cooperation." Then he said, "Oh, one last thing. Did you ever notice Fleisher writing in a notebook? I believe he carried a small blue spiral notebook."

Logan's brow wrinkled. "Can't say that I recall one."

"Well, thanks, anyway. If you should remember anything else, no matter how small it seems, I'd appreciate a call. Make it collect." Chris produced a generic card with the Seattle NTSB office number on it. Logan took it. "If I'm not in the office, leave a message and I'll get right back to you."

"Sure, Mr. Galloway, I'll do that."

I bet, Chris thought. "Okay, that's it then," he said. "I'd like to see the other two men now, if you don't mind sending them in." He checked the notebook he always carried. "That's Berensen and Johnson." Then he checked his briefcase for the files.

"Together or separate?" Logan asked.

Chris glanced up. "One at a time, please, Mr. Logan."

Bob Johnson was tall and pear-shaped. He was nervous, but that was relatively normal. He said nothing more or less than he'd said in previous interviews.

"So you think it was right around twenty minutes since the plane had been deiced?" Chris asked.

"Gosh, I'm not sure. Around that, I guess."

"Was it up to the pilot to ask for another deicing after twenty minutes had passed, or would you have reminded him?"

Johnson thought long and hard. "I guess it was up to Jim to ask. I was going to, you know, uh, suggest it, but I'd finished checking the fuel, so I guess Jim wanted to get going."

"Was that proper procedure?"

"Well, uh, sure, Jim knew what he was doing." Then he added, "Hell, he was the pilot."

He'd get nothing from Johnson.

He saw Berensen next, a young man with pimples and a tattoo of a military nature on his left forearm. He heard the same story again, exactly the same. Either it was the truth or they'd compared stories.

"Was Jim Fleisher a good pilot?" Chris asked.

"Oh, yeah, he was. Chief pilot. He had more hours than anyone around here. A good man."

"Do you think he made a mistake that morning?"

"I don't know. Coulda been the weather."

"So you think Fleisher shouldn't have taken off?"

"No, I didn't say that. Jim knew what he was doing. He'd flown in worse weather than that."

Exasperated, Chris stood and put his hands in his pockets. "All right, Berensen, that's about it. Thanks."

"You're welcome, Mr. Galloway, any way I can help." But he was out of that room so fast Chris almost smiled.

Damn. He was getting nowhere. He checked his notebook again—10:00 a.m., Madeline Vernon, Anna's roommate. Interesting. Maybe Miss Vernon could shed some light on this whole mess, although from her previous deposition, Chris doubted it.

He asked directions to the WestAir employee lounge where he was to meet the Vernon woman. On the way there he thought about the three men he'd just interviewed. They'd all been evasive, probably afraid for their jobs. And Chris knew they were caught on the horns of a dilemma: blame their boss and they got fired; blame themselves for lax maintenance and they got fired anyway. And none of them had really wanted to blame Jim Fleisher. So they were noncommittal and defensive. Chris understood their reactions—it was always the same story—but it didn't help his investigation any.

Madeline Vernon was sitting on a couch in the nearly empty employee lounge. She sat too straight, her feet together, her hands holding her purse in her lap. She was a lovely looking girl, striking, with a head of curling blond hair, but she seemed pale in her maroon uniform. Another nervous Nelly. God, he got tired of that reaction. As if a cabin attendant could in any way be blamed for the accident.

"Miss Vernon," he said, striding up to her and holding out his hand.

She stood, shook his hand and tried to smile. He could practically touch the aura of fear that surrounded her.

"I've met your roommate, Anna Parish," he said, trying to defuse her discomfort, "but then you probably know that."

"Um," she replied, "ah, yes, she said she'd talked to you."

"Shall we sit down? I just want to review your deposition, Miss Vernon. A few questions, that's all. Off the record."

"Sure." She bit her lip.

"Did you notice anything at all abnormal about the preflight routine that morning in March?"

"Uh, no, well, except we were a little late getting started because I, uh, think maintenance had to check the fuel or something."

"How late, do you recall?"

She thought. Her fingers played with the strap of her black leather bag. "Um, maybe twenty minutes or so."

"Did you notice when the plane was deiced?"

"I already answered all these questions. There was a court reporter and everything taking it down," she said defensively.

"I know, Miss Vernon, but I need to go over it again in case you remember something new, or in case I can get a new angle on things. So please be patient."

"All right," she said sullenly, "but I really wasn't paying any attention to deicing. That's not my responsibility."

"I realize that. I'm just trying to collect information. Now I know you were nervous that morning. It's in your deposition. Did you have any particular reason to be nervous?"

"No, not really. The weather, I guess. I'm just putting in too many hours. I'm going to quit flying soon, as soon as, well, I'm going to be getting married. I'm just trying to save some money. Then I'm going to be working the counter."

"I see. Well, Miss Vernon, I guess congratulations are in order."

"Thank you." But she didn't smile or meet his gaze.

"You weren't nervous about flying with Jim Fleisher, then?" he asked bluntly.

She looked up, startled. "No! I mean, I didn't say that, did I? Jim was a good pilot, one of the best."

"No, you didn't say that. I just wondered."

She shook her head vehemently. "Jim was very careful, very good. Please don't report that I ever said Jim wasn't."

"I'm not in the habit of putting untruths in my reports, Miss Vernon. If you say you trusted Jim Fleisher, then I believe you."

"Good."

"Ah, Miss Vernon, I've heard talk of a notebook that Fleisher kept, a journal of evidence against Lee Miller—"

"Did Anna tell you that?" she asked, paling.

"Yes, actually, Miss Parish did say something about it. Were you aware of such a notebook? Did you ever see it or hear Fleisher refer to it?"

Madeline was looking down, playing with her strap. She said nothing for too long a time.

"Miss Vernon?"

"Uh, what? Oh, a notebook." She shook her head, still looking down, her fingers white on the purse strap. "Maybe. I'm not sure. I really don't remember."

She could be lying. Chris wasn't sure. But her reactions were odd, too upset, too on edge, worse than Anna's. Maybe the crash had affected Madeline even more profoundly. In any case, he wasn't going to get a thing more out of her.

She looked up then and met his gaze, her expression puzzled. "Why did you take Anna out last night?"

He was taken aback; the worm had turned and the inquisitor was being questioned. He didn't much like it, either. "Call it a business dinner. Why do you ask, Miss Vernon?"

She seemed to realize the tone of her voice had been accusatory. She looked away. "No reason, I guess. I was only wondering."

But now Chris decided to press her a little. "By the way," he remarked offhandedly, "Anna Parish drove me up to the site of the accident yesterday."

Madeline stiffened. "She did?"

"That's right. It sometimes helps me to get a feel for what happened."

"I can't believe Anna would . . . would go there."

"Why not?"

She looked at him fearfully. "To relive it, my God. I couldn't do it. No way." Then her glance fell and she said, "Poor Anna. Did she...did she say anything, I mean..."

"What *do* you mean, Miss Vernon?"

"I..." She faltered.

Chris had the distinct impression she was hiding something. It was just a suspicion, not truly founded, but it created that itch in his head. He studied her for a moment and decided to drop it for the time being. He cleared his throat. "Okay, Miss Vernon, I have a couple of more questions now. Just a repeat of some you've answered before."

But Madeline was as defensive as every other WestAir employee. Actually he hadn't really believed Madeline could supply pertinent information, as she hadn't even been in the cockpit that morning, but he had to try. Even so Madeline remained inordinately nervous and fearful. He even detected a hint of hostility in her.

"I just want to tell you one thing," Madeline said as he finished his last question. "Anna was the bravest person I've ever seen in that accident. I was so scared I was paralyzed. I couldn't even think. But Anna pushed my head down, and she yelled to the passengers to get into crash position. She probably saved some lives, maybe even mine."

"That's good to know," he said.

"I just wanted to say that, to put it on the record. Anna deserves a medal or something," Madeline said earnestly.

"Have you informed WestAir's owner of Miss Parish's actions?"

Madeline looked away again. "No, he doesn't do that, give commendations."

"Perhaps your union . . . ?"

"Maybe."

"You could write up the suggestion and send it to your union representative."

"Yes, I could. I should do that."

"Anna's lucky to have such a good friend," he said carefully.

"Yes, we're very close."

It wasn't until Chris had left Madeline in the employee lounge that it occurred to him to wonder if Anna had ever told her roommate about Jim's ghost, and if Madeline was somehow trying to protect Anna. Maybe that was why she'd been so darn evasive.

The air traffic controllers who'd been on duty that day met Chris on schedule in an empty office in the airport's tower. Hal Radeky was short, heavyset and red-faced. He'd been the one monitoring flight 629 on the screen that day. The other controller was Ned Cochrane, a skinny scarecrow of a man with a gentle face.

"Nice to meet you, Mr. Galloway," Cochrane said. "I'm afraid I can't help you a whole lot."

"I appreciate your time," Chris said. "I'd like to know anything you can tell me about the accident, about WestAir's procedures, anything pertinent to my investigation. Since you boys work for the government, you're not in danger of getting canned, and I'd like your input."

"I hate to repeat gossip, but this is a small airport, and you can't help hearing things. If it'll help prevent another accident," Hal Radeky said, "it'd be worth it. I can tell you I never want to go through that again.

Watching that blip on the screen, all those people." He shook his head. "Awful."

They both agreed they'd heard talk of Lee Miller's management style, which caused resentment among his employees. Abusive language, pressure, threats. They'd heard the weathermen in the tower grumbling about Miller's insistence on reporting better visibility than they believed existed. They knew pilots often ignored legal minimums in landing. That they'd seen with their own eyes. It was a pattern, Hal Radeky believed, a pattern set by Miller. But, naturally, it was mostly hearsay. There was no proof, and as for the legal minimums, the pilots were at fault there.

"What about Jim Fleisher?" Chris asked. "What kind of pilot was he?"

Ned Cochrane answered. "He seemed to be pretty resistant to Miller's pressure. More resistant than most. I know they had arguments, but Fleisher was a real professional, a good pilot."

Chris studied both men's faces. "Did either of you ever hear of Fleisher keeping a journal, evidence to prove Miller was running an unsafe operation?"

The two air traffic controllers looked at each other. "Naw, I never heard that," Radeky said, "but that doesn't mean he didn't keep one."

"What do you really think happened that morning?" Chris asked. "Why did a good pilot fly his plane into that hillside?"

Hal Radeky shrugged. "I hate to say it, because Jim isn't here to defend himself, but I think he must have made a mistake. Something that wouldn't have mattered in dry weather, but did in the snow."

"He yelled something just before the crash," Chris said.

"Yeah, God, I'll never forget. Something like, 'That's not right!' Then, well, then some swear words," Hal said.

"Do you know what he meant by that?"

"No, could have been anything."

Inconclusive. It was still inconclusive. No answers. Hints maybe. Anna Parish had a point about Miller; it had been corroborated by Radeky and Cochrane. But all evidence still pointed to Fleisher making a fatal error that March morning. The thing that was still a big question mark, however, was Fleisher's statement on the voice recorder. "That's not right!" he'd yelled. Most of the Go Team who'd first heard the recording had agreed that Fleisher must have known he was going into the trees, and the shocked pilot had yelled the first thing that had come to his mind, either referring to the trees that shouldn't have been there or the plane's shaking. Yes, the Go Team had concluded Fleisher couldn't have been referring to anything mechanical because the plane's parts had been checked and rechecked a dozen times after the crash.

But Fleisher's words still beat at Chris. Why wouldn't the pilot have yelled, "The rudder's stuck!" or "Hell, where'd those trees come from!" Anything but "That's not right!" It didn't make a lot of sense. In fact, none at all.

One thing he could do, though, was keep that appointment with Lee Miller. He looked forward to it, in fact, because after all the hearsay and innuendos Chris had heard, he'd finally be able to judge the man for himself. He followed the directions Miller had given him to his house, back into town, then up the East Chewack Road, along another snaking river. The route traversed a beautiful valley, with horses grazing behind split rail fences, and the snowcapped peaks of Early Winters Ski Area off in the distance.

It would sure help if Fleisher's journal existed. Real evidence. Of course, the notebook could be a figment of Anna's imagination, a way of coping with the error her fiancé had made, a way of diverting blame. Hell, if she believed in his ghost, why not an imaginary notebook?

How could she have sat there and talked about a ghost as if such a thing existed? And how could he have listened to it straight-faced? It was like a kid's game, one in which you and a friend pretended to believe in Superman and you both talked about Superman as if he were playing the game with you. But that was kids pretending, not adults discussing reality. There were no such things as ghosts. It was all too obvious that Anna Parish was still in love with Jim Fleisher and couldn't let go.

As it had earlier that morning, the notion, once formed in his mind, made Chris lock his jaw in anger. What in hell was wrong with Anna? Why couldn't she accept Fleisher's death and go on as other people did? Why couldn't she—? He stopped the thought before it materialized. He pounded the steering wheel once with the flat of his hand. Hell, if he needed a woman that bad he'd do well to find one with a whole lot fewer complications. Last night had been stupid, unprofessional. He couldn't quite figure out why he'd done it, either.

On the other hand, Chris realized, the woman kept sneaking up on him from the corners of his mind. If it wasn't her face, it was her damn bookshelf and Fleisher's photograph. He saw her at the table in Three-Fingered Jack's. Soft, dark springing hair swept up casually. Hazel eyes—an interesting color, not yellow, not brown, not green. Dark lashes that laid fan-shaped shadows on her cheeks when she looked down. And at dinner, on top of that spectacular mountain she'd been all soft feminine curves. Great calves and ankles. A soft mouth, pale pink and sweet-looking . . .

My God, what was he thinking? How hard-up could a guy get? Leave it alone. Leave *her* alone. Get on with the damn investigation, he commanded himself.

Lee Miller's house was built of log, stone and glass, an elegant place. Perhaps the man was gruff and hard-nosed and difficult to get along with, but he had taste, or maybe his wife did.

"Mr. Galloway," Miller said, shaking hands, "you're late. I expected you at eleven-thirty."

"Sorry, some of my interviews ran over."

He followed Miller down a hall to an office. The man was burly and balding, a once-athletic guy gone to middle-age weight. His eyes were dark brown and sharp under heavy black brows, the eyes of a slim young man, oddly at variance with his appearance.

He gestured to a leather easy chair but sat behind his desk in the black leather executive chair. "So?" he said. "Ask away, Mr. Galloway."

"What kind of pilot was Jim Fleisher?" Chris jumped right in, not wasting time on niceties.

Miller steepled his fingers and pursed his lips. "A good pilot. He was pretty independent-minded, though. Jim and I had words from time to time, but he was a skilled pilot. Maybe a touch conservative, but I can forgive that."

"What did you and Jim have words about?"

Miller waved a hand. "Oh, technical stuff. I thought Jim was too fussy checking and rechecking things. His flights were late a lot. That's no way to run a business."

"Did you ever order Jim Fleisher to fly when he didn't want to?"

Miller frowned. "Of course not."

"Did you ever argue about it?"

"Maybe. Like I said, Jim was real conservative. We disagreed sometimes."

"What, uh, Mr. Miller, rather, *how* do you explain impressions I've gotten that there's some question concerning WestAir Express pilots having the final decision about whether to fly or not."

"Regulations state that the pilot-in-command has the final authority, right?"

"Yes, that's correct."

"Well, that's how WestAir runs."

"Did you order Jim Fleisher to fly that March day?"

"Lord, no. I wasn't even in the office. I was at home. Listen, if you're insinuating that I—"

"I'm just trying to get a handle on Fleisher's thought patterns, Mr. Miller."

"If a WestAir pilot wants to cancel a flight, he better have a damn good reason, not just because he doesn't feel like flying. I don't baby my crews. I have a business to run."

"What do you think happened that day? How do you yourself see it?"

Miller glared at him. "I'm waiting for your report, Galloway. I don't know."

"The air traffic controllers told me of pilots exceeding minimums while landing. They seemed to think you condoned it."

"If a pilot does that, he's in violation of FARs. I don't condone that," Miller said stolidly.

"What about training? Do your pilots get ongoing training and up-to-date manuals?"

"Well, now, I can't run full-time schools like the big carriers, but I order the manuals. They're available. And Fleisher trained the new guys. That was part of his job."

"How many hours of training do new pilots have in your Convairs?"

"Oh, I guess it depends. Five to ten, maybe. They're easy to fly."

"Five to ten. That's not much," Chris said.

"Hey, I can't afford to train up to maximums like the big boys. I've got a small operation here. I built it up myself, and I've been running it myself for almost twenty years. I never needed anyone's permission to run my airline the way I want to, and I don't need it now. Long as I stick to the rules, the minimum qualifications necessary for safety, and that's what I do, Galloway. And no FAA regional investigator's ever caught me doing otherwise."

"Right." Chris didn't like Miller's attitude. It showed aggression and impatience and callousness. Lee Miller had pulled himself up by his bootstraps, and no one was going to tell him what to do. Not even if his methods were detrimental to the public's safety. He'd push Miller's buttons a little, get the man's reactions. Why not?

"Have you ever heard talk about a notebook, a personal log Jim Fleisher was keeping? About procedures at WestAir?"

Miller waved a hand angrily. "You're referring to the buy-out, that damn acquisition corporation the employees put together? They're all against me. The balls of them trying to take my company away from me. They'll never do it!''

"I don't know about that, Mr. Miller. I'm referring to a personal record Jim Fleisher was keeping on what he considered dangerous procedures at WestAir.''

"Hell, how should I know?''

"It's missing. No one can find it," Chris said.

"Then how do you know it ever existed? Who told you about it?'' Miller demanded. "And what in the devil do you think he could have put in it, anyway?''

Chris sat stock-still, his light blue eyes unflinching while Miller postured and blustered. He imagined it was part of an act the man put on, either automatically or purposely. It meant to intimidate. Chris, however, found it fascinating.

"A notebook!'' Miller said, his hand rapping the desktop. "What kind of garbage is that? I suppose pretty Miss Parish was crying on your shoulder about it last night?'' Miller smiled grimly. "Oh, sure, I saw that. Poor bereaved girl. Hey, she's been trying that on everybody. Trying to get the blame off Jim Fleisher. The girl can't face reality, is all. A notebook! What bunk!''

"Miss Parish is naturally concerned," Chris replied easily.

"She better be concerned with her *job*,'' Miller pointed out.

"That sounds like a threat.''

"I don't threaten," Miller said. "I act. But I'll tell you, I don't like my employees fraternizing with government officials.''

"If you're referring to the dinner last night," Chris said, "it was strictly business. Miss Parish was the last person to see the cockpit crew alive.'' But he knew

Miller had scored a point. Hadn't he known the dinner was a mistake?

Miller leered. "Oh, well," he said, "I guess I can't blame a guy for making a date with a pretty girl. You don't have to explain to me, Galloway."

"That's right, I don't," Chris said, pushing down his anger.

"You got any more questions?" Miller looked at his Rolex. "Any more of my employees' complaints?"

"For now," Chris said pointedly, "that'll be it. Thank you for your cooperation. I do appreciate it." His tone was cool and impersonal.

"Anytime. Come on back and ask me some more questions."

"I'll be in touch if I need to speak to you again."

"Sure thing."

It wasn't until Chris was halfway back to Winthrop that his jaw relaxed and his pulse slowed. Oh, yes, Miller had really gotten to him, no doubt about it. He wouldn't be surprised, either, if Jim Fleisher had kept a notebook, not after that interview!

He glanced idly at the clock in the Taurus. It was 12:50. Holy cow, he'd forgotten! He was supposed to be on the 1:15 flight back to Seattle to meet Todd! He stepped on the accelerator, driving too fast back into town and then out to the airport. It was lucky things were close around Winthrop, or he'd never have made it. As it was, he had five minutes to spare as he grabbed his overnight bag from the back seat and slammed the car door behind him.

Chris walked swiftly into the terminal, went right to the gate, where he flashed his NTSB identification, and was ushered through with the usual forced courtesy. He was barely seated in the half-empty plane when the stairs were removed, the doors closed and the aircraft pulled away to head down the runway. He looked at his watch again—1:15 on the dot. Hell, you had to admire Miller's adherence to punctuality.

He hadn't had time to notice, but now he looked around, searching for a familiar face. The two cabin attendants were strangers, polite, smiling, attractive young women, but not Anna Parish. He let his head fall back against the seat and closed his eyes. It was better that Anna wasn't working this flight, much better. They would have had to smile and be polite and make small talk, awkward small talk. He should never have taken her out, never have let himself notice her vulnerability. Now it was time for his son, Todd, and he'd have his hands full there. Yes, it was Todd he'd have to concentrate on and not odd young women who believed in apparitions.

"Coffee?" the stewardess asked, leaning over him.

"Yes, black," he said. "Thanks."

Chris stared out at the bright May sky and the dark mountains below and went over everything he'd heard that day. He loosened his tie, undid the collar button on his shirt and tried to empty his mind of everything but the problem at hand—what had caused flight 629 to crash? His mind, however, refused to cooperate, and he found himself, much to his chagrin, staring out at fleecy white clouds and seeing Anna's face, her eyes, her pretty pink lips, imagining what the texture of her springing dark curls would feel like against his skin.

CHAPTER EIGHT

IT SEEMED LIKE AGES to Anna since she'd allowed herself an afternoon with the girls. Lunch, shopping, laughter and gossip. As she cleaned up the galley after the morning Winthrop-Seattle run, Anna actually found herself smiling, anticipating meeting her friend Cindy down by the waterfront for lunch. And Anna could always catch the late flight back to Winthrop, or even spend the night in Seattle if she wanted.

She checked her area one last time for the next crew, making sure she'd left the plane as she'd found it, then headed on through the movable ramp into the terminal of Seatac International Airport.

Lunch and shopping. Her steps felt light. For nearly three months it seemed all she'd done was grieve and try to pull the pieces of her life together. But now, well, maybe now she truly was coming out of that black cloud of pain and doubt.

Anna stopped by the WestAir office and signed out for the day. It was going to be a good day, too, seeing Cindy, an ex-stewardess who was now married and living in Seattle. Anna was glad Cindy had phoned early that morning—glad and feeling ridiculously young at heart as she stood on the curb and hailed a cab.

The weather in Seattle even cooperated with her mood, turning sunny and warm, not the usual rain and fog. It was going to be a beautiful day, nothing like the last time she'd been here when it poured cats and dogs and she'd been so upset about the NTSB interview. That was over; she'd seen Chris Galloway, and he hadn't been a monster, merely a lonely guy trying to do his job as well as he could. Oh, maybe he was somewhat lacking as a father, but he wasn't a *bad* person, just a man who had confused his priorities. Maybe it was a blessing that his son was coming to stay with him. It would force him to do his duty as a father. It would do him good.

Anna sat in the cab and wondered idly how that morning's interviews had gone for Chris, especially the one with Lee Miller. She wondered, too, if Miller would bring up the subject of their meeting last night at the Sun Mountain Lodge. Miller must have questioned that. Well, maybe at the very least Chris had asked a few questions today that he wouldn't have before talking to her.

The taxi sped along the freeway past the Boeing complex, and she remembered without consciously willing it how Chris had looked sitting at the bar last night. Clean features, wonderfully contoured over good bones. Deep-set, ice-blue eyes that watched the world with quick perception. Graceful hands and a strong neck. But he had also seemed tired, stressed out. She still wondered how he'd look if he let loose for once, really laughed, let it fly free.

Chris Galloway. Strange, how you met people and they weren't at all as you'd imagined. She'd spent time with a stranger, and he'd seen her cry, he'd seen her angry and defensive, yet they'd . . . well, she wasn't at all sure what had transpired between them. One thing was certain, last night had been more than an apology or a business dinner. Somehow Anna knew they'd both had an interlude from their troubles. She'd most likely never run into Chris Galloway again, but for those unexpected few hours she'd always thank him.

The taxi dropped her at the waterfront in the heart of Seattle. She saw the sign at the pier house: The Galley Oyster Bar. It was Cindy's favorite lunch spot, wonderful salads, creamy fish chowders, delicious oysters and affordable, too. The place was located out on pier 57 where there were shops and a bakery and other restaurants. Diners could sit and leisurely watch the ships and harbor ferries navigate the sound.

Cindy was full of gossip, as usual, and lunch was pleasant. The sun glinted off the water, and boats plied busily back and forth. Cindy told her where the best sales were, then sat back in her chair, smiled and looked expectantly at Anna. "Well, can't you tell? Don't I look different?"

Anna regarded her. "Did you get a perm?"

"No, dummy," Cindy said, beaming. "I'm pregnant."

"Oh, Cindy," Anna said, "that's wonderful. I'm so happy for you."

"I'm due in December. A Christmas baby. Oh, Anna, I'm so excited!"

And Anna was, too, but in the cab back to the airport that afternoon she felt her smile slip. Cindy pregnant. Everyone Anna knew was paired off, matched up, in love, starting families. Anna's mood slid another notch. God, it hurt. She *was* happy for Cindy, but she was sad for herself, sad and jealous, and she hated herself for being so small-minded. Oh, well, she'd manage. Maybe she'd be one of those old maid aunts whom everyone adored and leaned on, one who always had freshly baked cookies and lemonade ready...or was it hot chocolate? She smiled wistfully and tried awfully hard not to be angry at Jim for leaving her so bereft.

HE'D BE ON TIME, thank God. Chris checked his watch again, just to make sure. All he needed was to be late for Todd's flight, just when the kid was being shipped off from home like an unwanted puppy dog, probably against his will, too. He'd even have time to grab a late lunch and call the Seattle hotel to reserve a room for Todd. Maybe get back in touch with the rental agent.

He figured his son would prefer a separate hotel room. After all, Chris was practically a stranger. He'd never once since his divorce spent one night in the same room with his son. Pretty sad.

Okay, so he'd been a lousy father, but he'd make up for it. He'd get this investigation well under way, and then perhaps he could hand it over to someone else and take some time off.

He checked his watch again automatically, then stared out the window. It was a good thing it was off-season and WestAir flights were half-empty, because he really didn't want to be in the cockpit having to make conversation. He had too much on his mind right now. Mostly Todd. What *was* he going to do with the kid until he could hand this case over to someone? Chris worked long, irregular hours; he had to be ready to drop everything on the spur of the moment if the board members in D.C. wanted to see him. What would Todd do, stuck somewhere in a strange city? It was the worst possible scenario for a troubled kid. Helen should have her head examined for doing this; she knew Chris's schedule, and she knew how hard it would be for him.

Chris rubbed his jaw. A man couldn't turn his back on his own son, but how was he going to juggle his job and a kid? It wasn't as if he could send Todd to a day-care center or hire a baby-sitter. Hell, no, Todd was too old for that. Too old for a sitter but too young to be on his own. Good God, what was Chris supposed to do?

"More coffee, Mr. Galloway?" the stewardess asked.

"Yeah, I'll take another cup. Thanks."

"Oh, no trouble, Mr. Galloway. It's such an empty flight I've got all the time in the world."

They wanted to please; they always wanted to please Chris. The funny thing was, he'd just as soon be left alone and, no doubt, the flight crew would have preferred he'd taken a different plane. Ironic. There was a lot about his life that seemed ironic lately. He was a man used to being in control, in command of all that occurred around him. Yet inside, deep inside and well hidden from the world, Chris felt totally out of control. There was his son and the upcoming hassles. And there was now a new fact of his life he'd just become aware of—an emptiness. He hadn't known of its existence before Anna Parish. And that made him uneasy.

The stewardess moved on down the aisle, and from the back she could almost have been Anna. There were subtle differences, though. This girl was heavier in the hips, her hair longer, her way of walking not the same.

He allowed himself to wonder where Anna was now. In Seattle, he guessed, as she'd had that early flight. He hoped he didn't run into her. Last night had been a lapse in judgment. He'd left things in good shape, though, and told her goodbye. It was just as well he had, too, because for a moment when they were walking back to her car, Chris had almost asked if he could see her again in Seattle sometime. Almost. It had been half a bottle of wine and then that brandy. Good thing he'd caught himself.

He pushed his thoughts back to Todd. The emptiness Chris had felt was about to be taken care of, anyway. He could see himself introducing his son to people. "This is Todd, my son," he'd say, and he'd be proud as punch. That was what Todd needed—a father, a male role model. He was too old to be hanging around his mother all the time, and that was obviously the conclusion Helen had arrived at.

Sure, it was going to be a great summer. And when Todd went home to Helen he'd be a new kid.

The plane banked, coming in to Seatac Airport. Seattle lay below his window, undulating along its highways right up to the water. It was a beautiful spring day, the sun glinting off the choppy waves of Puget Sound like handfuls of diamonds. A wonderful day for Todd to arrive. Maybe they could go up in the Space Needle later that afternoon, see the sights, have a marvelous seafood dinner. Father and son.

The plane was almost down now, the ground rushing by on either side. Idly he looked out the window, watching the airport flash by at high speed. He noted the flaps in proper position, felt the contained vibration of the engines. They'd touch down any second now; yes, there was the first thump of the landing gear on the tarmac, a soft bounce, a second thump of the nose gear touching down. Chris checked his watch and reached for his briefcase, wanting to be off the plane quickly.

Then he heard a muffled retort. A gunshot, a blown engine, a piece of debris? Dozens of possibilities flashed through his mind, but there wasn't time to pursue the thought, because the aircraft lurched just then, throwing Chris back into his seat and flinging him sideways so that the seat belt dug into his hips. Then they were skidding, fast, out of control, and Chris had time to feel the adrenaline shoot through his body. The right wingtip caught on something. People yelled. Someone screamed. The plane careened off the runway, spinning, then stopped short as the wheels hit soft mud.

Chris flew forward, hitting his head and shoulder on something hard and unyielding. Pain flared in him for a split second, fierce pain that took his breath away, and he felt himself sinking, losing consciousness, unable to breathe. Everything was going black around the edges, and he was too weak, in too much pain to fight it. The last thought he had before he passed out was so very curious. Later, much later, he'd remember it in amazement. It was an immense regret that suffused his whole body—regret that he'd never see Anna Parish again.

CHAPTER NINE

ANNA SIGHED and deposited her two heavy shopping bags next to the WestAir ticket counter. She'd decided to catch a flight back to Winthrop that afternoon and save the expense of a hotel. And one thing was for sure—there would be plenty of space available. It was still off-season, after all.

But Ned, the ticket agent, was busy, his back to her while he spoke on the phone. "Oh, man," she heard him say in a low tone. "God, what a mess."

An alarm sounded in Anna's head. It was something in Ned's voice, the urgency she detected, the disbelief in his tone. When he finally hung up and turned back to the counter, her alarm grew. His face was troubled.

"What is it?" she asked. "Has something happened, Ned?"

He let out a long breath. "There's been an accident, Anna. It was 836, the Winthrop-Seattle run."

"Oh, my God." Anna paled and felt her knees turn to mush. It had happened again!

"They blew a tire out on runway 3A," Ned told her in a hushed voice.

Anna licked suddenly dry lips. "Who... Ned, who was working the flight? Was anyone... were there fatalities? Oh, God."

"Don't know yet. But the plane's intact. Skidded off the runway." He swore softly. "When's it going to end, Anna? When are they going to get that son of a bitch, Miller?"

But she wasn't listening. "Ned, can you punch up the passenger and flight crew list? I know you're not supposed to—"

"Sure, Anna. Don't worry about it." He collected himself and went to work on his keyboard, the green of the computer screen reflecting in his eyes. "Here it comes, flight 836."

Anna peered around the counter and he tilted the screen toward her. Pilot, Sid Laskey. Copilot, Eddy Sinouski, on and on. Anna knew the women working the cabin, Jill and Paula. Then the passenger list came up, passengers and the seat assignments given to them in Winthrop.

She must have stared at the name C. Galloway for a full minute before she realized what she was seeing. And then it was as if someone had driven a needle loaded with adrenaline straight into her heart. The blood drained out of her head in a rush and she gripped the counter.

"Anna? Is everything—" Ned began.

"Where?" she breathed. "Where have they taken them? What hospital?"

Ned didn't know. And it was another fifteen minutes before Anna could find out. She also learned that no one had been injured badly, or at least that was what people were saying. But reportedly there had been plenty of scrapes and bruises, a broken bone or two. She grabbed a taxi out front and headed straight to the hospital.

Chris. My God, she kept thinking. She'd wanted him to realize there were problems at WestAir, but not this way. God, no. Because Anna knew firsthand what it was like to live through a crash. Those last seconds, the awful, vast confusion, the horror. She couldn't fathom Chris Galloway having gone through that nightmare, too. If she'd taken a moment to examine the strength of her reaction, Anna might have realized it was far stronger than it should have been. But at the moment she could only wonder if the reports about the lack of injuries were wrong.

As the taxi moved through the traffic, the image of the WestAir plane skidding at high speed off the runway kept beating at her. The terror the passengers must have suffered; Sid, the pilot, trying desperately to control the aircraft as it lurched and careened. They must have thought it was going to flip over. Surely there had been that possibility. They would have seen flames in their mind's eyes, flames and explosions and screams of terror....

And Chris. The one-man crusader, wholly bent on passenger safety. What thoughts had shot through his head? What was he thinking now? Was Chris even conscious, aware of what had happened?

A spurt of loathing for Lee Miller coursed through her. A blown tire. Probably one of the mechanics had requested new tires months ago, and Miller had put that request on a back burner. Of course, he'd say he never received any such order. And the mechanic would suffer the blame. Or perhaps the mechanic never put in a request at all, afraid of disturbing Miller's bottom line.

At the hospital the front desk personnel were helpful. But then this hadn't been a flight carrying three hundred people, either. "Yes, Galloway, here it is," a receptionist told her. "Room 403. Take the first elevator to the left over there."

Then Chris was alive. They didn't put fatalities into rooms. But they *did* put badly injured people in rooms.

She walked rapidly down the corridor, her heart stampeding in her ears, her breath caught in her chest, starving her of air. It seemed so far, endless walls and doors and the muted clink of food trays, muffled voices of nurses, the overpowering antiseptic smell. She watched for the number, but it seemed always in front of her: 400, 401, 402—

There it was. She stopped short, shut her eyes and tried to take in a full lungful of air. How would she find him? Unconscious, mutilated, in agony?

An image of Chris, strong and tall and vibrant, filled her mind suddenly. She saw those clear blue eyes in his handsome face, the tilt of his lips when he tried to smile. It all came flooding in on her, his hand on the small of her back, the way he'd held her on that cold and windy hillside, the strong feelings that had stirred traitorously in her belly....

After a long moment, she reached out and pushed on the door to 403. It opened soundlessly, heavy and solid and wide.

"Mr. Galloway," someone was saying, "you really do have to stay in bed."

"Look, I can't. I have to—"

Anna stepped into the room and both occupants swiveled their heads toward her.

"Is he...?" Anna began. "I mean, am I allowed in here?"

The nurse regarded her for a moment, as if trying to decide whether Anna were friend or foe. "Yes, he's allowed visitors. Are you a relative?"

"Uh, no, a friend," she managed to say.

"Do you think you could convince him to stay in bed for the time being? I seem to be having trouble doing it," the nurse said curtly.

Anna shifted her gaze cautiously to the bed. Chris was propped up, his head bandaged, his arm in a sling. He was looking at her almost without comprehension, as if he couldn't fathom her presence.

"Chris?" she said timidly. He was there, in front of her, alive, conscious, talking. She felt every nerve ending in her body tingle with a wild mixture of relief and gladness as an unaccountable thought flew through her head: Jim had left her, but this man hadn't. He'd lived; his lifeblood still flowed.

She didn't know what to say then. The nurse was taking his pulse. Still, Chris seemed oblivious, wrapped in his own world of confusion and pain.

Anna took a tentative step closer. A part of her was checking him out, judging just how badly he was injured. Another part of her, one that she was trying desperately to subdue, was drinking in the sight of him, noticing the way a comma of sandy hair showed beneath his head bandage. Her knees felt rubbery all over again, and she was aware of her chest rising and falling too rapidly.

She glanced at the nurse, then back at Chris. She tried her voice. "Are you . . . are you all right?"

It seemed to take him a moment to focus and recognize her. "Anna?"

She smiled and felt her mouth tremble slightly. "*Are* you all right?" she asked once more.

"Yeah," he got out. "But what...?"

"I heard at the airport."

"And you came here," he said, regarding her for so long that she could only look down at her hands tightly gripping her purse.

"I was...worried," Anna said finally. "You...you look like you're in a lot of pain, Chris."

"A concussion," he said. "They tell me I have a concussion."

Anna glanced up swiftly to the nurse. "Is he in any danger?"

"Only from his own foolishness. He's got to stay here tonight at least. For observation," the woman said while she wrote on a chart.

"I can't stay," Chris said, and Anna knew that this wasn't the first time he'd told the nurse that. "My son's flying in. I have to pick him up."

"You're not picking anyone up," the nurse said, and gave Anna a meaningful glance.

"Look, let's cut this baloney. I have to pick my son up. A sixteen-year-old kid—for God's sake! I'll sign myself out of here," Chris said angrily.

He tried to push himself up then, and Anna saw him turn pale and break out into a sweat.

"Settle down. Somebody will meet Todd. Isn't there someone at your office I could call for you?" she asked.

He shook his head. "I can't think of a soul."

"Well, how about..." But she knew he was right. There was no one.

"Get this IV out of my arm," he ordered the nurse.

Anna hardly weighed the consequences before she spoke. "Okay. All right. I'll do it, Chris."

"What?"

"I said I'll do it. I'll meet Todd's flight."

"God, Anna, what can I say? If you can't do it, I'll..."

"I *said* I'd do it."

"It's asking a lot."

"Never mind that right now."

"Then you don't mind...?" He pronounced it "mine"; the drugs they'd given him were at work. His eyelids began to droop and his fingers twitched, going limp. She glanced at the IV in his arm. She'd bet it was loaded with painkillers. "Can't thank you 'nough, Anna, can't..."

For a few more minutes Anna stood next to his bed and watched him. In rest his face seemed relaxed, the worry lines around his eyes softened. His color looked better, too, and she listened to the soft breathing from his slightly parted lips.

She smiled to herself. Moments before he'd been an angry man, ready to take on the world to have his own way. But now... well, now he was quiescent, resting, a handsome man in his sleep.

She stood there for too long after the nurse left. Stood there and watched him and, against her better judgment, found herself comparing him to Jim. She tried not to. She tried to repress her thoughts, but they came of their own accord. Jim and Chris. Jim, gone now, a memory so painful that at times she thought her heart might break. And Chris. Practically a stranger, whom fate had thrown into her path.

Jim and Chris. Both men were strong, silent types. Hard workers who believed in their jobs, who believed their work mattered. At times Jim had been at least as single-minded as Chris, but whereas Jim could have gone on flying for many years, Anna couldn't imagine Chris tolerating the level of the stress from his job much longer. Either his body would give out or his mind would.

It was a curious thought that settled in her head as Anna stood in the dim room. Curious and unexpected: Chris needed her a whole lot more than Jim had. She sighed. Well, Chris needed *someone*. Maybe not Anna Parish, she decided, but someone to care about him, to care if he ate properly or got enough rest. To care if he—

Suddenly Anna forced her thoughts back to reality and glanced at her watch. Todd Galloway was due to arrive at Seatac in thirty-five minutes. She'd like to tell Chris she was heading to meet his son's flight, to reassure him. But he was out cold, his breathing deepening now, his face so relaxed . . .

TODD GALLOWAY didn't look at all how Anna had imagined he would. She'd pictured a miniature Chris, but the sixteen-year-old boy who emerged from the plane was an utter surprise.

Twenty or thirty years ago Anna would have called him a hippy. Today she guessed he'd be called a punk. He was a "radical dude," anyway, wearing black engineer boots, black faded jeans with holes in the knees, a dirty white T-shirt under a leather vest, some sort of an Indian bead necklace, and a long blond stringy ponytail halfway down his back. Sunglasses hid his eyes, but not his complexion. He was pale and had unattended acne. All Anna could think was, Oh, God, poor Chris.

After he was pointed out to her, Anna walked up to him slowly. She hadn't a clue how this young man was going to take the news of his father being injured and in the hospital. Would he be afraid? Would he cry? Probably not cry, but surely, after flying three thousand miles from home, he'd be very upset.

She was hardly prepared for his reaction. Todd Galloway snapped his gum and shrugged. "Yeah, so?" he said, looking disinterestedly around the concourse.

"Todd," Anna tried again, "your dad's in the hospital. He's got some serious injuries. His head's—"

"Big deal. Man, like I fly a zillion miles to meet the dude and he doesn't even show." He took off his sunglasses and eyed her from his six-foot height. "Who're you, anyway? A stew? I can't believe he sends a *stew* to meet me. Like, wow, I'm real impressed."

"Now, listen," she began.

"Oh, right, sorry. That was rude, wasn't it?"

"You're a very amusing kid," Anna said, just barely controlling herself. "You're so amusing, Todd, that I'm going to put it to you real straight. You have two choices here. Either you can straighten your act up for a minute or so and we'll go over to the hospital, decide where you're going to stay, or you can wing it out of here on your own. You seem to be a big boy, and Seattle's a fun city. I'm sure you'll do just fine." Then she added, "Got any money? The food's great here, but it costs."

Todd was completely silent, obviously unused to someone calling his bluff.

"Look," Anna said, "I'm waiting, kid. Either we go together now, or I'm out of here on the next flight to Winthrop. Your choice."

"Hey, man," he began.

"No, Todd," she said, "my name's Anna, not 'man.' I'm a pretty nice lady when people play it straight with me. But being a smart aleck won't work with me. What do you say?"

She got the shrug again and an ironic twist to his mouth—a stern mouth much like his father's. "Guess I'll cruise the city," he said, and began to saunter on down the concourse.

"Oh, boy," Anna breathed. What had she done? Chris was going to wake up and have a heart attack. The boy had come three thousand miles to visit, and Anna had driven him off. She'd played it all wrong. She knew nothing whatsoever about kids. Oh, Lord...

But Anna's fears were unfounded. Within a very few minutes Todd appeared again from the thick of the crowd. He was walking slowly, as if still nonchalant about the whole thing, as if he'd just "cruised" the city and found it dull.

"Hi," Anna said, "I'm glad you're back."

He shrugged.

"I really am," she tried, "because, well, because I'd like some company going back to the hospital."

He sort of bobbed his head noncommittally and let out a breath. "Okay. You're a pretty tough lady. Maybe I'll let you buy me dinner or something."

"The hospital first," Anna said, "then we'll see."

"Okay, dude...*Anna,* let's go take a look at my ol' man."

Chris was still out cold when they arrived. Apparently, seeing his father lying so helpless in a hospital bed, had its effect on Todd. The boy actually said, "Wow, he's real busted up, huh?"

"Yes, he is," Anna whispered, "but he'll be fine."

"When?"

"Soon. A week, maybe two."

"What am I gonna do till then? I mean..." He kept staring at his father.

"Well," Anna said, "we can get your dad's hotel key and—" But she realized she didn't have any idea where Chris was staying in Seattle. And even if she did, a boy his age shouldn't be left alone in a strange hotel in a strange town.

She recalled Chris mentioning having contacted a rental agent but not taking the time to look at the places. And she recalled her statement about priorities. Well, in this case, it sure would have been easier if Chris *had* bothered to get a house. "Look," Anna said, still quietly, "maybe we should call your mother."

"Oh, no way! Not a chance. She'd have a fit, man...Anna, I mean."

"Why would she have a fit, Todd?"

"Man, I don't know. I just know she'd be real mad."

"At you?"

"I don't know."

Anna let it drop. Plainly the relationship at home wasn't so good.

They sat for a time in Chris's room, wondering if he were going to wake up. Anna already knew she couldn't just leave Todd in a hotel, even if she did know which one. Maybe she should get him a room and one for herself. In the morning they'd see how Chris was coming along.

A couple of times Chris stirred, groaned in pain, then drifted off again. He was never aware of them in his room. The nurse checked on him and left. The doctor made a quick round, looked over the chart, then left. And all the while Anna sat there, wondering what to do with this pain-in-the-butt teenager whose hormones, from what she'd seen, were totally out of control.

"Think he's gonna wake up?" Todd asked her.

"I don't know," Anna replied.

"Should we stay?"

"I don't really know."

"We could leave him a note or something."

"Well, we could, I guess."

Todd was right. It was useless waiting for Chris to wake up only to tell him she'd gotten Todd at the airport. He probably wouldn't even remember in the morning.

"You want to write the note?" she asked Todd. "I think your dad would appreciate it."

"Sure," he said sullenly.

"I mean it. He told me about your coming for the summer, and he was really very excited."

"I bet."

"He was. I don't lie to people, Todd." She looked squarely at him. "Listen, go and borrow some paper and a pen from the nurses' station. We'll leave that note. Okay?"

"Yeah, I guess."

He was back in a couple of minutes, paper in hand. Anna gently prodded him to do the writing. It was important to her that Chris know the message was from his son. It was probably even more important for Todd to make this gesture, small as it was.

"Where'll I tell him I'm staying?" the boy asked.

Anna drew her dark brows together and thought. It was shortly after six. There *was* a 7:30 p.m. to Winthrop. The last evening flight. But what would Chris think?

Oh, what the heck. "Ever been to the mountains?" Anna asked.

"Huh?"

"I'm thinking we could fly up to Winthrop tonight, and you can stay with me at my house. It's crowded, kind of. But the couch is comfortable. What do you think? I'll make it your call.''

"How do you spell Winthrop?''

The flight seemed long and Anna was tired. The mishap with Chris's plane had milked her dry. And now Todd. It was a heck of a responsibility, this kid. Her cat was bad enough. But a real live kid—and one with a load of troubles, it seemed.

"They got any more peanuts?'' Todd asked, peering out the window at the evening-darkened Cascades. "Is that still snow down there?''

"On the higher peaks, yes.''

"Radical, man. I mean, Anna.'' Then he asked, "What's there to do in Winthrop? They got any movies? A mall?''

"No movie house yet and definitely no mall. It's really tiny. Kind of Old West but different. There's a ski area.''

"I skied once.''

"Did you like it?''

"Ah, I wasn't much good at it.''

"Takes practice, Todd.''

"And money, man.''

"Well, the kids in Winthrop work weekends and stuff up at the ski area. They get meals, a lift pass. You know.''

"Oh.''

"Do you work, Todd? I mean, when you're out of school?''

He shrugged. She was getting really used to that body language. "I did work at this drugstore at home.''

"And?''

"Ah, what the heck, I got busted stealing.''

"I see.''

"It wasn't a big deal. But Mom, like she had this heart attack or something."

"Um. Did you learn anything?"

"Yeah. Don't get busted."

"That's not what I meant."

"You mean, do I still rip stuff off? Nah. It's a pain."

"Why a pain?"

"What is this, the third degree?"

"No, I was only curious."

He fell into his peanut eating, and Anna let it go. He was a strange one, a mixture of seething emotions, battling one another at every turn. She'd seen ten different sides to this boy in the couple of hours she'd known him. It saddened Anna. A kid shouldn't be so darn mixed up. It was as if no one ever listened to him, really heard him. And Chris. She felt badly for him, too. It was his job now to deal with this confused teenager, a boy he barely knew. But, in truth, she realized as the plane banked on approach, it was Chris's problem. Not hers. She'd provide dinner and the couch, complete with cat and blankets. She'd show Todd where the bathroom was. Heck, he could wander around Winthrop for days and never find any trouble. Maybe she'd take him on a nice long hike, wear him out.

"That the town down there?" he asked.

Anna peered past his shoulder. "That's Winthrop."

"God, it's *small*."

"Oh, it's big enough for you, Todd Galloway," she said, and gave him a bright smile.

CHAPTER TEN

IT WAS LATE when Anna unlocked the door of her house and ushered Todd in. Not so very late in Winthrop, but certainly late enough in Syracuse, New York, where Todd had begun his journey that morning.

"Cool house," he said, looking around and picking up the cat.

"Thanks."

"You live here alone?" he asked, obviously trying to place her relationship with his father.

"Not exactly. I have a roommate, Madeline, and her, uh, her fiancé, Flip, but it's only temporary," she hastened to explain. "They're getting married next month and moving out."

"So how'd you meet my dad?"

"He's investigating a crash I was involved in," she said.

"Nice job he has, huh? Gory stuff all the time."

"He has an important job."

"Yeah, so he says."

"Now, young man, you're going to have to call your mother and tell her where you are."

"*Now?* It's late. She'll kill me," he said, plumping onto the couch, cat on his lap.

"It'd be much worse if she called tomorrow to check on you and heard your dad's in the hospital and you're nowhere to be found. Maybe she's even tried to call already."

Todd hung his head and shrugged.

"Trust me on this one, Todd. You just have to do it. Sometimes we have to do things we don't like, but that's part of growing up."

He rolled his eyes. "Man, Anna, you sound like my mother."

"Call her. The phone's there." She pointed. "And give her my number here."

Reluctantly the boy picked up the receiver. Anna waited until she was sure he'd dialed and the telephone was ringing on the other end. He seemed to sit there holding the receiver to his ear for a very long time, but she could tell when someone answered because Todd abruptly turned away from her.

"Mom? Mom, it's me, Todd." Then he waited for a moment, and Anna could see him shifting uneasily. "Mom, wait, I'm sorry I'm calling so late. I know I woke you up. I'm fine. There's this lady, I'm at her house, see, and she made me call." Silence, then. "Well, see it's like this. Dad was in a plane crash... No, he's okay, but he's in the hospital in Seattle, and he sent this lady to get me, and we flew to this town she lives in, and I'm at her house now." He shifted some more, his slender back hunching in tension. "I'll give you the number here, her name. Her name's Anna, Anna...?" He turned and questioned her with a look.

"Parish," she said.

"Anna Parish. She's a stewardess for WestAir," Todd told his mother. "No, I don't think so, Mom."

Anna couldn't help smiling. Todd's mother must be wondering who in the heck this strange stewardess was.

Finally Todd turned again, holding the phone out to Anna. "She wants to talk to you."

"I'm Helen Severin," came a woman's voice, suspicious, full of resentment.

"I'm Anna Parish. I'm, uh, a friend of Chris's."

"And you picked Todd up at the airport?"

"Well, there really wasn't anyone else. Chris couldn't leave the hospital."

"How badly was he hurt?" she asked, but there wasn't fear or sympathy in her voice, only a need to assess the damage.

"A concussion and a dislocated shoulder. He'll probably be released tomorrow," Anna said. "I didn't know what to do with Todd, so I brought him home with me. He has an airline pass, so it wasn't any problem."

"Yes, his father provides him with that at least. Funny how Chris always manages to have an excuse not to take on responsibility where Todd is concerned. It's typical of him," Helen said.

"Well, he really was hurt. I felt sorry for him, and there wasn't anyone else to get his son. As soon as Chris is out of the hospital, he'll take Todd and—"

"And what? Look, Miss Parish, I don't know how well you know Chris, but has he spoken about Todd, about any plans he may have? All I have is the phone number of the office in Seattle. I don't even know where he's living."

"Oh, yes, he spoke of Todd. He was looking forward to having him. I know he was going to figure things out, where they were going to live for the summer, and all that."

"For the *summer?*" Helen laughed. "I guess he didn't listen. I've sent him Todd for longer than the summer."

"Oh," Anna said, just now comprehending. But Helen Severin told her no more. Anna sensed the woman was embarrassed. Perhaps she felt like a failure where her son was concerned. Whatever. The one thing Anna did understand was that Todd had been sent to his father on a permanent basis. She wondered just how Chris was going to take *that* news.

"Thank you," Helen was saying to Anna, "for watching Todd. I'd tell you to ship him on back, but—"

"I understand," Anna said, "and I'm sure Chris will be out of the hospital tomorrow or the next day."

They said goodbye stiffly, and Anna put the receiver down and faced Todd Galloway. "So," she said, "you're here for good."

"Yeah." He shrugged.

"Want to talk about it?"

"Naw. It's no big deal," he said, rubbing the cat's ears, but Anna guessed he must have gotten into a whole lot of trouble to have been shipped off like that. It was still May, too, and she knew his school couldn't have been over for the year. Most likely he'd been kicked out. Great.

"You got anything to eat?" Todd was asking. "That meal on the plane, man, it wasn't much."

Anna fixed him two sandwiches, and then he attacked the cupboards. She kept trying to get him to open up, but he was all balled up inside. What she did learn, however, and only from a word or two, was that he didn't get along with his stepfather. No doubt there was little room for the teenager in Helen's new life. It was a too-familiar story. A divorce. A remarriage. Disaster for the children caught in the middle. No wonder the boy was acting up. He probably craved attention. And she wondered if Chris could provide that much-needed attention. Chris, who was so busy and tied up with his work that he barely had time for his own needs.

Todd fell asleep instantly after cleaning out the rest of the refrigerator. Anna kept the door of her room ajar and waited up, knowing Madeline and Flip would be getting in sometime soon, and they'd be pretty surprised seeing a strange body asleep on the couch. She'd have to explain everything to them—the accident and Chris and Todd.

Shortly after midnight they came in, giggling together, Madeline hushing Flip, closing the front door quietly. And then it was one in the morning by the time Anna had explained who the boy was and why he was there. But as they stood whispering in the kitchen, Flip was barely listening. Instead he was livid, furious at Lee Miller, blaming the man directly for the blown tire on that afternoon's flight.

"Damn that man," Flip kept saying. "You know he's too cheap to spring for parts! Damn him!"

"Shh," Madeline said, nodding toward the living room.

But Flip went right on with his tirade about buying Miller out before the man ruined a perfectly good airline, not to mention the lives of the employees and passengers.

It was almost one-thirty before Flip turned in, still growling. And then Madeline had to put in a last word while Anna sat at the kitchen table, head in her hands.

"Do you think it's wise to have Galloway's son here?" she asked Anna.

"I don't know. What was I supposed to do?"

"Anything. Anything but bring the kid here."

"He won't be any trouble."

"It isn't that," Madeline said. "It's his old man. Chris Galloway."

"So?"

"The man's the enemy, Anna."

"I don't quite see it that way," Anna said, sighing, tired of the whole thing. "Maybe Chris can help us."

"How?"

"I don't know. Maybe he'll find Jim's notebook. Maybe he can get some of the pilots to open up about Miller, go public."

"Fat chance."

Anna looked up sharply. "You know," she said, "if Flip or any one of the cockpit crews came forward, it would make a world of difference in this investigation. Maybe even in the buy-out bid."

"Well," Madeline said, turning toward the door, "I don't see that happening. What I do see is men like your Chris Galloway looking for convenient scapegoats. Like...like Jim Fleisher." And with that she left, and Anna had to wonder if Madeline wasn't one hundred percent right.

ANNA SLEPT LATE, woke and heard voices in the kitchen. It took her a moment of fuzzy thinking before she identified them—Madeline and Todd. Putting on her bathrobe, she joined them, yawning as she reached for a cup of coffee.

"Morning, Todd," she said. "I see you've met my roommate."

"Yeah," he said, eating toast and fried potatoes swimming in catsup.

"Oh, Todd and I are buddies. We let you sleep and I cooked," Madeline said dryly. "I guess we better buy some groceries. This kid can eat."

"Oh, I'm sure Chris will call soon and want him back in Seattle. Don't you think so, Todd?"

He shrugged.

Madeline caught Anna's eye over Todd's head and raised an eyebrow. Anna shook her head slightly. "Where's Flip?" she asked.

"Out jogging. He's still mad about that accident yesterday, trying to run it off."

"Did you meet Flip?" she asked Todd.

"Yeah, he's cool. Funny."

Madeline hid a smile.

"That's nice," Anna said. "I'll tell you what, Todd, why don't you shower now, so in case you have to take a flight to Seattle you'll be all ready."

With Todd safely in the shower Anna had a chance to talk to Madeline. "So he's not so bad, is he?"

"I see the family resemblance," Madeline said wryly. "They're both such charmers."

"This kid's been through it, Madeline. I feel sorry for him."

"I feel sorry for his mother," Madeline said, "but I'll be damned if I feel sorry for his father."

"I'm sort of surprised Chris hasn't called yet, to tell the truth. Don't they have breakfast early in hospitals?"

"You'd think so."

"I mean, what am I going to do with Todd? He'll be so bored here."

"Call Chris. Lay it on him. It's *his* kid," Madeline said.

And Anna did exactly that. She telephoned the hospital and asked for Chris Galloway in room 403.

"Oh, he's checked out," the desk nurse said. "The doctor let him go this morning."

"He's already gone?"

"Yes, ma'am. Left right after breakfast."

She put the receiver down. "He's gone," she said, turning to Madeline.

"So I gathered. Think he's on his way here?"

"I don't know *what* to think. I thought he'd call as soon as he woke up this morning. I mean—"

"Men," Madeline said. "They never learned to communicate."

"Funny." Anna sat at the kitchen table, thinking, sipping her coffee. "Well, for one thing, I *refuse* to sit around waiting for him."

"Thata girl."

"I'll just do my errands, take Todd along if he wants. Go for a walk. Take a drive..."

"Sounds like a blast." Madeline thought for a second. "Look, Flip and I are flying his Cessna to Vancouver to see his parents. You want us to take Todd along?"

Anna stared at her. "You'd do that? Flip would do that?"

Madeline raised her shoulders and let them drop. "What're friends for? It'll get him out of your hair. We'll be back tomorrow. Let his father stew. Hey, he'll probably thank you for getting rid of Todd for a day."

"Oh, Madeline, don't be mean. Chris really wants this to work with Todd." But Anna was beginning to wonder about that.

"He can start making it work tomorrow. You know Flip's folks have that great house on the island with a sailboat and all. There'll be so much to do, he'll forget about being a juvenile delinquent for a day," Madeline said.

"The Akers won't mind?"

"No, they're too busy with their tennis game to notice."

"And Flip?"

"Oh, Flip will be glad to do you a good turn. After all, he's been living off your generosity for weeks."

"Friends don't ask for paybacks," Anna said quietly. "Listen, Madeline, I wanted to talk to you." But Madeline was carrying dishes to the sink, her back to Anna, and didn't say anything.

"Madeline?"

"Hmm, what?"

"You want to talk? It's not often I get you without Flip around," she said lightly.

"About what?"

"Oh, anything. Have you been...ah...sleeping better lately?"

Madeline turned and eyed her. "Fine," she said. "I'm sleeping fine."

"Good," Anna said, not believing a word. "I'm glad to hear that." And the knowledge of what they didn't mention hung between them. It was as if they were both playing a game, the object of which was to spare the other pain, as if by not saying its name it didn't exist.

Todd came in then, his long hair wet and hanging down his back. He sat down silently, picked up a magazine and began leafing through it, as if nobody else were in the room. Madeline rolled her eyes and turned back to the dishes.

"Well, guess I'll get dressed," Anna said to no one in particular, but Todd never looked up.

She showered in the tepid water that was left after Todd's bath and cast about for ways to handle the boy. He wasn't enormously pleasant to be around, although she'd seen glimmerings of a more decent person in him. She needed to do some errands in town and wondered whether she should ask Todd if he wanted to tag along or whether he'd rather stay here. She guessed she'd ask him to go, anyway, and hope that he preferred staying here. And then, what if he didn't want to go to Vancouver? What would she do with him until Chris decided to take over? Lord, that man was irritating!

By the time she got dressed, Flip had returned, Madeline had spoken to him and they were presenting their plan to Todd.

"You got your own plane?" Todd asked Flip, showing enthusiasm for once.

"Yes, and we're going to visit my parents, Maddy and I. Thought you might want to come along. Just for a lark, you know," Flip said. "Have you got some ID? A driver's license will get you into Canada for the day."

Todd scowled. "Nah. No license. But I've got my passport."

"You're *sure* you don't mind?" Anna asked Flip.

"Nah, the plane holds four, so what the heck?"

"What if your dad comes for you, Todd? What should I tell him?"

Instantly the sullen look was back on the boy's face. "He won't care, man. He's busy."

His reply was so full of carefully denied pain that Anna wanted to shudder.

As it turned out, Todd did decide to tag along with Anna until Flip and Madeline were ready to go.

He didn't say much at the grocery store, just looked around with undisguised disdain, as if to say, "What a rinky-dink operation this is." He was barely civil when Anna ran into a couple of old friends and introduced him. He looked superior in the hardware store and didn't laugh or even smile when Benny James, the owner, said something meant to be amusing about his long blond hair.

But when Anna drove out East Chewack Road to pick up fresh milk at Edna's dairy, his nose was practically pressed to the car window.

"Pretty, isn't it?" she asked.

"It's okay."

"Different from back East, I guess," she tried.

"Yeah."

"There's a lot of hiking and camping and fishing around here. Skiing in the winter, like I told you. Horseback riding. Do you do *any* of those things, Todd?"

"No."

"What *do* you like to do?"

"Nothing. Hang around." He shrugged. "I live in a city."

"Well, maybe you could try some of those things with your dad. He told me he used to do stuff like that when he was young."

"Yeah, he told me all that camping stuff. Boring."

"Not so boring."

His thin shoulders moved noncommittally under his black T-shirt, and his chin was thrust out.

Anna gave up. Todd wasn't her problem; she didn't have to entertain him.

She collected her two quarts of milk from Edna, the kind in old-fashioned bottles with a bulb at the top where the cream collected. When she got back into her car, Todd was staring out across the fields. "*That's* what I want to do," he said with a measure of ferocity in his voice.

She looked. Edna's son was out there, driving a tractor, hauling manure. "What?" she asked, not understanding.

"*Driving.* I'm sixteen. I want to drive."

She looked at him. "Well, sure you can drive. Your dad'll teach you."

"Oh, right. When he's around. Right. And what state would I get a permit from? I don't even know where I live anymore!"

He was correct about that. He needed to be a resident of...somewhere, didn't he? "Oh, Todd, I'm sure Chris will take care of it. Don't worry."

But he ignored her. "And where am I going to go to school? Nobody tells me. I get booted out of school for some bum rap and I gotta leave all my friends and come to this...this hick town."

"Oh, I'm sure you'll be going back to Washington, D.C., with your dad. That's where he lives."

"He doesn't *live* anywhere, man."

He was right again. And Chris really was going to have to do something about that. But meanwhile...

"I'll tell you what, if you promise not to snitch on me, I'll let you drive my car a little. It's a country road here, no traffic. The worst you can do is go into the ditch, I guess."

"You would? Oh, man." He straightened up and looked at her. "Is this car a stick shift or what?"

"Stick, four forward speeds. It's easy. Now wait till I get out of Edna's driveway and you can try. You know how to let the clutch up and give it gas?"

"Well, I drove a friend's car. Once."

Once. Oh, boy.

She negotiated the driveway and pulled over to the side of the road. "Okay, let's switch. Now adjust the seat. The rearview mirror. Now first gear. Oh, not that way! All right, there, that's better."

He jerked the car, stalled it, tried again. His concentration was fierce, total. He muttered and gripped the steering wheel with white fingers. Anna was sure he never heard a word she said. Eventually the car jerked and bounced down the road without stalling.

"Second gear now, straight down, easy, there, let up the clutch, give it gas. No, too much. Okay, that's better."

He stared straight ahead except when he looked down to shift, and then the car swerved all over the road. Anna held her breath, let it out slowly. He was in second, then third, going too slowly for third, lugging the protesting engine. He was smiling, though, grinning widely, oversteering and pressing the accelerator unevenly, but thrilled with himself.

"I'm driving," he said. "Man."

"You certainly are. Oh, watch that rabbit. Yes, there, no! Put the clutch in or you'll—"

The car stalled. He glanced at her in panic. "You forgot the clutch," she said. "Start again. Clutch, start the car, first gear, let up the clutch, gas, no, a little more. There, that's better."

And they drove like that all the way to the outskirts of Winthrop where Anna, weak with relief, took over.

Flip and Madeline were waiting outside.

"Sorry I'm late," Anna said. "Todd, run in and get your bag."

"How's it going?" Madeline asked.

"Oh, God, I just gave him his first driving lesson," Anna breathed.

"Brave woman," Flip said. "I'd rather fly anyday."

"So would I."

She drove the three of them to the airport and let them off at the terminal where Flip kept his own car and plane.

"See you tomorrow. I'll tell your dad where you are. He might want to call," Anna said. "Have fun."

Todd looked at her shyly. "Thanks, Anna, for—" he looked around to make sure no one was listening "—you know."

"Be polite to the Akers," she said. "Don't be a pain."

"We'll take good care of him," Madeline said. "Don't worry."

"Come on, young fella. You ever read a map? Maddy's lousy at it," Flip said.

Driving home, Anna saw the red-and-white Cessna fly overhead, bank and turn northwest. She waved automatically, even though they couldn't see her. Whew, a free day. A day to deal with Chris if he ever showed up. She'd go home, fix a sandwich, relax a little, clean up the house. Go for a walk maybe. Let her poor old car recover from this morning's session.

The phone rang just as she got inside her house with the two milk bottles. Cradling them in one arm, she grabbed the receiver. "Hello?"

"Anna?"

Her heart sped up treacherously. "Yes?"

"It's Chris. Listen, I'm sorry as hell about your having to deal with Todd. Is he okay? Has he been a problem?"

"He's fine." She just couldn't start explaining everything right now. "Where are you?"

"I'm still in Seattle. Anna, I'll be in on the three o'clock flight. Could you pick me up? I hate to impose, but I'm not supposed to drive for a couple of days. Hey, I'm really sorry to put you in this spot, but I—"

"Chris, you never even called, and we had no idea where you were!" She sounded too angry even to her own ears, but she couldn't help it.

There was silence on the other end for a moment. "Anna? I did try to call. Was Todd upset? Has he given you some trouble?"

"It's not just Todd."

He sounded bewildered, in pain, still groggy, confused. "Look, let's sort it out when I get there. Is that okay? Tell Todd I'll see him in two hours. I'm really looking forward to it. Anna, if you can't pick me up, I'll just take a taxi. Is that okay? If you're not there, I'll..."

"Oh, for God's sake, Chris," she said angrily, and hung up on him.

CHAPTER ELEVEN

IT WAS THE LAST THUMP of the plane's tire on the runway that got Chris. He should have taken one of the painkillers they'd given him when he checked out of the hospital. But he'd braved it, needing to stop by the NTSB office before his flight and, above all, wanting to be a hundred percent for Todd. His martyrdom had backfired. Instead of being alert and cheerful, Chris was ash-white and in agony. His shoulder felt as if someone had been pounding on it with a ballpeen hammer, and his head was throbbing to beat the band.

He was a long time unbuckling his safety belt. "Mr. Galloway," the stewardess asked, "are you all right? Would you like one of us to—"

"I can make it," Chris breathed. "I'm fine." He rose from the seat, felt a wave of dizziness sweep him and wished he were anywhere but in Winthrop and about to face his son and Anna.

Chris managed the metal stairway and stepped onto the tarmac, holding on to the end of the rail for a long moment. He wasn't even sure if Anna were going to meet his flight. She'd sounded, well, mad. And then, of course, she'd hung up on him. He was in no condition to figure out why she'd acted like that. Sure, taking Todd had been a terrible imposition, but she'd offered, hadn't she? Or had that been drug-induced wishful thinking?

But Anna *was* there. As Chris started toward the terminal, he spotted her. She was waiting just outside the door, the sun striking her head, turning her mass of dark curls to chestnut. She looked nervous, perhaps because of the way she was gripping her purse to the abdomen or her rigid stance. Still, the pain in his body evaporated for a split second as he approached—she looked so pretty, so lovely and vulnerable standing there. Among many things it was that edge of need in Anna Parish that drew him against his better judgment.

He was saying the words, "Hello, Anna," even as his gaze imprinted her image in his mind indelibly. He knew that he'd always recall her framed by the doorway, her hand raised to shade her eyes, a soft breeze molding her beige skirt to her hips and thighs, a single lock of escaping hair blowing across her cheek. Slim fingers, translucent skin...

"Hello, Chris."

He forced himself back to reality. And with reality came the sharp pain in his temples and shoulder.

"My God," Anna said, bridging the distance between them, taking his good arm, "you look dreadful."

"Why, thanks." He managed a lame smile, then grimaced.

"I mean it," Anna said, "you're a mess. You never should have checked out of that hospital, Chris Galloway. That was pretty stupid."

He was in no mood to argue. He could only follow her lead through the terminal and out to her car and allow her to press him carefully down into the passenger seat.

"I'll go get your bag," Anna said. "Do you have your ticket? The claim check?"

He reached into the breast pocket of his sport coat beneath the sling. "You shouldn't have to carry my bag," he began, but the acute pain in his shoulder and head made talking impossible. He felt foolish and helpless.

While Anna was in the terminal he gathered his thoughts enough to wonder why Todd hadn't accompanied her to the airport. He sure hoped the kid wasn't being a nuisance. He mostly hoped he wasn't going to have to discipline Todd right away. At that moment Chris couldn't have disciplined a two-year-old much less an errant teen.

Anna lifted the hatchback on her Subaru and tossed his bag in. When she closed the trunk door, Chris was rocked by a jolt of pain. She slid down into the driver's seat and shoved the key into the ignition. "You know," she said, shooting him a look, "you could have called the house this morning."

"I *did* try to call."

"Oh? When? Certainly not when you woke up and found the note."

"Well, I—"

"You went to the office first, didn't you?"

"Yes, I did. I couldn't get on a plane until this afternoon, and I figured I'd call you from the office." Now Chris was beginning to simmer.

"You don't get it," Anna said. "Your job's important, Chris, but I think Todd is *more* important."

"I already told you I tried to call."

"Three hours after you got the note?"

"No. Hell, maybe it *was* hours. I don't remember. Listen, I know my responsibilities."

"I wonder," she said darkly.

Chris would have retorted, but he thought better of it. First, maybe she did have a point, and she'd been an angel of mercy with Todd. He could hardly argue that.

Anna backed out of the parking space, then shoved the gearshift into first. He paled as the car surged forward. "Sorry," he managed to say, "I assumed you'd—never mind. It was wrong of me not to phone the second I woke up."

And he thought he heard her mumble, "Men."

Anna drove in silence, her face set in unbending lines. He wanted to ask her just exactly what was eating her, but wisely he kept quiet. And the pain, he couldn't have dealt with Anna's problem rationally even if he'd wanted to.

It was Anna who first brought up the subject of Todd as she pulled into her driveway. "Aren't you even wondering where your son is?" she asked accusingly.

"Well, yes, but I assumed—"

"He's in Vancouver."

"He's *where?*"

"Vancouver. Madeline's boyfriend took the two of them up to see his folks. They're going sailing, stuff like that."

"But..." Chris began, confused.

Anna turned to him and said sharply, "But nothing. You didn't call. You didn't anything. It was a nice opportunity for your son to see a very special place with two really good people. They were kind enough to offer, so I said yes. If it was wrong of me, well, it's too late now."

"No," Chris said, "it wasn't at all wrong. I mean, it was good of you and your friends to take care of

Todd like this." Pain coursed through his head. "I...I appreciate all you've done, Anna, and..."

But she was helping him out of the car. "Look at you," she said, "you're an absolute wreck. How *could* you have checked out of the hospital? Oh, never mind. Can you make it inside?"

"Sure, sure."

She took care of him. A nurse couldn't have been more attentive, especially that old hag who'd been on his case. Oh, yes, Anna was a far cry from that woman. Anna was, well, an angel, a beautiful angel with the most lovely hands and touch. She made him stretch out on the couch and propped a pillow under his arm. She got his head just right on the armrest and pulled off his shoes. And the whole time she shook her head and grumbled about what a fool he was. But still she tended to his every need. A veritable angel.

Chris was embarrassed. Worse, he was humiliated. He'd always been independent, able to care for himself, certainly able to kick off his own shoes. But each time he tried to move, pain seared his nerves like a hot iron until his brow broke out in a cold sweat.

"Okay," Anna said, arms akimbo as she stood over him, "where are they?" She looked irritated, but her tone was soft.

"Where are what?" he asked hoarsely.

"Your pain pills. I know they gave you some. They must have. And it's real obvious you haven't taken one."

"Coat pocket," he said, "but I really don't—"

"Nonsense. You're taking them and that's an order."

She got his pills. She got an ice-cold glass of water. And then she watched him swallow a Demerol, as if she suspected he might try palming the big white pill.

"Now give it a few minutes," Anna said, "and maybe you'll feel like you're going to live."

"God, I hope so," he admitted, closing his eyes and breathing deeply.

He must have dozed off. When he awoke, his head was groggy and the pain was dull. His vision swam a little, but he felt oddly carefree. Disoriented, he sat up like a drunken man and looked around for Anna. He couldn't see her, but he could hear pots clanging in the kitchen. He blinked, trying to focus.

He tried his legs. They were rubbery, but they worked, and he went into the kitchen, holding on to the doorframe for support.

She hadn't heard him. And despite the shadow of pain lurking in his body, he felt a smile pull at the corner of his mouth. Anna was bent over, way over, searching for a pan in a low corner cupboard. Her skirt was pulled skintight over her derriere, and he found himself drinking in the sight like a young fool. When she straightened, she had to adjust herself, skirt, bra and all. Chris was utterly spellbound. He wished for a crazy moment that he could become invisible and watch this woman for an entire day and night, many, many days and nights, in fact. A notion struck Chris then, swimming around in the haze of his brain: was that what Jim Fleisher did?—watch Anna day and night?

"Oh," she said abruptly, her hand flying to her breast, "you scared the life out of me!"

Chris tried to straighten. He licked incredibly dry lips. "Sorry," he got out, "I must have dozed off."

"Well," Anna said, "you better sit down. You look a little shaky." She nodded at the kitchen table that was near a sunny window. Geraniums graced the outside sill, and long shadows fell across the lawn. "Want some coffee or tea? Maybe tea would be better."

"Coffee, please."

He felt as if he were in a kind of heaven, somewhere between reality and drug-induced lethargy. Everything moved in slow motion. Anna moved in slow motion. Oh, yes, especially Anna.

"I'm making us dinner," she said. "Something easy. I hope you feel like eating."

And then he remembered. "I think I better get a room, Anna. I mean—"

"I think you're sleeping right on that couch tonight where I can keep an eye on you," she said, leaving little room to argue. "It's not the most comfortable, but it's not bad, either."

"Are you...?"

"I'm positive."

So he watched her cook dinner, each movement isolated in that maddeningly pleasurable half speed. She'd raise an arm to reach for a measuring cup on a shelf, and her blouse would stretch across her bosom enticingly. Then she'd stoop, picking up a dropped spoon, and those panties would wink at him from their hidden place. She stood at the stove and sink, her dark head bowed slightly, one knee bent. He watched her intently, hungrily, aware that his thoughts were out of control, aware also of a desire growing inside him that was becoming more compelling by the moment.

"More coffee?" Anna asked once.

"Oh, sure, thanks."

He never searched for words. They seemed out of place in her peaceful little kitchen. He merely watched, his lethargy dragging him along on its own journey. He saw odd little things about Anna that he'd never noticed before. There was a small dimple in her left cheek, and she wore pearl stud earrings in delicate pink lobes. Her neck was long and graceful, a white column against her springing dark hair. Her nose was larger than he'd first thought, not too large for her face, though, fine and straight. And Anna's mouth. She had a beautiful mouth, a bit pouty-looking when she was concentrating.

Nice legs, too, Chris thought as he sipped his coffee and watched her move around the kitchen. Shapely legs with trim ankles.

His gaze traveled up, lingeringly. She was quite a woman, with facets that kept him guessing. He'd seen her soft and yielding, her spirit broken. He'd seen her angry and defensive. He'd seen her at her best and worst, and always he'd found her honest, caring, warm. It bothered Chris more than he dared to admit that this special woman was mourning another man. And worse, she still *loved* Fleisher.

Carefully he pushed aside the unwanted thought and went back to watching Anna.

By the time dinner was ready, his calm was departing. The pain was still dulled, but every so often he was again experiencing jolts when he moved too quickly. Chris decided he didn't mind the stabs. What he minded was the return to reality.

Anna put a bowl of salad on the table. "You look a little more alive," she commented, going to the refrigerator for the dressing.

"Guess I am waking up."

"Want another pill? It's been four hours or so."

He shook his head. "Maybe later."

Anna served them both salad, stirred something on the stove, then sat down, taking up her fork. She cocked her head. "How *is* the pain, Chris, really? I mean, we could drive over to Dr. Carson's and have him check you out."

"I'm fine. Really I am. I just feel like a fifth wheel around here. I really do think I should get a hotel room."

"Let's not argue about that again," Anna said. "We'll discuss it in the morning."

He finished his salad and ate the beef and vegetable stew she'd made as if he were starving. She dished him out seconds and shook her head. "You do eat poorly, Chris. I hope you'll try harder with Todd around for... for the summer."

"You mean three squares a day?"

"And not chocolate bars for breakfast, either."

"I guess I'm going to have to try, aren't I?"

"Yes, you are." She studied him for a minute, then said, "Todd called his mother last night."

"He did?"

"Yes. I made him do it. I thought she might have told him to call when he got into Seattle. Anyway," Anna said, "she would have worried."

"I never even thought—"

"I know you didn't." Anna sounded irritated again, and Chris began to wonder if she hadn't been all along. He might have been too out of it to notice. "Anyway," she told him, "your son seems like a good kid, *underneath.*"

Chris raised a sandy brow.

"What I mean is, he's got problems. It's as if he acts up just to get adult attention."

"He didn't do anything . . . ?"

But Anna waved him off. "No, no, he was fine. I'm just saying I get the feeling he's desperate for attention. For *love,* Chris."

Chris wasn't at all sure he understood. Not entirely. "You know," he said, pushing his plate away, "I'm pretty new at this father business."

"It scares you," she ventured.

Instinctively Chris was ready to flat out deny it. But then, after a moment's reflection, he said, "Yeah. Yeah, I guess I am afraid."

"Seems natural. I would be, too."

Chris smiled wryly. "Women can handle it. I'm not sure I can."

Anna sighed. "You can if you really want to. You only have to listen to Todd. To really hear what he's saying." She stood and began clearing the table. Abruptly she stopped and gave him a long, hard look. "Sometimes," she said, "we think we understand a person, but somehow we get it wrong. Maybe we all need to listen and trust a little more." And for the life of him Chris couldn't comprehend why her statement seemed more directed at him than his son.

He finally took a cup of coffee into the living room while Anna washed the dishes. He'd offered to help, but in truth Chris was pretty much of an oaf around a stove or sink. And besides, with one arm helplessly in a sling . . .

"Well," Anna said, a damp dish towel still in her hand, "that's that."

"It was excellent." Chris felt like rising when Anna sat opposite him in an easy chair. "You've gone to an awful lot of trouble for me, and for Todd. I don't know how to—"

"It's all right. I still feel dreadful about that plane mishap. It never should have happened, Chris, never."

"It will be investigated, Anna."

"Oh, sure. It'll take months, and then some feeble excuse of a report will be filed and Lee Miller will get away with it again."

"Don't jump to conclusions," he said.

"I know how he works, Chris. That tire was shot."

"Maybe," Chris said carefully, not about to admit to her just how thoroughly he was going to pursue this case.

She got up then and began moving around the room restlessly. His eyes followed her from window to lamp to bookshelf, where she stopped, seemingly absorbed in the photographs there. Something sharp stabbed him in the gut before he shoved it away. Fleisher again, always Fleisher.

She came across the room to stand before him, her brow drawn in a frown, her soft pink lips in a worried pout. "Can you do something? You were on the plane, you were hurt..."

"I have no personal knowledge of any wrongdoing, Anna. I can only testify to what I witnessed."

She stood there, frowning down at him, her arms crossed, and her closeness was like a deluge of ineffable sweetness showering him, making his skin tingle.

Anna seemed to realize their close proximity then, and she moved away, tidying something, straightening things. He kept watching her, unable to stop, feeling his head and arm now, the flaring pain.

"Shouldn't you take another pill, Chris?" she asked, collected once more. "If you don't, you'll be up all night."

"In a minute," he said, still studying her.

She cocked her head. "What is it? What are you looking at?"

He almost said "You." Instead he got out "Nothing. I guess I was just thinking."

They talked quietly for a time, a single lamp in the corner lighting the room. Anna told him about her day with Todd and about Flip, Madeline's boyfriend, a WestAir copilot. It irked Chris that here he was, laid up, and another man was out doing things Chris wanted to do with his son. But his injuries would heal. And he and Todd would find that place for the summer and begin to know each other again. Maybe it could be like Chris and his own dad—good times, companionship, understanding. How had so many years slipped away?

The pain got bad around ten. Maybe it was the swelling in his shoulder. Maybe it was the concussion. All Chris knew was that the jabs of occasional pain turned into a steady throb. He sat back on the couch, paled and let out a low groan. "Damn it," he said between clenched teeth.

Anna came to her feet. "You're taking that pill, Chris." He gave no argument this time. "Do you want to change into pajamas?" she asked. "Will you need any help getting into them?"

"Pajamas." He tried to smile. "I don't own a pair. I just sort of sleep, well, in my—"

"Okay," she said quickly, "you need something, though. Something easy to get on over that arm. Just a minute."

She went into the other bedroom and returned soon with a pair of blue pajamas over her arm. "I knew Flip had a pair. Madeline gave them to him for Christmas. Don't worry. He's never had them on. I guess he, ah, sleeps like you do."

In the bathroom Chris changed slowly, awkwardly, painfully. He felt foolish and useless, seeing himself in the mirror with the bandage on his head. His face was pain-racked, old-looking. He took the pill she'd given him, gathered up his clothes and returned to find her making up a bed on the couch.

Under her careful ministrations Chris stretched out. She tucked a blanket around him and adjusted the pillow, her cool hands brushing his feverish flesh. The pill began to take hold. His senses dulled. There was still her occasional touch, a whispered word, and a fresh, warm scent as she bent over him one last time to check his bandage. He drifted into sweet oblivion as the scent lingered and languished in his swimming brain.

ANNA SAT BENEATH the soft pool of light from the lamp and watched him. She wasn't at all sure if he were asleep or if the drug had again taken him into that place of hazy dreams. But she felt safe sitting there unobserved, and she marveled at the circumstances that had brought this singular man into her life and her home.

The blown tire on the plane, Anna thought. She owed Chris's presence in her house to a near disaster. And what if that tire hadn't given out? What if she hadn't been in the airport at the time? Anna didn't necessarily believe in fate, but she was changing her attitude lately.

Chris stirred, rolled onto his shoulder for a moment, then eased off it onto his back. He was talking a bit in his sleep, occasionally making incoherent sounds. She watched him intently and listened to the male timbre of his sleeping voice. Jim used to talk in his sleep once in a while. . . .

Anna rubbed her eyes and decided to sit for a few more minutes until she was certain Chris was comfortably at rest. She admitted to herself that she was hesitant to turn in for another reason, as well: she was enjoying watching him. He'd kicked the blanket off one leg, and she could see the long, tapered muscles of his thigh beneath the pajamas.

Her gaze traveled over him leisurely. She took in the strength of his neck and the leanness of his hips under the blanket, his flat belly and mussed sandy hair. She'd known him as a vital man, competent, capable, in charge. But she'd seen the hidden Chris, too, the man who was afraid of the responsibility of fatherhood, the wounded man who worked too hard, needing to be indispensable. And that side of Chris Galloway pulled at her heartstrings and allowed her to do the little things for him that Jim had always pooh-poohed.

She shook herself. It was too soon to be thinking such things. She wasn't even over Jim yet. So much remained to be done still. And there was the nightly fear of his presence, that crouching fear that she'd awaken and find him hovering nearby, his eyes sunken, pleading, begging her to help.

She couldn't think about Chris in terms of a relationship. Still, he *was* there, in her life, in as much need as she was. And she could no longer deny the physical attraction. It had become too real, an aching pulse deep inside that persisted despite its inappropriateness.

Anna rose and snapped off the lamp. Silently she went into her bedroom and undressed, pulling her nightgown over her head in the half-light from a bedside lamp. She folded her blouse and hung up her skirt. But her thoughts were on the man resting just a few feet away on the couch. What if he *could* find Jim's notebook? It had to be somewhere. It wasn't with the wreckage of flight 629. It wasn't still at the site of the crash. The coroner's office had assured her they had found nothing remotely like it. So where was that damn notebook?

Anna pulled the sheet and blanket up to her chin and turned off the bedside light. In the next room she could hear Chris mumble something and stir. She listened for a time until he settled back into sleep, and then she rolled over, facing her window. The notebook was somewhere. It was either misplaced or someone had it. Chris simply had to press. He had the authority to turn the hangar where the wreckage was, and even the coroner's office, upside down. He had the pull to find it. The question was: how hard would he try? If he didn't truly believe her, he might not really try at all.

Anna's eyes closed slowly, drowsily. Tomorrow she'd talk to him again, do some pressing herself. If Jim's notebook could be located, then maybe, God willing, the poor soul could find his rest.

Her eyes snapped open. Something was wrong. The digital clock blinked 3:00 a.m. A breeze was stirring the branches on the big cottonwood outside, and one branch scratched at her window. There was moonlight, Anna noticed as she held her breath, spilling across the floor, and the cat stood in its swath, frozen there on the carpet.

She saw it then—a faint, faint light near the corner closet—and gasped as her stomach shifted. As she watched, lying rigidly, the light began to pull in upon itself, taking on definition. It wavered and flared and began to solidify. And then he was there, his form seeming to pulse in places, to ebb and flow in the moonlight. The cat growled and ran from the room, its fur on end. But Anna couldn't move. She could only stare, her heartbeat pounding in her ears, her breath coming in short, frantic gasps.

His face took shape. Mouth, nose, eyes. He was as pale as death. Pale and bloodless. But his eyes . . . oh dear God his eyes. Gray, sunken and accusing.

It was as if an inner voice spoke to her then, a whisper from a dark, hidden place in her brain. *Find it, Anna. Find it,* the voice said. *Find it.*

She forced her eyes shut and then opened them abruptly, praying it was a dream, but knew it wasn't. And when she saw him still there, her heart pounded even more furiously while panic grasped her in sharp talons and propelled her out of bed, every fiber of her being crawling in fear.

Somehow she banged open her door and made her way to Chris's side. Frantically she shook him, crying, "Wake up! For God's sake, wake up!" And then he was on his feet, and she was dragging at his arm, pulling him toward the bedroom, toward the ghastly proof of her sanity. "There!" she began, standing behind him on the threshold. "There! See...." Behind her the cat growled fearfully. But the room was utterly still, black and empty. The ghost of Jim Fleisher was gone.

CHAPTER TWELVE

SILENCE HUNG in the air for a moment, a stunned silence, and then Anna moaned. "He's gone. Oh, God, he's gone."

Chris was still groggy with sleep and the hangover effect of Demerol, yet he was singularly aware of Anna's presence, of the way she sagged in disappointment. It was as though his body reacted to her on a visceral level despite his brain's fogginess. It didn't occur to him at the moment how sensitive the situation was. There was only the empty room, the darkness and the woman standing so close to him, full of despair.

He wanted to ask "who?" But the word refused to form on his lips. He knew exactly who she meant. Jim. Her dead lover Jim Fleisher.

"He was here," she whispered. "He was right here. I wanted ... wanted you to see ... to believe me."

He couldn't say a thing. Anything he could offer would sound wrong. And he wasn't ready to say, "I do believe you."

They stood in the darkness, and the silence embraced them. Chris became aware of the situation, acutely aware of being in the middle of this woman's bedroom, her bed mussed, the scent of her filling the air with sweetness. She was standing with her back to him, her head bowed, her shoulders bare and gleaming in her skimpy nightgown. He could imagine the silkiness of those shoulders and arms, the warmth of her skin . . .

"Oh, Chris, why?" Anna breathed, and her hand went to her mouth. "Why is he doing this? Why?"

"Anna," he finally asked, his voice husky, "could it have been a dream? Have you considered—"

But she shook her head. "No. He *was* here. I was awake."

"Okay" was all he could offer. "It's okay." And he drew her around to face him in the night. He was aware of her eyes glistening in the moonlight and her lips quivering. He drank her in, from her smooth shoulders to the outline of her breasts beneath the nightgown. He didn't allow himself a thought when, with his good arm, he encircled her waist and brought her up against him.

"Oh, Chris," she said, "I'm not crazy. I'm not." And she sobbed softly into his chest. His lips brushed the crown of her head, and he shut his eyes, his groin tightening.

He kissed the top of her head, and when she stirred, his lips were against her temple, lowering to touch the bridge of her nose. His heart began to beat a quicker cadence as her scent, so female and honey-sweet, drifted around him. He was aware of Anna melting against him, of the rapid rise and fall of her breasts where they pressed into his chest, and he had a moment of hesitation, just a fleeting moment when he drew back a fraction and met her eyes in the moon glow. And then he was lost.

"Anna," he whispered, an ache deep in his loins. He lowered his head toward her mouth. Her hands were on his chest now, hesitant, uncertain, barely holding him away. And then his mouth was covering hers, parting her lips. He felt those warm lips tremble for a moment before she responded. Then her hands were slipping around his waist, and he could feel the tautness of her nipples against him.

White-hot, glorious agony ripped through Chris. He twisted his mouth to hers and drank her in, and Anna pressed herself to his hardness, clinging, longing.

Moonlight speared in through her window, bathing them in silver, and they clung together, thigh, hip, chest touching, searing. She fitted against him perfectly, soft curve contoured to his hardness. His breath rasped in his chest with difficulty.

He forgot the time. He forced away the danger signal that lurked somewhere in his brain. He even forgot his bad arm.

Until he raised it to pull her closer.

The hot passion turned instantly to a bolt of pain spearing his shoulder. He drew away, hunched over and gasped, sweat popping out on his brow.

"Chris..."

"Whoa, give me a second," he breathed, waiting for the agony to abate. And when the pain began to ebb, awareness seeped into his mind. He'd come into Anna's room...something about Fleisher...and then... How had he let it happen? Holy...

"Chris, are you all right?" she asked.

"My shoulder," he mumbled, still hunched over. "I'm sorry. I—"

"No, no, it's my fault," she insisted shakily.

She looked away, apart from him, and hugged herself.

"I shouldn't have done that," he said lamely.

She straightened and met his eyes. "I asked for it. Don't apologize."

They faced each other across a growing chasm, more distant every moment, and between them lay a rift that was yawning and black and full of unspoken words. He couldn't touch her now, even though she stood before him. She was too far away.

"Are *you* all right?" he asked.

She gave a small laugh. "I'm fine, just fine. I'm sorry I bothered you. It was a dream, a bad dream." She paused, then asked, "Is your shoulder...? I mean, is it hurting?"

He tried to smile, to match her retreat into the impersonal. "Only when I move. It's fine," he said, unconsciously echoing her words.

"Oh, good. Well, then..."

"Will you be okay? Can you go to sleep now?"

"Yes, sure. You, too. Good night."

He left her room and heard her close the door behind him. Suddenly his head hurt, his shoulder ached, his feet were cold on the floor. He felt as if he'd lost something precious. He lowered himself onto the couch and pulled the cover up. He felt her on every part of his body: his hands, his lips, his chest. Wherever he'd touched her he was branded, his skin super-sensitive. It was a poignant pain, a phantom sensation, as if she still lay with him in the darkness. He couldn't believe that a minute ago he'd been in her bedroom, kissing her, and now... How in hell had he let that happen?

IN THE MORNING the tension between them became almost too sharp to deal with. They were polite to each other, hideously polite.

"More coffee?" she asked.

"Yes, thank you."

"How's your shoulder?"

"Oh, much better, thanks."

They didn't use each other's name, as if that would be too intimate, but kept everything civilized, superficial. He felt like a damn fool. Yet how could he forget the smell, the taste of her? It was as if his innocence was gone forever, his life skewed from the course he'd set it on. And Anna? He didn't know, couldn't tell. Her hands didn't shake, she met his gaze openly, she seemed untouched. Yet he knew in his bones that she'd been affected. It was a scary time, that morning, both of them on the brink of something. Either could choose to plunge forward or back off. Both of them knew it, and it was there between them, beckoning and repelling.

"Would you like more toast?" she asked, sitting across the table from him in a white terry-cloth robe. Her neck rose like a column from the collar, almost as white, slim and milky. Her lips curved deliciously up at the corners even when she didn't smile. He couldn't tear his gaze from that adorable quirk.

"No, I'm full. That was good."

"Thanks."

It went on like that until Chris could no longer meet her eyes. "Well," he said, "I've got some work to do. I better—"

"Work? I mean, are you up to it?"

"Nothing strenuous," he said. "A couple of phone calls."

"Calls?"

"About the notebook," he said. "Fleisher's notebook."

"You'll start asking around?"

He ignored the hope in her voice. "I already told you I would. I intend to keep my word."

"But you don't really believe it exists, do you." It wasn't a question.

"Listen," Chris said, again meeting her gaze, "my job requires me to look into every last detail that might have affected a plane or a pilot. Every last one. I don't know whether or not Fleisher kept a journal, but if he did, I want to see it."

"So you can close the files."

"Yes, so I can close the files and know that we left no stone unturned."

"I see," she said dejectedly.

"I hope you do."

"Well," Anna said, "I guess I'll have to settle for that. Anything that works, even if you think it's a wild-goose chase."

"Anna..." He used her name and knew abruptly that it *was* too intimate; it brought everything back.

She made a gesture in the air. "No, that's all right. I don't care what you think as long as you look for it." She hesitated, then raised her eyes to his, those limpid, tawny eyes that were full of questions. "How will you do it? I mean, try to locate the book?"

"I'll start with the coroner in Seattle."

"I already spoke to his office," Anna said. "I got nowhere."

"I believe a call from me will have more effect."

"I'm sure you're right," she said dryly, then rose and piled the dishes in the sink. "Well, I'm going to take a shower. Feel free to use the phone. Whatever."

"Thanks."

A few minutes later he could hear her in the bathroom taking a shower as he sat at the kitchen table finishing his coffee. He shut off the image that began to coalesce in his mind and forced himself to think of

Todd. He wondered how Todd and Anna had gotten along, how Todd had reacted.

He still had the few scrawled words of the note that his son had written in the hospital. Anna and Todd. How very curious that things had worked out this way. And what in hell would he have done if Anna hadn't been there?

He knew now he should have had a place in Seattle all set up and ready to go to; Todd could have gone there for the night. Still, Chris didn't feel he'd acted as badly as Anna seemed to think. Todd was growing up, the boy would be a man soon, and things sometimes happened. The boy had to learn to deal with that. Women were just too protective, worrying over too many details. Chris was going to get things on the right track with Todd, and it sure would be nice if Anna would just let things run their course.

He stood and went to his jacket where it hung over the back of a chair and got the pain pills out of the pocket. He'd take half of one just to blunt the edge. He'd taken the sling off to sleep, and if he kept his arm still, close to his side, it was okay. It was only when he forgot and moved the arm too quickly that pain resulted, like last night, but maybe that had been a propitious interruption.

She came out of her room dressed in a denim skirt and a crisp white blouse. Neat and prim and pretty. Her dark hair was fluffy and loose, pulled back behind her ear on one side. He had a sudden vision of Anna in an old-fashioned dress, all lace and ruffles and a high neck with her hair piled on top of her head and a big hat with feathers. She'd look perfect that way, he realized. A lady. Beautiful and distant and self-contained.

"I'll be gone running errands for an hour or so," she said as he chased the whimsical dream from his head. "Can I get you anything?"

"No, nothing. I'm fine."

"You better take one of your pills," she said, "before you start hurting."

"I took one already."

"Oh, good."

"Don't worry about me. Just do what you'd normally do. I'll be out of your life this afternoon. You've done enough for Todd and me."

She swung her purse strap onto her shoulder, checked inside and pulled out her car keys. "It's no problem. I haven't done much. If you find that notebook, you'll repay me a hundred times over."

The morning sun striped the floor when she opened the front door, gilding her, framing her head with a bright halo, outlining her in gold. "Well, I better get going. See you in a while."

Chris nodded and watched until she disappeared out of the driveway.

He showered and washed his hair awkwardly with one hand, wincing as the soap stung the cut on his head. He dressed slowly, pulling the shirt sleeve cautiously up over his bad arm, working it over the elbow. He could tell his shoulder was better already. Stiff and sore as the devil, but not screaming with agony when he moved. He'd live.

He had work to do, though. Getting his files out of his briefcase, he found the coroner's telephone number. He was only too well aware of the confusion that reigned at a crash site. People's belongings were strewn everywhere, and rarely did every item get returned to its proper owner. The cleanup crews tried, the coroner's office tried, everyone tried his best, but sometimes it was simply impossible to figure out what belonged to whom. Oh, yes, Chris had been on enough Go Team investigations, the first to arrive at the still-smoking ruins of an aircraft. The horror never left you. Clothes, pieces of the aircraft, seats, suitcases—everything lay in a jumble.

A notebook such as Anna described could easily have been lost, misplaced, trod underfoot, thrown out. It could also have been returned to the wrong survivor or family of a deceased passenger.

He settled himself in the chair next to the telephone, careful not to jar his arm. It took five minutes or better to get the medical examiner who had handled the March WestAir disaster on the line. And when Chris did get him, the man was curt and testy.

"Yes," Dr. Sullivan said, "I handled the March case. You've got the files, Galloway."

"What I don't have," Chris said, "is a small blue spiral notebook that belonged to the pilot, Jim Fleisher."

"If it was on him, it was returned to the family. We're very careful."

"I understand," Chris said, knowing Sullivan wasn't going to like this. "But the notebook's missing. I need to locate it. I'm afraid that means—"

"You've got to be joking," the man said. "Do you know what you're asking? There were hundreds of items recovered, hundreds. Hell, it took six weeks to sort through everything and—"

"I *do* understand, Sullivan. I wouldn't be requesting this search if it weren't vital to the ongoing investigation."

"Weeks. It'll take weeks to go back through the records." Sullivan made a derisive, snorting sound.

"Yes, I know," Chris said.

"You can't really expect—"

"I can make it a formal request from the NTSB if you want."

"Damn right you will," Sullivan said hotly. "If I gotta pay an assistant to go back through every last record, I want it in writing."

"Fine. And Sullivan," Chris said, "*weeks* isn't going to cut it."

"What?"

"I'm sorry, but this is very important. I'll expect that list of belongings and disbursement as soon as possible."

There was a moment of silence. "You say your name's Galloway?" the man asked.

"That's right."

"Who's your boss? I really think—"

"I'm the boss, Dr. Sullivan. As soon as possible, if you will, the finalized list."

Sullivan hung up.

"My," he heard behind him, causing him to start, "you sounded pretty dangerous." It was Anna, standing in the living room with a bag of groceries in her arms.

"Sometimes I have to push to get results." He almost shrugged, then remembered in time. Instead, he stood, went to the couch where his sling was lying and slipped it on carefully.

"Who were you talking to?" Anna called from the kitchen.

"The coroner in Seattle."

"It's a lot to ask, isn't it? I mean, so many small items, especially when you don't really believe—"

"You're right," he said sharply. "I don't believe the damn thing exists. I've talked to a lot of people now who knew Fleisher, and no one ever saw him with a notebook."

Anna let out a breath. "So I must be crazy then."

"I didn't say crazy. But I think maybe you... Listen, after last night I don't know what's—"

"You mean Jim." She was angry now herself, that telltale red staining her cheeks. "You mean you think I'm really off my rocker." She put down the can, placed her hands on her hips and cocked her head. "You know, Chris Galloway, you're so cocksure of everything, aren't you? Sure of what's right and wrong, what's truth and lie. How wonderful it must be to be so sure."

"Look, Anna, I didn't mean—"

But she couldn't be stopped. "Anything to get your job done, to get those pure facts of yours. If you'd believe me about Jim, if you'd believe he wants us to find that notebook and prove—"

It was the way she said his name. Jim. Reverently, lovingly. Jim. He cut her off. "I'm sick of hearing about your Jim," he said in a low, hard voice that he only used in official situations. "Jim is *dead*. He's gone. He doesn't *want* anything. Can't you get that through your head, Anna? What's the matter with you?"

"There's nothing the matter with me," she choked out, drawing herself up.

He had to get out of there, had to flee the rage that was building in him, to get away from Anna and her proud pain, her love for a dead man. He walked toward the door, feeling how she hurt but unable to stop himself. "Okay, there's nothing the matter with you," he couldn't help saying, "but you're in love with a dead man, and I'll be damned if I'm going to fight a ghost to have you!"

He pushed open the door and grimaced as pain shot through his shoulder, then banged the door shut behind him and walked swiftly down the flower-bordered walk.

ANNA CONTEMPLATED Chris's announcement all morning. He wasn't going to fight a ghost to have her. What a strange thing to have said but, nonetheless, each time the words tiptoed through her mind her heartbeat quickened. She was afraid to let herself analyze his statement, afraid to let go, to trust, to hope again. She was afraid to remember last night. To recall the feel of his warm body against hers, the touch of his lips, the special scent of him. She couldn't let herself dwell on it. They'd kissed, and passion had ignited between them, but whether it meant anything at all, Anna didn't dare contemplate. She cleaned up the kitchen and living room, did a load of wash and tried not to think about Chris Galloway at all or to wonder where he'd gone.

He returned in the middle of the afternoon, opening and closing her front screen door quietly, sitting on the edge of the couch as if deep in thought. Anna came out of her bedroom where she'd been doing spring cleaning in the closet. "Hello, Chris."

He looked up. "Oh, hello." He started to rise.

"Did you . . . ah . . . go for a walk or something?"

Chris nodded.

"Your shoulder's okay? Your head?"

"I feel better than I have, in fact," he said.

"Good, that's good. They say fresh air—oh well, you know what they say." She smiled too quickly.

It was terribly awkward. Last night had been, well, Anna thought, an unexpected occurrence between them. She tried to chalk it up to need, to loneliness. But then his words of that morning sneaked through her brain again, his jealous, irrational statement about fighting a ghost, and her heart began to beat a fast, steady rhythm. She stood in the bedroom doorway and felt shy and confused.

"Ah," Chris asked, "mind if I get a cup of coffee?"

"Oh, I can get it."

"No, no, go on with whatever you're doing. I can do it." He nodded toward the kitchen.

"You're sure?"

"Positive." Then he asked, "Say, when do you suppose Todd will be in?"

"Um. It depends on Flip, of course, but I'm sure he won't fly in after dark."

"No, probably not," Chris concurred.

A moment settled uncomfortably between them, and Anna finally held up the vacuum cleaner attachment she'd been using and smiled. "Well, back to spring cleaning. If you need help with the coffee..."

"Oh, I'll get it. You go on."

Chris had his coffee and read that week's issue of the *Methow Valley News* while Anna gave her closet the most thorough cleaning it had ever seen. Despite her furious efforts to blank him out of her mind, she kept thinking about Chris in the very next room. And then she'd think about Jim. Once she stopped and stared, fascinated, at the corner where he'd appeared. A chill ran from her insides to her skin, raising goose bumps. Bright afternoon sunlight spilled through the window and lit the corner, gilding the little wooden chair that sat there. How could he have been there? What insane quirk of nature could produce such a thing?

She put away the vacuum and wondered again if she was going crazy. Maybe something in her brain had been jarred in the crash, creating a lifelike image—a hologram—before her eyes.

Anna closed the broom closet door and bit her lip. Okay, if she were crazy, then what about Madeline? And the cat. The cat had seen something in her bedroom, too. Maybe Madeline was missing her marbles, but not a *cat*, for God's sake. She walked past Chris, whose head was still bent to the newspaper, and into the kitchen. She just couldn't go out there and face him again. She couldn't stare at those ice-blue eyes, that austere mouth, and pretend nothing had happened. She stooped and began tidying a low cupboard, anything to keep from facing him.

At four-thirty Flip, Madeline and Todd arrived. Anna saw them pull into the driveway in Flip's car, and she saw, too, who had been at the steering wheel.

Oh, no.

She willed Todd to climb out of the driver's seat before his father heard the car and went to the front door.

"Is that a car?" Chris called from the couch. He folded the paper and put it on the coffee table, beginning to rise.

"Oh," Anna said from the kitchen door, "geez, I don't . . . let me look. You just sit still, rest." *That kid.* She peered outside. The three of them were all in the driveway now. It was impossible to tell who'd been behind the wheel. Anna cursed herself for opening that can of worms with Todd.

The trio thumped across the front porch as Anna said, "Why, it *is* them," and laughter floated through an open window. She turned to Chris. He was standing and watching the door; he looked as nervous as a caged animal.

"Hey," Flip said, pushing the door inward for Madeline to enter, "home from the wilds of Canada."

"Hi," Madeline said, seeing Chris. She indicated the overnight bag in her hand and headed straight for her room without giving a backward glance.

And Todd. At first he said nothing, looking as uptight as his father. Finally he cleared his throat, shuffled his feet and said, "Wow, man, you're covered in bandages."

The two just stood there facing each other. Flip winked at Anna and followed Madeline into the bedroom. But Anna wasn't sure whether to pull a disappearing act or not. Maybe these guys needed a mediator or something.

"Hi, Todd," Chris said, his good hand in his trouser pocket. He looked as if he wanted to embrace his son. Or at least he looked as if he knew he should do something—shake the boy's hand, pat him on the back, whatever. But Chris just stood there awkwardly.

Silence filled the room to bursting.

"Well," Anna said, "how was your trip, Todd?"

"It was cool. I mean, Flip even let me take the controls of the plane once. Like, it was really something."

Anna wondered what Chris was going to say to that news, but he didn't even blink. Maybe he believed in boys having an adventure once in a while. Maybe he was too tongue-tied even to comment.

"Did you go sailing?" Chris asked him.

"Yeah. But it got cold and real windy. It was okay, I guess."

"How about some sodas or something?" Anna asked. "Are you thirsty?" She looked from one to the other tall, stiff-backed male.

"I'll have one," Chris said, and nodded at Todd.

"Yeah, me, too."

She made her escape. But not out of earshot.

"Sit down, Todd," Chris offered.

"Man, does all that *hurt?*" Anna heard Todd ask.

"Sometimes," Chris replied. "That's quite a mop of hair you have there, son."

"I'm not cutting it, man."

"I didn't say anything about cutting it, did I?"

"Nah, I guess not."

"Well," Chris said, "I'm very sorry I wasn't at your gate in Seattle to meet you."

"Not your fault, I guess."

"I suppose it wasn't."

Anna returned with the Cokes and placed them on the coffee table. She sat down next to Chris and then wondered if she hadn't placed herself in the enemy camp from Todd's point of view. Too late now, though. She sipped on her own soda and couldn't help recalling Todd's mother on the telephone, the woman's lecture on how Chris habitually avoided his responsibilities. Thank heaven it wasn't her problem, this thing between Chris and his son. It was absolutely none of her business, and a person would be insane, not to mention wrong, to interfere, to butt in between a father and son. But still it nagged at her, and even if she didn't dare say anything more to Chris, she worried about Todd and how Chris would handle him. It put a wedge between her and Chris, an ugly shadow, one more barrier to their relationship.

"You know, man," Todd said, "this town isn't half bad. I was wondering, well, it's like this, man . . . Dad. Mom said you'd help me get my driver's permit, and like, the office is probably open today. If we're going to stay here—"

"Stay here?" Chris raised a brow.

"You know, in Winthrop or wherever I was—"

"What makes you think we're staying here, son?"

"I thought—"

"My work's in Seattle. Temporarily."

"Oh." Disappointment. "Where are we gonna live, then? I mean, how long are you gonna be in Seattle?"

"I don't know exactly," his father replied, and he rubbed his jaw absently.

"I mean," Todd said, "like for the whole summer?"

"I don't—"

"Where am I gonna go to school? I mean, school starts in August some places."

Anna shut her eyes. *Here goes . . .*

"School?" Chris was clearly baffled.

"Yeah, school, you know," Todd said, "the place that's got books and teachers, you know, man."

The look on Chris Galloway's face told it all. He hadn't a clue before that moment of what Todd's mother had pulled. Not an inkling.

"I mean," Todd was saying, "I gotta go to school, don't I?"

"Well, yes, of course," his father said uncertainly.

"In Seattle? Or are we gonna be living somewhere else?"

"I..." Chris glanced at Anna for help. But there wasn't a thing she could do. She shrugged apologetically, and Chris shifted his gaze back to his son. "We'll figure it out, Todd. I promise I'll make arrangements—"

"Sure," the boy interrupted. "You'll have me in six schools next year. I know how it is. Big-time NTSB investigator."

"No," Chris said, shaking his head slowly in denial, "I won't. Something can be worked out."

"Yeah, I bet." Eyes the color of Chris's glared back at him in defiance.

"Listen," Chris said, "I *will* work it out. And if you want to know the truth, this is the first I've heard that you're going to be living with me on a permanent basis. Helen didn't—"

"Bummer, huh?" Todd threw out, still staring.

"No," Chris said, "it's not a bummer. It's a surprise. In fact—" he leaned forward, grimacing as he moved his shoulder "—I'm glad you're with me."

"Sure."

"I mean that. I really do mean it."

Todd was silent.

"We *will* work it out," Chris finished, as if trying to convince himself.

Anna drove them over to the lodge where Chris had stayed before, but Todd kept nagging his father about a "real" place to live and where he was going to get his driver's permit.

"Seattle, I suppose," Chris told him twice from the front seat.

"So when are we gonna go to Seattle, then?"

Chris began to look exasperated. "Soon. Tomorrow, maybe the day after. I have some work to do here, son."

"What work? Isn't your office in Seattle?"

"Yes. But there's some missing evidence I'm trying to trace." He looked at Anna. "It's something that might have belonged to the pilot of flight 629. I have some more searching to do here in Winthrop."

"Swell," Todd mumbled. "So you gotta fly back and forth. What am I supposed to do with myself?"

"I . . ." Chris began, but Anna intervened.

She pulled up into the lodge's parking lot and set the emergency brake, took a deep breath and decided to plunge in, despite having told herself to stay out of it. She prayed she wasn't going to do either of them irreparable harm. "Listen, I don't mean to butt in, but maybe there's a solution that would work for both of you. For a few weeks, anyway. Want to hear it?"

Chris laughed humorlessly. "I'd like to hear just about anything right now."

"Okay," Anna said, "this is it. There's this cabin down the road from my house, belongs to some people called the Ledbetters. It needs a lot of fixing up, but nothing that can't be done in a day or so. And I'll bet you could rent it by the week or month real cheap."

"But I've got to be in—" Chris began.

"I know," she said, "Seattle. But not all the time. And the thing is, Todd would be perfectly safe in Winthrop by himself for a day here and there. I'm around, so are Madeline and Flip. In Seattle, well, it's a big city. A sixteen-year-old boy can't—"

"Oh, man," Todd said, disgusted.

But Chris put up a silencing hand. "Maybe Anna's right. You would be fine here for a day or so if I'm in

Seattle." He drew his brows together. "I can always have files sent up here from the office. I could do a lot of my work by phone if I have to."

"You mean," Todd said, "we'd really *live* in Winthrop?"

Chris turned to look at his son in the back seat. "You bet we will," he said. "And if I get this case wrapped up by midsummer, I might just tell the NTSB I'm taking some time off. Hell, I've got months of back vacation time due me."

"And I can get my driver's permit right here?"

"Real soon," Chris said, "we'll go to the driver's license bureau and get you all fixed up. It's a promise."

"Wow."

"Now be a good kid and get our bags out of the back, will you? I want to talk to Anna for a minute. Okay?"

"You bet. Sure. *All right, man!*"

"I wanted to thank you," Chris said in that raspy voice of his that ran over her nerve endings like a cat's tongue. "I'm not always this helpless. It's just that—"

"Oh, really, Chris, never mind. It's for Todd," she said quickly. "I'll call the rental place tomorrow and get you fixed up. A kid needs—"

"Anna, Todd and I are going to be okay."

She heard the edge of annoyance in his voice but couldn't look up from her lap. She'd see those clear blue eyes, the curve of his lips. Anyway, Todd was *his* problem; she had problems of her own. And she'd sworn to stay out of it.

"Listen," Chris said, "I do appreciate your help."

"But I'm a busybody, I know," she said.

"I wasn't going to say that."

"Oh, yes, you were. Okay, I know. It's none of my business. My intentions were honorable, though."

"Well, thank you. Helen handed me a pretty big surprise. But don't, well, don't think I'm helpless. We'll manage just fine. I'm a big boy, Anna."

"I know."

He stirred beside her, but she couldn't look. He was too close. She could feel his body heat, hear his breath sigh in his chest. Another second and she'd scream. She couldn't bear it.

But he was only getting out of the car, and she closed her eyes and drew in a grateful breath. "You've done too much," he said.

"Oh, well, us locals like to pitch in and help. You'll see tomorrow. You'll have more helping hands than you can use."

"I look forward to it."

"Well," Anna said, finally giving him a quick smile, "till morning."

His gaze met and locked with hers for a long moment. "Till morning, Anna." Then he closed the door and was gone.

CHAPTER THIRTEEN

CHRIS AWAKENED with a start, an aching shoulder and that sense of not knowing just where he was. A hotel. In Winthrop. Todd was in the adjoining room, and Anna Parish was only a few blocks away. He put his good arm over his eyes for a moment and realized she'd be in her nightgown most likely, the filmy material barely concealing her thighs, hips, belly, breasts...

He sat up straight and punished himself mentally. It was happening too fast. His life had been turned upside down in the space of a week. First a woman and then Todd. Damn, he barely knew who he was anymore, much less where he was headed.

Chris took a shower, alternating the water from hot to cold. He forced himself to think about the business at hand: moving into the house with Todd was top priority, but then the WestAir case wasn't going to wait forever, either. He'd made a couple of promises in the past few days that a part of him regretted and another part feared. He'd told his son they were going to be living together, and he'd see to it that Todd wasn't moved from school to school. Right now the task seemed monumental. And Anna. He'd promised to look into Fleisher's missing notebook. If there even *was* one, Chris thought derisively. Still, he'd said he'd check thoroughly, and that meant pressing the coroner in Seattle again if need be, as well as having the

NTSB Go Team boys pick apart the wreckage all over again. It wasn't just for Anna, Chris knew. The notebook issue had implanted itself in his brain. If it existed, it had to be located.

A thought struck Chris as he toweled off and carefully slipped his arm back into the sling. If the notebook were found, and if what Anna and others had said about Miller were true, it was possible that Fleisher himself had fallen victim to the very tactics he'd hoped to expose.

And just how was Anna going to handle that knowledge?

Chris collected Todd from the adjoining room, and they breakfasted together in the hotel's dining room. The boy sure could eat.

"*More* pancakes?" Chris asked when the waitress took Todd's second order.

"I'm starved, man. Say, how tall are you?"

"I don't know. Six-one or so."

"Like I'm still growing. I'm just under six feet now."

"So eat up," Chris said, smiling, sipping on his third coffee. "You wouldn't want to be shorter than your old man."

"No way," Todd agreed.

The morning was crazy. Anna, with Madeline's help, had gotten the key to the Ledbetter house and had opened it up by the time Chris and Todd had finished breakfast. And then there was the move. The place truly was a wreck, even by Chris's standards, and his and Todd's suitcases sat by the front door while Anna fussed.

"It's going to take all day," she said, casting around, her work shirt sleeves rolled up. "And that bathroom. I'll have to see if Daryl can't stop by and shore the darn plumbing up." Then she was off, marching down the street to get mop and buckets and "gallons of detergent," as she put it.

"Geez," Todd said, walking through the tiny two-bedroom cabin. "It's a dump."

"Yeah," Chris agreed, "I suppose it is."

"Maybe we should have gone to Seattle."

Chris put a hand on his shoulder. "It's going to work. Right here, Todd."

"If you believe in miracles, man."

The miracle began to happen by noon. Anna had been right. Neighbors had obviously grown curious and were turning out to help, introducing themselves, pushing up sleeves. Todd met a boy his own age, and together they cleaned up the yard and the patio that was out back by a little stream. *Talk about miracles,* Chris thought.

Maybe what the kid needed was a little less nagging and more freedom. Chris knew Helen; she'd probably ridden the boy day and night, ridden him so hard he'd rebelled. Chris guessed he'd just have to experiment— today freedom was working. So be it.

The plumber finally showed up to fix the toilet and shower. Anna, Madeline and Julie Frye from across the street cleaned until the place actually smelled like a hospital, and Flip, with a trip to the hardware store, helped Chris replace two broken windows.

At twelve-thirty Chris plumped down onto the sprung couch that was now covered with one of Anna's Indian blankets. His shoulder was done in.

"Hey, man," Todd called, "Larry thinks there's fish in this stream. Hey, Dad, come on out! Where are you?"

But Anna called back from the kitchen, "He's resting. He'll be out later."

Later turned out to be three minutes. Chris didn't mind, though, because for the first time in years his son seemed to have found an interest. There were small fish in the clear water running behind the house, but as for eating size...

"Let's catch some," Todd said, walking up and down through the undergrowth, staring at the water. "We could barbecue them tonight." He turned and looked at his dad. "Can we catch some?"

"Sure," Chris said, "see if your friend has a pole." The blessing was that Todd had forgotten, for the moment, about the driver's permit. Tomorrow, though, the kid would remember.

It was Flip who mercifully saved Chris from the madness of domestic chores. "I'd say it's time for a beer. How about you, Chris?"

"Thank God," Chris muttered.

"Oh, no," Madeline began, yellow rubber gloves on her hands, "we've still got to—"

"Let them go," Anna said, coming out of the bedroom. "We'll just make them fix dinner and do the dishes tonight."

"It's a deal," Flip put in, nodding Chris toward the door.

"You really don't mind?" Chris asked Anna.

"No, I don't. But I'm serious about dinner." She put her hands on her hips.

"Dinner it is," Chris said, "even if it has to be in a restaurant."

"Deal," she said.

"Deal," he returned, and for an instant something passed between them, a poignant sort of sharing that came from trust and understanding. He followed Flip down the street and wondered about that, wondered if, after all, Anna had come to trust him. It seemed dreadfully important.

The beer tasted great. The hamburger just as good. And Chris liked Flip Akers; he was easygoing and smiled readily and genuinely. But most of all, Flip wasn't the least bit nervous around Chris, as were most airline employees he'd come across. No, Flip was good-natured and sharp. Chris found himself more than a little curious as to how Flip and Madeline managed— Flip so outgoing and Madeline, well, Chris would call her withdrawn, high-strung. One thing was for sure: she didn't like or trust Chris Galloway.

"Another beer?" Flip asked, draining his long-necked bottle.

Chris shook his head. "I took half a painkiller earlier. I better make it coffee."

"Shoulder still hurt?"

"Not much. Well," Chris admitted, "it can get bad."

"I bet." Flip waved at the waitress. "That was a helluva near miss in Seattle you went through. Must of given you a few second thoughts."

"Oh, yeah, one or two. And, believe me, we'll get to the bottom of it." You bet, Chris thought, whoever was responsible was going to pay.

"Um." Flip ordered the beer and coffee, then turned back to Chris. "You know," he said, "the tire on that plane was bum." Then, seeing Chris's carefully expressionless face, he added, "I know, I know, the NTSB will make that judgment. But between you and me, pal, Miller could kill a whole lot more innocent folks before someone stops him."

For some time Chris studied the young copilot sitting across from him. Finally he made up his mind. "Flip, you could go on record, you realize, with the authorities."

"And lose my job?" Flip laughed lightly. "That's what would happen, you know. And maybe I'd lose my license, too, if the FAA decided I'd broken FARs, even if it was under pressure. No thanks, pal."

"Not necessarily. Of course, I can't promise anything, but I know of many instances where cockpit crews have come forward with information and nothing happened. Their cooperation, believe me, was greatly appreciated."

"Maybe, but if you ask me it's a big gamble."

"Look, if you feel that way, we can talk and I'll keep it off the record. You've got my word on that."

"Does that make me a snitch?" Flip asked sarcastically.

"Not hardly," Chris replied. "It makes you a hero to the flying public."

It was slow going, but finally Flip began to relax and trust Chris, and a world of information came gushing forth.

"Then there was the time I was flying with Jim Fleisher and—"

"I had no idea you copiloted flights with Fleisher," Chris said over his second cup of coffee.

"Oh, you bet," Flip replied, "a couple of times. You know, filling in on vacations, sick time. Anyway, Jim had decided to can our flight. The winds were bad, whipping around so you couldn't tell what direction they'd come from next. Anyway, Miller was up in his office, and he's got this window that overlooks the runway. So he calls the tower and has the controllers patch him through to Jim." Flip smiled and shook his head, remembering. "Miller was ticked off real bad. It was over the Christmas holidays, and we were shuttling passengers in and out of Seattle by the drove. Anyway, Miller's yelling over the intercom for Jim to take off in between gusts. Jesus, it was impossible to tell when the next bad gust was going to tear down the valley."

"What did Fleisher do?" Chris asked gravely.

"He told Miller where to get off and sat on the end of the runway for another half hour. Maybe more."

"And this is all on the cockpit voice recorder?"

"I guess it must be."

"Did the tower overhear that conversation?"

"They must have. But with commercial flights coming and going and all the private planes—it's a zoo at Christmas. I'm sure they were busy with other planes bucking the wind."

"How about the mechanics?" Chris asked. "Did you ever hear Miller lay into any of them in person?"

"All the time," Flip said. "He'll march right onto the tarmac and say stuff like, 'You there, boy, what's wrong with that filter? Don't you know this plane's gotta be in the air in fifteen?' And the poor mechanic usually stuffs the filter, or whatever it is, back in so the plane can board up and take off."

"You've *heard* conversations like that?" Chris was astounded. Oh, he suspected things like that went on all the time at the smaller commuter lines, but to hear a copilot admit it . . .

"Sure, I've heard it go on," Flip said. "The man's got a one-track mind—bottom line."

Chris whistled softly between his teeth. "Okay, let's get back to Jim Fleisher. From what I've heard he was a really safe pilot. He stood up to Miller when he had to.''

Flip nodded. "He did.''

"But flight 629. It took off in that storm. Even the copilot—''

"Len.''

"Yes, Len, was troubled. How do you figure that?''

"I liked Len," Flip said, "but he really was a wimp in a lot of ways. New at the game. I wouldn't put too much stock in the stuff he said that day.''

"So you believe Fleisher deemed it safe to take off.''

"Oh, yes, Jim—'' He hesitated.

"What is it?'' Chris asked carefully.

"Jim was a super pilot. The best. But...'' He paused again, weighing his words. "I don't know.''

"How do you mean that?''

"I don't mean that he thought he was invincible or anything, but he knew the skies, the area around here. He knew these mountains as well as any man.''

"You think he misjudged the weather?''

"I don't know," Flip said. "I'll never believe it was pressure from Miller to run the flight on schedule. Not with Jim. But...''

"But Fleisher missed something, didn't he?'' Chris said in a low, hard voice.

"Yes. He had to have. I just can't believe it was the goddamn weather.''

Flip had a third beer. By that time he was reminiscing about Fleisher as if they'd been bosom buddies. He talked eloquently about Jim's many attributes and what a special person he'd been. Chris listened silently, a ball of resentment growing in his gut. He was jealous of a dead man! How in hell was he supposed to compete with Mr. Super Pilot himself? But more relevant—and he had to work hard to keep his mind on it—was his growing certainty that Fleisher had made a fatal error that morning in March. And Chris had to find out what it was. When he did, though, just how was Anna going to take the news?

"And Anna and Jim were such a great couple," Flip was telling him. "They really were."

"I'm sure they were."

"Anna's real special, too, you know."

"Yes, she is."

"She's been a little upset lately," Flip said carefully. "She told you."

"Uh, yes, she—"

"Madeline's got a problem, too. The same problem," Flip said, averting his gaze.

This was getting over Chris's head. "How's that, Flip?"

"Because—hey, can you keep this to yourself?"

"Why, sure."

"I mean it. Madeline would die if she knew I told you. And, well, I know you've got to be thinking Anna's some kind of a wacko."

"I do?"

"Of course, that ghost stuff. You know, Jim's spirit floating around her room." Flip made waving motions with his arms.

"Go on."

"This is a secret, right?"

"Right. You've got my word on it."

Flip let out a breath. "Madeline says she's seen him, too."

"Who?"

"Jim. That's who."

"His . . . ghost?"

"Yep."

"Oh, my God." Chris sat back hard in his chair. Madeline, too? Then . . . but it couldn't be. It wasn't possible.

"I know," Flip said. "I know. It's crazy. Some kind of mass hysteria."

"That, my friend, is an understatement." And for the rest of the afternoon Chris just couldn't get Flip's revelation out of his head. Both women had seen Fleisher. That simply couldn't be possible.

Chris didn't have to cook dinner at all, not that he would have even known where to begin. Luckily, as it turned out, Flip was a pro on the outdoor barbecue. He rushed off to the store at five, marinated chicken in his own teriyaki sauce, shucked ears of corn with Todd's help and whipped up a huge bowl of coleslaw.

They ate outdoors in the wooded backyard, the adults seated on old lawn chairs on the stone patio, while Todd and his new friend tried their hands at fishing. Occasionally Chris rose and helped Todd with a tangled line or showed him where to cast, but for the most part Chris quietly listened to the adult conversation and watched Anna.

She'd changed earlier from her work clothes into a white skirt and a sleeveless, cherry-red tank top that seemed to reveal more than it covered. Or maybe that was just him, Chris thought, observing her as she stood near the barbecue, talking to Madeline.

Chris glanced at the boys, who were moving downstream with their lines, and then back at Anna again, to her shower-damp mass of hair that she'd loosely pinned up, to her softly curving shoulders and the outline of her breasts. Through the golden evening light that danced with tiny insects and dust motes, Chris studied Anna, his brow furrowed, his body tensed as if expecting a blow. Something was happening to him, something utterly out of his experience. Every time he even glanced in Anna's direction his nerve endings seemed to leap beneath his skin, and that tightening in his groin grew unbearable.

He sat in the rickety old lawn chair, his back still warmed by the late sun, and asked himself exactly what it was he was feeling for Anna Parish. He felt as if he were walking on loose stones in a wide, rushing river. How long he could keep his footing, Chris had no idea. And where a plunge would take him was a mystery, too.

"Yo, Dad!" Todd's voice came, disturbing his reverie. "Dad! I think I got one!"

Todd had indeed hooked a small brook trout, so small that Chris had to throw it back. "Thanks," Todd said dejectedly. "I'll never catch another one and you throw it back."

Chris explained, as best he could, about helping nature along so that in the future there would still be fish to catch. "Does that make sense, son?"

"I guess so." The two boys finally gave up fishing and, stuffed with Flip's meal, headed off to town to "hang out."

"He'll be fine," Anna said, coming up behind Chris. "He really can't get into trouble here. They'll probably just go to the pinball palace or T-shirt shop. No big deal."

"I wasn't worried," Chris said. "The kid's got to grow up sometime and take on a few responsibilities."

Anna cocked her head.

"What?" Chris asked.

"I wonder," she said, lowering her eyes. "I just wonder if that isn't a cop-out, Chris. Don't get mad, but—"

"I'm not mad," he stated quietly, but in truth he was beginning to wish Anna would let him and Todd seek their own level. She sure could be—he searched for the word—motherly.

"I didn't mean to—" Anna began.

"We're doing our best," he said firmly.

"I suppose you're in charge now," she said, and her hazel eyes looked both doubtful and reassuring at the same time.

Something was changing between them, something intangible but real. She was easier with him, softer, and he admitted, grudgingly, that she was wonderful with Todd. He asked himself if he didn't prefer the previous, convenient distance between them to what might come. He already had Todd to worry about, and this WestAir case was far from closed. Did he really need another complication?

Abruptly he caught himself. What was he thinking? Anna wasn't interested in an old, shopworn NTSB investigator. Hell, no. She had those loving memories of hers, memories of the spiffy, perfectionist pilot Jim Fleisher. The man's man. What would Anna want with Chris Galloway?

Madeline was asking him something from the back door. "Want a beer or wine?"

He shook his head. "No, thank you."

He watched her disappear inside again and wondered for the hundredth time at what Flip had told him.

Unbelievable. *Both* women, seeing the same dead pilot. Absolutely insane. As Flip had said, it must have been a form of mass hysteria or something. A psychiatrist would know. Sure. There was a simple explanation. Still, what a crazy situation—Jim Fleisher's spirit appearing to two women.

Anna came out of the house and sat down next to him. "That was a great meal."

He laughed. "Thank Flip."

"Well, you're the host."

"So I am. Strange, isn't it?"

She stretched her legs out in front of her and looked up at the night sky. Her throat glistened whitely in the faint light, and her profile was carved alabaster. "The moon's coming up," she said, turning to him.

"It's a very nice moon," he replied.

"Um."

And as he watched the half-moon rise over the Cascades, he wondered just who Anna would choose to sit with if she had the choice. Himself, or Jim Fleisher?

THE DAY BEGAN innocently enough. Later Anna would think over and over that it was all her fault. She should have behaved differently, more maturely. But at the time she wasn't thinking at all. She was reacting.

Chris stopped by around ten the morning after he and Todd had gotten settled. He looked, Anna noted with pleasure, somewhat relaxed, dressed more casually than she'd ever seen him in a pair of jeans and a plain white shirt, cuffs rolled up to his elbows, bad arm and all.

"How was your first night in your new house?" Anna asked, holding up the coffeepot.

"Sure, I'd love a cup," he said, and sat at her kitchen table. "The first night was fine. I slept pretty soundly, in fact."

"Well, moving's always tiring." Anna poured him a mug and then went to the sink. "Todd seems to like the place," she said over her shoulder.

"Kids his age can manage just about anywhere."

"Um, I remember."

After a short silence, he said, "I wonder if I could borrow another blanket, just until I can pick up a few things in Seattle. I know it's imposing—"

"Oh, but it isn't, really. We have lots. Winters can be downright brutal, so I keep extras in the hall closet." God, she was rattling on, nervous, she realized. Why did Chris always have this effect on her?

"Well, thanks, I do appreciate it." He cleared his throat and sipped the steaming coffee. "Flip and Madeline around?"

"No. They went biking early. I guess Flip has a flight later."

"Um . . . I wanted to thank them for all their help."

Anna finished tidying up and dried her hands. She pushed her hair behind one ear and sat down across from him. "Where's Todd?"

"He's still sacked out. I left him a note."

"Oh."

"Anna . . ." he began, looking at his mug. A muscle worked in his jaw. "Listen, there's something . . ."

She smiled and cocked her head. "Well, what? Don't keep me on pins and needles."

"Oh, maybe I . . . never mind."

"No, tell me, Chris. I hate it when people do that. Whatever it is, tell me." She was still smiling. "You want to borrow some sugar, right?"

"Not exactly." His eyes rose to meet hers.

"Then what?"

He continued to regard her solemnly for a moment, apparently deciding something. "It's about the other day. I feel I owe you some sort of an explanation or—" he frowned "—call it an apology."

"An apology? For what?"

"My rash behavior."

"When? Oh," Anna said, waving a hand negligently, "you mean Todd, about your not calling from the hospital. It's all right. You were hurt and—"

"Anna," he said firmly, "it's not about Todd. It's about my storming out of your house like an ass. I...I...ah, said some things that—"

"Oh, Lord," Anna whispered, remembering, wishing with all her heart he'd just let the whole thing drop and forget it. He'd said he wasn't going to fight a ghost to have her, and Anna still had no way to cope with that statement. She didn't *want* to cope with it. Not yet. "Look, let's forget the whole thing. Do you want some more coffee?" She stood quickly and began to walk toward the counter.

"Anna." Chris caught her arm. "I want to explain."

"Please..."

"No, I'm not going to pretend something wasn't...isn't...going on."

"Nothing's going on, Chris. Not a thing." She looked down at her imprisoned arm. He released her. "I can't...I don't want to discuss this."

"What about me? Maybe I want to."

Anna's lower lip trembled. "I can't help...I can't be responsible for how you feel. I barely know how I feel myself."

"And that's the point, isn't it?"

"Oh, God."

"No," Chris said in a deep voice, "don't turn away from the issue like this, Anna. I need to know."

Anna whirled to face him. "Need to know what?" Her tone was high, shrill, and she felt her control slipping. She knew what he wanted to know. She knew and, Lord help her, she was afraid of the truth, afraid to look it in the face.

"About Fleisher," he said. "I want to know how you feel about him."

"Feel about him?" Anna cried. "How should I feel about him?"

"You know what I'm asking."

"Can't you see how much this is upsetting me?"

Chris nodded slowly, pensively. "Yes," he said, "and what I see tells me you're still emotionally involved with the man."

"Of course I am! I told you, it's his notebook. It's—"

"It's *not* his notebook," Chris ground out. "It's a whole lot more than a simple notebook."

Anna could feel tears begin to burn behind her eyes. She averted her face.

"You still love him," Chris stated flatly. "You aren't even making an effort to let go, are you?"

"What a joke!" Anna blurted. "And just how am I supposed to let the man go when he still visits me!"

"That's your story."

"Oh, right, you're always so damn right!"

"About this I might well be."

Again Anna whirled to face him. "You don't know anything about me. You don't know what it's like to have someone you love be killed like that. You don't know what it's like to have that person come back and—"

"Why won't you give me a straight answer?" Chris demanded. "I asked you if you still love the guy. Do you?"

"I...I..."

Abruptly Chris came to his feet. "I believe I already have my answer. You have to do what you have to do, Anna, and I'm sorry if I was holding out false...hope. I should have known better. I knew all along how you felt." He strode to the back door.

"Chris," she began, desperately trying to collect herself, "don't...don't go like this."

"Look," he said, his voice hard, "I only came over to get this all straight. When I said that the other day, I really didn't know exactly why myself. Now I do. I guess I was starting to like you a little too much, Anna. I asked for this, and I got it."

"Chris," she said, her voice a plea, "I just need more time. I'm not ready...I'm not ready to—"

"I get it, all right." He left then, closing the screen door firmly, and all Anna could think was that she should have kept her cool and lied to him.

CHAPTER FOURTEEN

FOUR DAYS WAS an incredibly long time. Ninety-six hours, thousands of minutes, every one of them full of misery and self-reproach and longing. Anna had been struck dumb by the enormity of Chris's absence, struck deaf and dumb and blind. She couldn't sleep. She hurt all over. Tears filled her eyes at odd moments.

She couldn't even be mad at him, because he hadn't done anything wrong. In fact, he'd been absolutely right. They *had* been getting to like each other too much—or at least Anna had been getting to like Chris entirely too much. And it had scared her, threatened her pleasant memories, her comfortable mourning for Jim.

She had to admit Chris might be right. Maybe she did still love Jim. Anna stopped in midstride. She was dragging the garden hose around to the front of the house to water the lawn, and she had stopped in her tracks, struggling with the thought. She *had* loved Jim, yes, but did she still? He was dead, and the man she'd loved was certainly not the sad wraith who visited her. *You can't love a dead man,* she told herself. *You can only love his memory.*

Oh, God, maybe Chris was right. Maybe it was time to give Jim up, to let him lie in peace and try harder to turn her life outward again. Not to forget, to go on.

She wanted to tell Chris what she was thinking, how she was suffering, how she missed him. She wanted to sit with him and hear his husky voice and feel his blue eyes on her. She wanted him near.

But it was over between them, and it was better that way. She just wasn't ready for the roller-coaster emotions Chris had raised in her. She couldn't handle it. But she missed those feelings, nevertheless, and she felt empty inside, lost, bereft, sad.

Chris was so close, just down the street. She could walk by, bring some tulips from her garden to put in a jelly glass from his sparsely stocked cupboards. Drop in casually. And she knew he was there because Todd had stopped by often enough and filled her in on the Galloways' new life.

He'd burst in the door a few days ago, elated. "I got my permit! See? Here it is. Permanent address, it says. See? One-eleven Bluff Avenue, Winthrop, Washington, Okanogan County."

"Great, Todd. That's super."

"Yeah, and he let me drive home, too."

"And you did all right?" she asked.

"Aw, that rental car is an automatic, no fair. It's a boat. But I drove great, yeah, really, man."

"You didn't...ah, tell your dad about...?"

"No, that's our secret. I promised," Todd said soberly. Then he smiled. "But he was sure surprised at how good I did. Man, I'm telling you."

"I'm glad it worked out," she said, dying to ask how Chris was, how he looked, how he felt, if his shoulder hurt, if he was eating well. But she didn't.

"And dad took a few days off, you know. Sick leave, he said. See, his shoulder still hurts and he gets these headaches."

"Oh? He's not feeling well?" she asked, deliberately casual.

"He's okay. We went hiking yesterday, and he got really out of breath. Said he was in bad shape." Todd laughed. "Yeah, he's getting old."

"So how's the house?"

"It's fine, I guess. He makes me keep my room neat. Bummer."

She smiled, wondering just how neat the two men really were. Maybe she should offer to—

"So, anyway, there's this baseball team here," Todd said. "I'm not bad, so my dad talked to the coach. I guess it's a city program or something. Anyway, I'm the relief pitcher. We have practice every morning. That's hardball, man, not softball," he said with great seriousness.

"Oh, sure, I know the difference. You pitch overhand, right?"

"Yeah, that's it."

"Well, sounds like you're settling in."

Todd was silent for a moment, obviously thinking over something he'd wanted to say. Anna stood quietly, waiting for him to speak.

"Uh, Anna, well, this is sort of personal," he finally said. "I mean, Dad's been grouchy and I, well, sort of got this idea something…I mean, did you guys have a fight or something?"

Oh, Lord. "Not a fight, Todd." *Don't lie to him,* she told herself. "Sort of an agreement to disagree, I guess you'd call it."

"Why?"

She concentrated harder on her hands. "Oh, reasons."

"Come *on,* Anna. I'm not a baby."

"Well, things were moving too fast. We decided to slow down," she said awkwardly.

"Slow down?" Todd laughed. "More like stop, I'd say."

"Todd, it's hard to explain—"

"Geez! That's what he said!"

Her heart froze. Todd had spoken to Chris about it. Of course, he would have noticed. He would have—

"Well, I think you're both dumb, man. You could be friends at least, couldn't you? I mean, man, it's not like we've got all these friends out here!"

He'd left then, and Anna had puttered around the house, weeded the garden, cooked herself something light. Madeline and Flip were both working again after their short break, but Anna had only had one round-trip flight that week; it was still off-season. And now, with both her roommates in Seattle for the day, Anna felt lonely, yearning to see Chris, wondering about him, worrying, torturing herself. And Todd...he was right. They were both dumb. They'd both jumped into something too fast.

She hosed off the front walk and saw nothing in the rainbow spray but Chris's face that night at the barbecue. They'd sat out behind his house and watched the moon rise. He'd been studying her closely, and when she turned to meet his eyes, his expression had been so serious, so intense.

Julie Frye came out of her house down the street. She waved and yelled, "Hi!" Anna waved back.

A blue car came around the corner and pulled up in front of Anna's house. She looked, then looked again. Todd was driving.

He popped out of the car, a wide grin on his face. The first thing she noticed was that his hair was cut. Not exactly a crew cut, but shorter.

"Todd! Does your father know you've got his car?" she asked.

"Yeah, man. He said I could drive around a little to practice. Wow, what a kick."

"You know that's a rental car. You have to be over twenty-one to drive a rental car. Are you both out of your minds?"

Todd shrugged. "What can happen in this little town?"

"God knows."

"Well, my dad says it's okay, so I guess it is. I'm being careful."

She couldn't help but note the way he said "my dad," the possessive, proud way he said it, shouting to her, to the world: "I have a dad, and he cares about me." Still, Anna questioned the wisdom of letting the kid have so much freedom. Was this just a way for Chris to avoid disciplining the boy? Couldn't Chris put his foot down and say "no"? Or was she being horribly female, and meddling again? After all, Todd seemed to be doing well. He seemed happy, well adjusted, a different kid from the one she'd met at the Seattle airport that day.

"You got a haircut," she said.

He put his hand up. "Yeah, it was cut it or not play baseball."

"It looks nice."

"It's okay, I guess."

"Uh, how's your dad?" Casually she watered the flowers and the grass, sweeping the hose back and forth. "Any more headaches?"

"He's okay. Said he was on vacation, but he's been on the phone a lot."

"A workaholic, huh?" But all she could think was that he had a phone and he hadn't called her. But then why should he?

"Yeah, I guess so," Todd said.

"Is he going back to Seattle soon?"

Todd gave that familiar shrug again. "He didn't say. But he likes it here. Says he sleeps real good. And, you know, we went shopping for groceries. I drove both ways. He says it hurts his shoulder to drive."

"How fortunate he is to have you around."

"Yeah."

"So how *is* baseball?"

"We have a game this weekend. In Twisp. I'll probably get to pitch some. I have a good fastball, the coach says. It's kinda fun. The girls come to watch us practice."

"Wow, Todd. I didn't know there were any girls in this hick town," she teased.

"Yeah, there're a few," he said nonchalantly.

"Well, I'm glad you like it here. Has Chris...has your dad decided if he's going to stay after the investigation's over?" She felt foolish and so transparent, pushing.

"Aw, he just gets uptight when I ask him. I don't know. I guess he doesn't want to think about it yet."

I'll bet he doesn't, Anna mused.

Todd drove away in the blue car, slowly and sedately, she noticed. Chris sure was giving him a lot of responsibility. She only hoped it didn't backfire. Oh, God, she wished she could stop worrying about Chris and Todd! She didn't need it. She had plenty of problems of her own.

Enough, she told herself. *It isn't your business.* But Jim and his notebook were. And it sounded as if Chris was working again.

She wondered if he'd heard from the medical examiner. She was dying to know if anything had been found. Would Chris tell her one way or the other? Should she ask him, use that as an excuse to drop in?

No! He didn't want to see her. That was plain. He'd ended it between them, whatever "it" had been. Not a relationship, not an affair, not exactly a friendship, either. It had been an ephemeral thing at best, undeniable but so very fragile, and it had shattered under rough handling. She would only be prolonging the agony if she weakened and called him.

For the past few days she'd thought about Jim when she lay in bed at night. She'd tested her feelings of guilt the way you'd worry a sore tooth with your tongue. There was a slight twinge, yes. It was still there, but it was fading. She'd shed her tears, she'd mourned, she'd suffered the visits of Jim's spirit. She'd paid her dues. He was dead and she was alive. She was doing everything humanly possible to find Jim's journal and prove him innocent. As long as she held true to that, she felt no guilt. But how singular it was that the very man who could help her vindicate Jim was the one who would... But she stopped herself there. She wasn't going to think about the future. Not yet. Still, she missed Chris's voice. She missed his presence, his own special smell, the way he stood, the way he moved, the way he looked at her with those blue, far-seeing eyes. She wanted to make sure he ate well and rested and took his pain pills if he needed them. Who washed his clothes, his and Todd's?

She wanted him close to her, comforting her, seeing the truth of her. She wanted to talk to him about how she felt. She craved him as a junkie craved drugs, and it was so hard not to drive by the little house or walk by and knock on the door or call.

She held herself back by sheer willpower. Day and night it was a constant fight, her mind switching back and forth: I will. I won't. I have to. I can't. Yes. No. Do it. Don't you dare. A constant dialogue inside her head, arguing, hoping, beseeching, yearning. It was exhausting and debilitating and agonizing.

The coroner—she tried to focus on that, hold on to it. The list of personal effects. Was Jim's notebook there? Had some poor, bereaved family received it by mistake? Could it be traced?

If Chris had found out anything, he would have called her, wouldn't he? He knew how important it was to her. He wouldn't just let her sit and stew, would he?

She wished she was scheduled to work. Anything to occupy her mind. At last she decided to drop everything and went for a hike in the mountains. It didn't help.

That night she lay in bed tired from a long hike—physically tired, but her mind still raced. And every time car lights swung across her window she wondered, Is that him?

But night was also a time for Jim. It was at night he'd appeared to her. And she lay there tense, confused, more than a little afraid, at his mercy.

She recalled with bone-chilling clarity the night he'd come from that dark and shadowy place beyond the grave. He'd known Chris had been sleeping on her couch. And he'd come.

She rolled over, willing her limbs to relax. But the struggle persisted. Jim and Chris. Death and life. She'd always miss Jim Fleisher, but the emptiness and loneliness couldn't go on forever. Jim had to free her. He simply had to find his peace and let her go.

The next morning there was a knock at her front door. Todd, Anna thought, with another installment on the Galloway saga. She rose from where she'd been sitting reading the paper and finishing her coffee. She wore shorts and a T-shirt and no shoes. It was going to be hot out. Maybe she'd go to the pool, ask Todd to tag along, she was thinking as she went to the door.

"Early, aren't you?" she said, opening the door.

But it was his father. He had a carefully dispassionate expression on his face, and he took her attire in swiftly, from the top of her head to her bare toes.

"Oh, I'm sorry," she said quickly. "I thought it was Todd. I..." Her voice died, and a hot flush crept up her neck. *He's come back* was all she could think, and her insides shivered with fear and gladness and confusion.

"I *am* early. Should I come back later?"

"Oh, no, no. Come in." She gestured with her arm, feeling foolish, her heart thumping too fast against her ribs.

"Are you sure it isn't too early?"

"No, it's all right. Coffee?"

"You know my weakness," he said, not meeting her eyes.

She studied him for a moment. "You aren't using the sling. And no bandage on your head. Todd said you were getting headaches. I wondered—"

"Sometimes Todd talks too much."

Shakily she poured him coffee, wondering where to go from there. She was glad he was here, terribly glad, but she was afraid to show it. He'd see it in her eyes, though, in her face, in the joy bursting from her skin, and she was afraid he'd take fright and retreat. "I...uh...see that Todd seems to be having a good time. Baseball and all."

Watching her, Chris nodded.

"And he got his hair cut. Was that your idea or the coach's?"

"Both."

"Um. Well, he looks good. Better."

"Yes."

She sat on a stool at the counter, crossed her legs and hooked one foot around a rung. Nervously she pushed her hair back. "He showed me his permit. He's awfully excited about driving."

Chris shrugged—that male Galloway trait. "All boys like to drive."

"Yes, they do," Anna said, interlacing her fingers around her knee.

Chris was moving around her kitchen, prowling, restless. It occurred to her that he might be as ill at ease as she was. But he was braver. He'd come to her first. Neither of them said anything for a time, too long a time, until finally Chris stopped, took a gulp of coffee from the mug she'd poured him and raised his eyes to hers.

"I couldn't stay away," he said. "I tried but I couldn't."

"Oh, Chris..."

"I'm sorry I pushed you like that the other day. I shouldn't have. It was childish. I was jealous."

She closed her eyes and felt tears burn behind her lids. Sad tears, happy tears—she wasn't sure which. "I missed you," she said in a choked voice.

"You did." It wasn't a question.

"Yes, I did. Horribly. I was going to come by a hundred times."

"You were."

"Yes. Oh, Chris, I'm sorry. It was my fault. You deserved an answer and I didn't give you one."

"If you...care about a person, you compromise, you talk, right? You don't deliver ultimatums, Anna," he said carefully.

"Yes," she whispered.

"So...I came here to talk, to discuss things calmly. I won't push you. I know it's too soon for you, but I can't—" he looked down at his coffee mug, frowning "—just let you go."

"I'm so glad. I...I wish I'd done it days ago. I wish I'd had the courage," she said, smiling through her tears.

"You don't hate me? You aren't angry?"

"I tried to be, but it didn't work," she confessed.

"Okay. Fresh start, then?"

"Sure, fresh start."

He looked at her for a time soberly, considering. Then he drank some of his coffee and put the mug down on her counter with a thump. He stood in front of her, tall in her cozy kitchen. "Actually," he said, "I had another reason for coming to see you." He put his hands in his pockets in that way he had and thrust out his jaw. "I've got some news about Fleisher's notebook."

Anna closed her eyes and whispered a prayer, waiting.

"Anna, I'm afraid it isn't very good news."

"Oh, no," she whispered.

"Look," he said, "it's a bizarre story. Just give me a minute and I'll try to explain. Something—maybe a notebook—was taken from the medical examiner's office a couple of days after the crash. It was an item belonging to Fleisher, but we're not sure what it was at this point."

"How . . ." She fell dutifully silent.

"It happened like this. The front desk receptionist gave whatever it was to an FAA official. He signed for it, the whole nine yards. But—"

"Surely all you have to do is ask him and—"

"That's the hitch. The official doesn't exist. The name the man used was phony. If he flashed an ID, that was fake, too. And the receptionist who, by the way, took a maternity leave only a few days later, can't recall much more about the incident. She's back at work now and—"

"So *that's* why," Anna said. "That's why no one at the office remembered anything being taken."

"Exactly. And the girl can't really be blamed. Dozens of documents and potential evidence items were signed for by both the FAA and NTSB the week after the crash. What surprised me is that the girl remembered at all."

"I wonder why she did," Anna said pensively, her brain working overtime.

"A fluke." A muscle worked in Chris's jaw as he paced, his hands in his trouser pockets. "I asked her that myself and she said the investigator, whoever it really was, left Fleisher's possessions scattered on a counter when he was through. I guess she had to straighten it all up and repackage everything. She said she recalled the incident because she was feeling so rotten that day."

"Chris," Anna said, "could she identify the man? I mean . . ."

But he was shaking his head. "How is she going to identify someone who—" He stopped short and spun around to face her. "What are you thinking?"

"Miller," Anna said in a low voice. "It must have been Lee Miller."

"Anna, you can't just—"

"Oh, yes, I can. You bet I can!" Her cheeks felt hot and flushed, the sure, gut knowledge of the identity of that official hitting her like a slap on the face. "It *couldn't* have been anyone else. I know it. And so do you." She bit her lower lip. "Chris, you could show the woman a photo. You could—"

"Anna," he said sharply, "even if you *are* right, he's not going to have the notebook. He'd have destroyed it."

But she shook her head slowly. "Not necessarily. Not Miller."

"No? Why not?"

"Nixon," Anna said suddenly. "Remember the Watergate tapes? Remember how he kept them kind of like a trophy or something?"

"So?"

"Ego, Chris. Maybe Miller's ego is just as big."

"And maybe it isn't."

"You could try," she said in earnest. "It can't hurt to try at least."

For a long moment Chris studied her. Finally he said, "It's a real shot in the dark, Anna. You realize that."

"But you'll *try*. You'll show that woman a photo. Maybe she'll remember. And if she does, then we could—"

Chris held up a warning hand. "One step at a time, Anna."

"Oh, Chris, if I could just get my hands on Jim's notebook. If I could prove to you and everyone else—"

"Prove what?" His tone was guarded.

"Prove everything is Miller's fault. Prove—"

"And what if the notebook is found and it proves nothing, Anna? What if—" But he stopped, a deep frown crossing his features. "Anna," he said, taking a step toward her, "I know you believe in your heart that Fleisher is seeking vindication. But what if it's something else. What if Fleisher is really at fault?"

"I'll cross that bridge when I come to it. I know you don't believe his...spirit exists, but it does. And, well, I can't believe Jim would be coming back like this for nothing. I mean, he has to *know* his book exists somewhere. That's why he keeps coming and coming."

"Anna," Chris said, letting out a long, exasperated breath, "don't you know how that sounds?"

She nodded, averting her eyes.

"Then you know I can't go marching into a judge's chambers and ask for a search warrant based on...based on the appearance of a dead man." He ran his hand through his hair. "I'm sorry, but even if the receptionist can ID Miller—if it *was* Miller—I still don't know...."

"Facts," Anna said under her breath. "It's all those facts of yours, Chris Galloway. Don't you ever play a hunch? Listen to your heart instead of that unbending brain of yours?" She tried to smile, but it was a rueful attempt. "I suppose you can't. I suppose it's just like any habit. It's too hard to break sometimes."

He moved up behind her and touched her on the arm. "Call it a bad habit of mine. I just hate to see..." He let his voice trail off.

"That notebook exists," Anna said quietly. "And somehow, I don't know how, but somehow I'm going to get it."

He ran his finger along a tendril of her hair, and she shivered with the sensation. "That's *my* job, Anna, not yours."

She turned to face him. He was so close she couldn't breathe. Her blood ran hotly in her veins, and she could feel her face flush again. "Will you at least try to find the notebook?" Her eyes searched his with a kind of desperation. It mattered so much. Somehow everything was tied together, Jim's notebook, Chris, her own feelings, her very sanity.

"I said I would, Anna, and I'll do my best." He met her gaze calmly.

"Would you...would you do this for anyone? Or is it just for me?" She held her breath, wanting his answer yet fearing it.

He averted his eyes and gave a little laugh. "You ask hard questions, lady." He hesitated, then looked back at her. "I don't know. I honestly don't know. I hope I'd treat everyone the same."

She touched his arm. "Well, thanks, thanks for helping me."

"I'm just doing my job, Anna," he said gravely.

She walked back to his house with him because he asked her to and because she couldn't bear to let him go yet, now that he'd finally come to her. Something had been clarified between them. A decision had been made. Their relationship had shifted. He'd come to her. And now they had to find their way, fumbling and inexpert and slow perhaps, to the next step. Anna knew this instinctively and walked beside him in the warm June sun, frightened but tingling with delight, caressed by his voice, his nearness, the touch of his leg brushing her hip.

What would happen now? She didn't know, but it *would* happen, and she was ready. Chris was ready. It was there, ripe, ready to pluck and taste. She was poignantly aware of every sensation—the warm air, the fragrant breeze, the aroma of newly cut grass, a dog barking, the cries of children playing. Chris next to her, his head bent as they spoke, his hands in his pockets.

Carefully, in wordless agreement, they spoke of inconsequential matters: Todd, his house. Safe subjects. Whenever their eyes met, a jolt of electricity passed between them, a current so strong that the tiny hairs stirred all over her body. She moved in a haze of euphoric knowledge.

The house, however, brought her back to reality with a jolt. Her first response was to laugh.

"What's the matter?" Chris asked defensively.

"Do you really want to know?"

"Well, it's a little . . . messy."

"It is that." She looked around. Dishes were piled by the sink. Bread crumbs littered the counter. Empty cups and glasses and plates of dry bread crusts sat on the table. Todd's sneakers lay on the floor, dirty socks draped over them.

"It's okay. It's relaxed," he said. Then he looked around, plucked a jacket off the couch and nudged Todd's shoes aside with his foot. "I don't think it's so bad. I kind of like it. Homey." He collected some glasses and put them on the counter next to the sink.

Then he stood there for a minute as if thinking. "Anna..."

"Um?" She was stacking dishes, emptying cups.

"Flip told me about Madeline, about her seeing—" He ran his hand through his hair and looked away. "God! I can't even say it. I feel like a fool."

"What, Chris?" But she knew. She knew.

"Madeline has seen Fleisher, too."

"Yes, I know." She tried to sound matter-of-fact, but her blood surged in her veins. "I can't believe Flip told you. He thinks we're both under some kind of hypnosis or something."

"Yes, he mentioned that. You know, he told me to try to help you out, so I'd believe you."

"Well, did it work? Do you believe me?"

Chris moved around the room, picking things up, putting them down. He rubbed his jaw, his back to her. "I'll be damned if I know *what* to believe, Anna."

Arms folded, she leaned against the sink, watching him, waiting, her heart beating slow drumbeats in her ears.

"I just don't know how to figure it."

"And that bothers you, doesn't it?" she suggested.

He turned to face her. "Yes, I like everything in neat tidy boxes, if you want to put it that way."

"Oh," she said. "What about...us, Chris? How do we fit?" She couldn't believe she'd said those words, dared him to examine the "thing" that had formed between them like a brewing storm. She held his gaze, but it was so hard, so humiliating. What if he...?

Slowly, purposefully, Chris began to move toward her. The tension in the small room pulsed like a living beast as he neared. Anna held her breath, her lungs on fire, ready to explode. He kept coming. And then he was there, standing over her, so close, the intensity in his blue eyes almost a white-hot glow.

"Chris," she whispered, trying to catch her breath, searching for a reality that was fast slipping away, "this is crazy."

Slowly his hands came up to cup her face. "Maybe we're all crazy," he said, and Anna closed her eyes and felt his lips descend onto hers.

She knew she was lost then. The final step had been taken. She was in a strange place, beset by new sensations: his lips on hers, his hands in her hair, his chest hard against hers. There was no going back, nor did she want to.

He kissed her, moved his mouth on hers until she was breathless, her belly knotting with an ache, a need, a hot pulsing. He drew back then, and his gaze questioned her silently, speaking to her soul: *Anna, is this what you really want?*

In answer she drew his head down, stroked the back of his neck, opened to him like a flower. *Yes,* her soul replied, *this is what I want.*

"Todd?" she whispered.

"Baseball."

She smiled, a shy, secretive smile and buried her face in his chest, drawing in his scent.

"Oh, God," he moaned, his hands hard on her back, her hips, her shoulders. He brought her face up to his again and kissed her hungrily, twisting his mouth to hers, parting her lips in a demanding, urgent kiss that rocked her senses until she sagged against him, clinging. Then he was leading them, pulling her along toward the bedroom door. Anna stumbled over a sock or something and laughed, clutching his hand, but he brought her up against his chest again and silenced her with his lips.

They clung and kissed and searched each other with dazed and hungry eyes until they reached his bedroom and a small reality came rushing back.

"You sure?" he breathed, holding her shoulders, and in reply Anna nodded.

For a moment he left her then, and Anna saw the unmade bed, the sheets familiar ones she'd loaned to him. He closed the door and pulled the shade down. Heat and stillness and a dim golden light filled the room. She pulled her T-shirt over her head and stepped out of her shorts. He looked, drawing in the sight as if he'd never seen a woman before.

Half-naked, Anna moved to him and unbuttoned his shirt, pulling it out of his pants and spreading her fingers on his chest. Then he pulled her close and took her mouth in a long, sweet kiss. "You're beautiful," he said against her lips.

She did feel beautiful then. She felt adored, worshiped, loved. She loved this man, this laconic stranger with all his problems. She wanted him and needed him and nothing else mattered.

He had a long, slim body, smooth, muscular. He was utterly different than Jim, she dared think. Narrower, fairer, exciting, needing her. They stood in the warm, gilded light, and he made love to her with his hands, his mouth, his entire being. Small kisses on her mouth, her chin, her neck, nibbling her skin in sensitive places, caressing her, long strokes from neck to waist, unbearably sensual. Arousing.

Carefully, her two hands in his, Chris pulled her toward the bed and eased her down and across it until her shoulders were on the far edge and her head hung back so that he could kiss her neck, her collarbone, her shoulder. He kissed one breast, then the other, circled the nipple with his tongue, breathing on her skin until she quivered with sensation, losing herself, feeling her mind flee while her body stayed and responded.

He spoke, murmured in her ear, asked, did she like this or that? How did she feel? Would she touch him there? Her breath came quickly, and she moved mindlessly against him. He rose over her, entered her with a throaty sigh, and they moved together.

Slowly she felt sensation building inside her, a molten liquid that ran down her limbs, making them tremble with excitement. Her breath came in tearing gasps, moans, whispered words. Quicker, they moved together in a swift rhythm, yearning, longing to reach the apex, his hands gripping her, urging her on. Then she arched under him and cried out, and her body shook in an exultation of feeling, and he filled her hard and powerful and gave himself to her completely.

She came back into her body still breathing hard, her heart beating a mad tempo. Chris lay on her, sprawled in damp exhaustion, his face close to hers, his eyes closed. She stroked his hair, loving how he felt, the satin of his skin, the sweat on his back, the long, naked man-shape of him.

"Mmm," he said, "I can't move."

"Stay," she whispered. "I like you just where you are."

He moved on her, heavy, relaxed. "It's been a long time," he murmured. "I hope you weren't... disappointed."

She smiled. "Oh, no, not at all," she said in a parody of courtesy. "You were quite satisfactory, Mr. Galloway."

After a time, he raised himself on his elbows and studied her with shadowed eyes. "I told you, I don't go in for relationships. I mean, I haven't. I don't want you to think I do this with every stewardess I interview." A crooked smile tugged at the corner of his mouth.

"I believe you."

"You're very special, Anna Parish."

"So are you."

"I think—damn it, my shoulder is killing me." He shifted to one side, supporting himself on his good arm.

"As you were saying?"

"I think...I think I'm falling in love with you, Anna."

"You *think*, but you're not sure," she said with a smile. "Spoken like a true bureaucrat."

"It's happened pretty fast," he said soberly.

"Yes, it has. I *think* I love you, too. But we have time, Chris. We don't have to decide everything now."

He leaned over and kissed her lightly. "We have to damn well get up and get dressed before Todd gets home for lunch. That's what we have to do."

"He'll notice, won't he?" she asked.

"Todd? I don't know. Are teenagers that perceptive?"

"You bet." She paused. "Will you tell him, Chris?"

"Oh, God, give me some time. Not yet, Anna. I...uh...this isn't easy, this father business."

"You seem to be doing just fine."

"Do you think so?"

She pulled his head down and kissed him. "I think you're good for Todd. He needed you."

"Like *I* needed *you?*" Chris asked.

"No, different, but just as necessary."

"I've got to get up."

"So do I."

"I want you again, Anna." He groaned and rolled away from her. "What in hell's going to happen now?"

"Todd will come home, and he'll eat lunch, and you'll ask him how baseball was."

"God, you're so beautiful," he said wonderingly, his eyes drinking her in before his mouth lowered to hers in a last, lingering kiss.

CHAPTER FIFTEEN

"NO WAY," Chris said, checking his watch. "The car stays right here, Todd."

"But I'll bring it home tomorrow after the game. I'll leave it in the city lot while we drive in the van down to Wenatchee and—"

"No. It's 6:45 already. You better get on down the hill before you miss the van entirely."

"Geez, man."

"Look," Chris said, "we're pushing our luck as it is, letting you drive a rental car around by yourself. Be a good kid and don't nag me at this ungodly hour, or I'll say no every time."

Todd picked up his baseball mitt and frowned. "Man, like you're starting to sound parental." He headed toward the door.

"I hope so," Chris said. "Now get going. I'll see you tomorrow night when I get back from Seattle. Okay?"

"Yeah. Sure."

"And behave yourself in that motel tonight. In this neck of the woods they string kids up for wrecking motels. Got that?"

"Sure they do."

"Bye, Todd."

"Bye, man...Dad." And he was gone, off to the baseball tournament.

Chris yawned, poured himself a cup of coffee and marveled at the wonders of being a father. Already he'd found that Todd responded well to a light hand. The boy wanted to make his own decisions and seemed pleased with the results. Chris crossed his fingers. He sure hoped he'd gauged Todd correctly. It would kill him, Chris admitted to himself, if Anna had been right all along about too much freedom being bad for Todd. But so far so good. The new union was working better than Chris could have hoped. In fact, he was feeling a strong bond forming. Father and son. It was good, difficult at times, but good.

How had it happened that two good things had arrived at the same time? Two good but difficult things: Todd and Anna. Anna and Todd. God, life was strange, he thought as he stepped into the shower. It was awful and wonderful, and he couldn't decide which took precedence. But then maybe it was what you made of it. And that was where things turned really hard. He hadn't any idea where he was headed with Anna Parish or, for that matter, where Anna herself was going.

And what about Fleisher? Chris couldn't envision himself sitting down with Anna and getting that issue straight. It just wasn't in his nature. But Fleisher, or his imagined spirit, was still very present in Anna's life. It killed Chris to think she continued to love the dead man. It killed him and made him want to reach inside her head and wipe the memory clean.

He pulled on his trousers and buttoned his shirt, leaving it hanging out. Anna. The sun wasn't even up yet and he was craving her. He felt like a man drugged with love. He strode out into the dawn and headed up the street toward her house, and he knew he was hooked. Fleisher or no Fleisher, Chris couldn't give her up.

It was early. A dog barked somewhere, intruding on the stillness as Chris tapped quietly on the screen in her bedroom window. What was he doing? In a few hours he had to be in Seattle, for God's sake. He felt like a fool, a damn idiot as he stood there peering in, hoping she'd wake and hear him. Maybe he should retreat, get the hell out of there before the whole neighborhood heard him.

But Anna came to the window before he could run. And then he wasn't sure if he shouldn't tell her this was a stupid idea. But she looked so lovely, sleep-drowsed and warm, that sudden obsession overcame his doubts.

"Come around to the back door," she whispered through the screen, motioning with a slim arm.

"You sure?" Chris whispered back.

She nodded and smiled, and his blood began to boil.

Chris pulled her to him right in the kitchen. He could feel the warmth of her skin through the filmy nylon she wore, her curves, the flesh of her hips and buttocks.

He kissed her thoroughly, and they went hand in hand to her bedroom. Leisurely Chris drew her nightgown off her shoulders, and when it slipped over her breasts and hips and thighs, he kissed and held her. A part of him knew they were both using each other to fill a void in their lives; and yet Chris knew, as well, that this unquenchable need had shifted, altered and had become something more: love. He kissed Anna and stroked her breasts and pulled her down to him on the bed and knew they were fast approaching a new crossroad. Once again they could go either forward or backward. He drew a nipple into his mouth and felt a wave of sheer pleasure flow through his body as she moaned, clutching him. Before he lost himself in her soft, warm flesh one last stab at reality pierced his mind: if he did find Fleisher's journal, would its contents free Anna at last, or would she be forever bound to the dead man? He entered Anna and felt her arch up to meet him, and a strange, ugly notion filled his brain. He was purging Fleisher from her, branding Anna with his own body, driving the dead man from her soul.

He thrust against her and felt Anna's response. His lips to her throat, he uttered, "It's me you want. Tell me it's me, Anna."

For a moment he could feel her swift break back to reality. "I want you, Chris. I . . . I love you," she whispered, and he found her mouth and kissed her long and hard as they both lost all sense of time and space and rode that wondrous wave to its crest.

"Look, Sullivan," Chris said as he stood in the coroner's Seattle office, "I appreciate all you've done to expedite this investigation. I know what a pain in the butt it's been, but I still need to interview the girl myself."

Sullivan muttered. "She's weeks behind, Galloway. You think all we have to do around this joint is run back and forth for you government people?"

"Like I said, Sullivan, five minutes of her time. That's all."

Again the medical examiner grumbled under his breath. "You know, you're never going to win any popularity contests."

"Oh," Chris replied, "is that a fact?"

The girl was shy and timid like almost everyone Chris interviewed. You'd think he was an income tax agent, for God's sake.

Chris was fed up with the whole routine. He was sick to death of the unwarranted suspicion in their eyes, of the misplaced guilt they suffered. He spoke to the receptionist softly, trying to allay her fears, but got nowhere. She'd been eight and a half months pregnant back in the beginning of March, overworked and taking medication for some complication in her pregnancy. She only remembered a man flashing an ID in her face, saying he was FAA, then proceeding to dump Fleisher's possessions from a sealed plastic bag onto a counter.

"Did he seem to be searching for something specific?" Chris asked her.

She didn't recall. "The phone was ringing off the hook, Mr. Galloway. You know, all the families of the victims. Then there was the usual everyday stuff. You can't imagine how busy we can get around here."

"I do know," he said, "and I appreciate it." He took a folder out of his briefcase and opened it. Three photographs stared up at him. Two belonged to NTSB officials and the third was Miller's, procured from a newspaper file. "Okay," he said to the girl, "I'd like you to look at three photos I have here and tell me if anyone is familiar."

She took the pictures but gazed up at Chris anxiously. "Am I...am I in any trouble over this? I mean, he showed me ID, Mr. Galloway, and I wouldn't know what an FAA identification card looks like, anyway."

"You're in no trouble whatsoever. Now the pictures?" He nodded, containing his impatience.

Chris waited, watching her carefully as she examined each photograph. She did pause for a moment or two when she studied Miller's, but there was no true recognition in her eyes.

"I...I'm sorry," she said, handing them back, "but no one seems familiar. I'm sorry, Mr. Galloway. I was just so darn busy."

"That's all right," he said. It was too much to hope that she'd recall. And besides, he wasn't convinced himself Miller had stolen the notebook. That was Anna's theory. He let out a breath of disappointment nevertheless. "But you do remember the man taking something, possibly a notebook?"

"Something," she said. "I don't know quite what. He signed for it, though," she added quickly.

"Yes, I know," Chris said. "Thank you. You've been very helpful." When she was gone, he sat on the edge of Sullivan's cluttered desk and frowned. The last thing he'd told Anna that morning was that he'd call right away with the news, good or bad. He pulled out his wallet and NTSB credit card and picked up Sullivan's phone. "Damn," he muttered.

ANNA TURNED in that night feeling let down and dejected. It wasn't Chris's fault, of course, but when he called with the bad news she hadn't been able to hide her disappointment. She lay there alone, missing Chris Galloway, wanting him there to hold her, to comfort her, to tell her that somehow he'd keep searching until Jim's notebook was recovered.

She put an arm over her forehead and sighed. How could she give herself fully to Chris until she was free of the past? "Oh, Chris," she whispered, "what are we going to—"

It happened suddenly, before Anna could finish her thought. The strange, unearthly light filtering through her eyelids. Her heart quickened instantly, and she knew, even before she dared to open her eyes, she knew.

The form materialized in front of her, pulling together from wisps of light and shadow. It was Jim, formidable in his uniform and pilot's cap. He had an awful stillness about him, an unblinking quiet that made her hair stand on end.

She lay there, afraid to breathe, afraid to move, but her fear came from the unknown, not from any dread that she was in danger. This thing, this phantom, shouldn't be here. It couldn't be here, but it was. She bit her lip hard to prove she wasn't asleep. It hurt. No, she wasn't asleep, but Jim, his eyes shadowed, his stillness absolute, stood in front of her, even though it wasn't possible.

"Jim," she whispered, but the figure didn't move or answer her. "Jim," she said again, louder, raising herself on her elbows. "What do you want? What do you want from me?"

Nothing, only the backlit figure, a statue, a mannequin, and yet Anna felt something emanating from it. A vast sorrow so deep that there was no plumbing it, a cold horror of guilt and misery and jealousy. She felt it inside her, and she moaned and put her hands over her face.

Moments later when she took her hands away he was gone. The room was dark, empty, as if nothing had ever been there. But Anna still felt that awful burden of anguish, and as she lay there in the dark, bathed in a cold sweat, she wondered if it wasn't hers alone. Maybe she conjured up Jim to share it with her, to ease her mind, she thought, casting about desperately for a rational explanation.

Then she felt with her tongue for the place she'd bitten her lip. Yes, it was there. She hadn't dreamed it. She'd been awake.

EARLY THE FOLLOWING morning Madeline came into the kitchen, looking haggard and disheveled in an old bathrobe. "God, is that coffee?" she croaked, running her fingers through the tangled mass of her blond hair.

Anna just stared.

"Please," Madeline said, "the coffee?" She looked away.

Anna poured her friend a mug and then pressed her down into a kitchen chair. "Want to talk about it?"

"He...he won't leave me alone," Madeline moaned.

"Flip?" But Anna suddenly knew. It wasn't Flip.

Madeline gazed up at her through sunken eyes. "I'm going to be haunted for the rest of my life! Oh, God! What does he want! Why *me!*"

Quietly, an arm around Madeline's shoulder, Anna said, "He came to me last night, too. He wants us to find his notebook, Mad. He wants to be avenged."

"So what! Why am I being tortured! Oh, Anna, I'm going crazy!" She put her face in her hands and sobbed, and to add to the confusion Todd rapped at the back door just then. "Oh, hell," Madeline said, her head snapping up, "look at me."

Anna let Todd in. She even fixed him hotcakes while he went on about his dad leaving the rental car at their house with a note: "Pick me up at the airport this evening, flight 847, 8:50."

"Can you believe it?" Todd asked. "Dad's letting me drive all over while he's in Seattle. Mom would have locked me in the attic, man, like she didn't trust me with my bike or nothing.''

"Or *anything,*'' Anna put in, giving Madeline a look.

"Yeah, well, I think my old man is pretty cool.''

"Amazing,'' Anna said.

"It sure is,'' Todd concurred.

Anna looked at Todd, really looked at him, and listened to what he was saying. Hadn't she once told Chris to listen to his son, really listen? Well, she'd failed to follow her own advice. Todd was enthusiastic, happy, proud. He talked about his father constantly: "My dad did this or my dad did that.'' She hadn't realized until this moment just how much Todd had changed from the slouching delinquent she'd met at the Seattle airport. And all along she'd doubted Chris's ability to be a father. She couldn't have been more wrong, and she was suddenly relieved and thrilled that she'd been so misguided. She'd have to tell Chris. Oh, yes, she'd have to tell him as soon as he got back.

Todd ate and talked about yesterday's baseball tournament in Wenatchee. He bragged about getting to pitch in a whole game because his arm was stronger than John Meyers's was. "Man, I struck out two dudes in a row.''

"Swell,'' Madeline said, pouring herself another coffee.

Todd looked up from his second stack of pancakes. "Say, where's Flip?''

"He's in Seattle on a flight,'' Anna put in.

"Too bad. I thought he might wanna go fishing or something.''

"Maybe when he gets back,'' Anna said. "In the meantime, until Chris gets in tonight, why don't you clean up your room and do some dishes? Surprise your father."

Todd shrugged. "Aw, he wouldn't notice."

"You're probably right," Anna said. Then, feeling Madeline's eyes on her beseechingly, she asked, "Would you like to do me a favor?"

Todd looked up.

"I need a few groceries. Maybe, if you drive real carefully, you could go to the store for me. Of course, if you don't want to..."

"Sure. I'll go. But I don't have any money."

"I'll give you the money." Anything, Anna thought, to get him out of there for a few minutes. Madeline looked as if she was going to scream in about three seconds.

"He's an okay kid," Madeline said when Todd was gone, "but teenagers scare me. They're so...so *dumb*."

"That's a nice thing to say," Anna said, "when you were one yourself not so long ago."

Madeline made a face, then sighed. She pulled the tie on her bathrobe tighter and began pacing the kitchen. "What're we going to do, Anna? What're we going to do about Jim? I really can't go on like this. Maybe we should both... you know..."

"Go to a shrink? Madeline, forget it. It didn't do any good. They don't believe us." She pushed her hair back. "There's a reason this is happening. There has to be a reason. God, Madeline, I can feel all these awful feelings coming from him. Terrible feelings. Sadness, guilt—" she swallowed "—jealousy."

Madeline hugged herself and shivered.

"I don't know how I know it, but I do." Anna lowered her voice to a whisper. "He's jealous."

"Of what?"

"Of us, because we're alive. Oh, this is so ridiculous." She turned around and put a hand to her forehead. "How can I be saying these things? A ghost, jealous."

"Go on. You were going to say something else."

"He's jealous." Anna averted her eyes. "That's all."

"What are we going to do?" Madeline asked in a hushed voice.

"We could find his notebook ourselves." Anna went to the kitchen window, folded her arms and stared into the middle distance.

"But you told me just yesterday that Chris said the coroner didn't know who—"

"But *I* know who has it, Mad," Anna said, her brow furrowed. "Miller's got it."

"He might have destroyed it. He probably *did* destroy it."

"If he destroyed it, don't you think Jim would know that?" Anna asked fiercely.

Madeline winced.

"I don't know how or why this is happening to us. I don't know how Jim can . . . exist. But he does somehow and he knows. He knows Miller took that notebook."

"Oh, great." Madeline plumped down into a chair. "So why don't we just ask Jim where it is?" She laughed a little hysterically.

Anna shrugged. "There aren't answers to everything. I don't know why Jim doesn't somehow lead us to it. Maybe he has. I don't know. Maybe we aren't listening."

Madeline swore and waved a hand in the air. "I can't take this anymore. Let's just go ransack Miller's house.

Hell, if we get caught, I can go to prison and maybe Jim won't find me there!''

"Not his house," Anna said quietly.

"What?"

"I said, I don't think it's in Miller's house."

"What're you...?"

"His office, Madeline. He'd have locked it away in his office at the airport."

Madeline laughed, scoffing. "Oh, right. You know that."

"I *feel* it."

"Oh, you 'feel' it. So now what? We ransack his office?"

"Yes."

"You're kidding."

"No. I most certainly am not joking about this." She caught Madeline's eye. "Listen," she said, "this is really important to me."

"I know."

"Do you? Do you know what's happened between me and Chris?"

"A blind man can see it, Anna," Madeline said, shaking her head. "And now you want... well, you want Jim to go away."

"Yes," Anna said, "I do. I really do. I never thought I'd say that. But I've fallen in love."

"Is it... the same? I mean... oh, never mind."

"No," Anna said, "I want to tell you. I can't really tell Chris. Not yet, anyway. But it's not the same, Madeline. Jim, well, Jim was so strong. He never really needed me. Oh," she said, waving a hand, "he needed me in some ways, I know, but not my... my strength, my support. Chris needs me. We're good together."

Madeline looked away. "Do you think—now, don't get mad—but do you think Chris really loves you? I mean, maybe you'll get him back on the right track and find out he doesn't really love *you*, just your support, you know?"

Anna gave a short laugh. "Don't think I haven't thought that a dozen times. I believed it, in fact, up until a few days ago. And then...then you just know it's changed. Madeline, he *does* love me."

"I guess you know."

"I do." Anna smiled. "I really do. And that's why it's so important to find Jim's notebook. I'm...I'm not really free yet. I know how crazy the whole thing is. I know it's impossible for Jim to be...to be still here, but we both know somehow he is. And he isn't going to go away, either. Not unless—"

"We prove Miller's at fault."

"Yes." Anna nodded.

"So we get into his office. Oh, brother, there must be another way."

"There isn't."

"But...but can't Chris just get a search warrant or something?"

Anna shook her head. "Not without that reception-ist's word that it was Lee Miller who actually took the notebook."

"Oh, great."

"A minute ago," Anna said, "you were going to break into Miller's house."

"I was kidding."

"But *I'm* not. What do you say? Will you help me?"

"You're asking me to help you break into Miller's office? What if we get caught?"

"We'll face that when and if it happens."

"What if it's locked?"

"We'll take along a crowbar."

"A crowbar."

"Yes."

"Oh, great."

"*Will* you help, Madeline?"

Her friend was silent for a full minute. Finally she looked up at Anna. "You really think Jim will leave us alone if we can find that notebook?"

"That's what he wants," Anna said with assurance.

"Oh, boy."

"*Will* you?"

"I . . . I guess so. Yes," Madeline said, beginning to nod in earnest. "Yes, I'll do it. When do you want to pull off this caper?"

"Tonight. After dark."

"Oh, geez, why didn't I think of that? At night. Of course. We'll go and commit a little breaking and entering. No big deal."

"It's to vindicate Jim. To get Lee Miller, Madeline. If we can prove he runs a dangerous operation, we'll be doing everyone a favor."

"And Jim will leave us alone," Madeline muttered under her breath.

"*Who* will leave you alone?" came a voice at the screen door.

Anna whirled around. It was Todd, grocery bag in hand. "And just how long have you been standing there?" she asked sternly.

But the boy gave her that casual shrug. "Just drove up, man, why?"

"No reason," Anna said slowly, watching him. "No reason at all." She caught Madeline's eyes for a moment before taking the groceries from his arms.

"I got some cookies," Todd said, and sat down for the duration.

CHAPTER SIXTEEN

ANNA BENT over her coffee table. One hand was on her hip, the other fingering items she'd laid out on the table. "Okay," she said, mostly to herself, "flashlights, extra batteries, screwdrivers, pocketknife, hammer, crowbar—"

"Oh, God," Madeline whispered, "this is insane."

"Oh, and leave your wallet here," Anna said, still stooping, ignoring her friend. "Just in case."

"Just in case of what?"

Anna shrugged.

"I see, no ID so the cops won't know who we are. Right," Madeline said. "That'll keep us out of the electric chair. But maybe just one credit card so we can jimmy the lock or something, huh?"

Anna didn't bother to answer. Madeline was as keyed up as a runner before a race. So was Anna. Neither of them had eaten dinner, nor could they sit still.

"Thank God Flip isn't here," Madeline said. "He'd kill me."

"He'll be proud of you when it's all over," Anna said.

"Yeah, he can bake me a cake with a file in it."

"I wish it'd get dark," Anna said, looking out the window and biting her lip.

"What if we can't get in? What if he's there? What if we can't find anything?"

"We'll get in. And he won't be there, and if we don't find anything . . . well, we'll look somewhere else."

"Why am I doing this?" Madeline asked, walking to the window, then back to the couch, wringing her hands.

"You know why."

"When will it be dark enough?" Madeline asked distractedly.

"Soon."

"I'm out of my mind. We're both out of our minds."

"You want out? I'll go alone. I'll—" Anna began.

"No. No. I'm too scared. He'd haunt me. Oh, God, why me?"

"It'll be fun," Anna said staunchly.

"Fun!"

"An adventure," Anna said. "I'm sick of being a victim. It's time to do something."

"How will I look, getting married in a striped prisoner's suit?" Madeline asked.

"Terrific. Especially with your mom's gray lace."

"Oh, God, is it dark enough yet?"

When they couldn't bear waiting another moment, they got into Anna's car, two women in jeans and dark jackets, their hair pushed up under dark caps. Anna's pockets were heavy with tools that jabbed into her sides as she drove.

"I'll park right in the WestAir lot. Everyone's used to seeing my car there. I want it close in case we have to get out of there in a hurry," Anna said breathlessly.

Madeline moaned quietly.

"No one will be there. It's off-season. No one works at night this time of year. The last flight will be just about in, and all the baggage guys will be busy over in the terminal. There's a whole building between them and us. No one will see us."

"We'll be real quiet, keep the blinds drawn," Madeline said. "Security at that place is terrible, anyway. Miller's too cheap to put in a security system."

"Lucky for us."

"Right."

"You have the flashlight?" Anna asked.

"You asked me that twice already."

"Oh."

She drove slowly, her hands gripping the steering wheel, her mouth dry, her heart pounding madly. But she was sure of herself and dizzy with a kind of exhilaration. Oh, Lord, she thought, if Chris ever found out. "What'll I tell Chris?" she asked, abruptly panicked. "Where'll I tell him I got the notebook?"

"Anna, geez, let's worry about that when you get it. We'll think of some story."

"I don't want to lie to him. I hate lying."

"Oh, breaking and entering is okay. It's lying a little that's bad," Madeline said, arching a pale brow.

"In this case, yes. Miller stole Jim's notebook. He lied and stole. I feel perfectly justified in getting it back like this."

She turned into the airport. It was dark, the main parking lot nearly empty. There were tall streetlights on, but all they did was illuminate in faint circles. A slim sliver of a moon rose over the mountains, shining faintly into Anna's eyes. "Oh, my God," she said, "what if there'd been a full moon?"

"Beginner's luck," Madeline muttered.

Anna drove to the right, around the side of the terminal to the WestAir employee lot. A few cars remained there—the night crew, the mechanics on duty, a couple of others. She parked in the middle, hoping to be unobtrusive but not too far from Miller's office.

They both sat there for a while once the car was turned off. All Anna could hear was the ticking of the car engine as it cooled. She was sweating.

"Well?" Madeline asked shakily.

"Okay," Anna said, but nothing more came to mind.

"Okay, what?"

"Look around. See anybody?" Anna asked, craning her neck to check out the area. Something sharp stuck into her ribs. The crowbar.

"No, nobody."

It was dark in the lot. Anna could just make out Lee Miller's office, up the stairs on the second floor of the WestAir building. She'd been in his office a few times . . . when she was hired, for meetings, once after the crash. The building was deserted for the day, locked up, its windows all dark. Perfect.

"Okay," she said again, then took a deep breath. "Let's go."

They both got out of the car and closed the doors quietly. Looking around like criminals, they walked swiftly toward the outside metal staircase that led up to Miller's office. It was warm out, and Anna felt sweat gather between her breasts and under her arms. She had a sudden, desperate urge to rip her jacket off so that she could breathe. Her forehead prickled with perspiration. Her knees felt weak.

Up the stairs. They were metal and clanged dully, no matter how careful Anna was. She stopped at the top, Madeline crowding her, and looked around again. No one, nothing, no sounds, no movement. There was only the sigh of the night breeze and the chirp of crickets in the grass that bordered the parking lot.

"Let me try," Madeline whispered. "I brought my credit card."

Anna stood there, vigilant, holding the flashlight, throbbing with adrenaline, while Madeline slid her card along the crack, trying to push the bolt in, muttering and mumbling, wiping sweat off her forehead while she struggled.

"I can't get it," Madeline whispered. "Damn. Switch off the flashlight."

"The crowbar . . . ?"

"It'll make too much noise," Madeline hissed in the blackness.

"We'll have to. Wait a minute." Anna was looking right at the ledge above the door, a darker horizontal line of shadow. "What if . . . ?"

"What are you doing?"

Anna reached up, stood on tiptoe and felt along the ledge.

"Hurry up!" Madeline urged.

"I am. I—" Yes, there it was, a flat metal object that slid along the ledge under her fingers. "Got it!" she whispered.

"The key?" Madeline asked in awe, her face a pallid oval in the darkness.

"Probably for the janitor, or maybe Miller's just lazy. Leaves it there all the time," Anna said, pushing the key into the knob and turning it one way, then the other.

Click.

They slipped inside, two sweating wraiths, and closed the door with a quiet snick behind them.

"Oh, my God," Madeline breathed, "we're in."

Anna switched on her flashlight, keeping the beam low. "Where would he put it?"

"I'll take the desk. You do the filing cabinets," Madeline whispered hoarsely.

A terrible pang of guilt struck Anna as she stood there in the middle of Lee Miller's office. She shouldn't be there, she had broken the law, this was a terrible thing to do. She forced it down; more than her feelings were at stake here. Jim had come back from the dead to get her into this office. She had to do it: for him, for herself, for Chris, for all those people who'd flown and were going to fly.

Hurry up, she told herself, heading toward the filing cabinets.

They said nothing as they worked. The room was inky, cut occasionally by beams of light held low, guarded carefully. Anna's heart knocked against her ribs, and she felt short of breath.

"Shh!" Anna hissed once, and they both stopped dead and switched off their lights. Madeline sobbed once in the blackness, a sob of terror. But nothing moved, no noise came to their ears. "I thought I heard something," Anna whispered, "but I guess not."

"Don't do that to me," Madeline whispered back.

Methodically Anna rifled the files, not reading the papers, looking for a notebook, going through each drawer from front to back. "It's blue, remember," she said. "And maybe it's in a manila envelope. It could be. I don't know...."

"Nothing here," Madeline replied. "Not so far."

They found nothing in the desk, nothing in the files. Anna was close to tears.

"Maybe it isn't here," Madeline said dejectedly. "Maybe he has it somewhere else. Maybe he destroyed it and Jim doesn't know."

"No, it's here. It has to be!" Anna saw the closet door then, a dark rectangle in the corner. "Come on."

They squeezed inside the closet, closed the door and turned on their lights. It was hot and musty. The air was stale. A worn air force bomber jacket hung on a hook—Lee Miller's jacket. There was a shelf above a row of hooks. Madeline stretched and shone her light, picking out an old hat, a can of oil, an umbrella.

"Nothing," she said.

Back in the corner of the closet, Anna's flashlight beam struck something, a metal box. On her knees, brushed by the gossamer threads of cobwebs, she pulled it close and examined the lid. It was locked.

"Hurry," Madeline whispered. "God, this is spooky."

Anna pulled a screwdriver out of her pocket. Her heart was hammering, sweat blinding her. She swiped at her forehead with her forearm, then stuck the flat edge of the screwdriver under the lid of the metal box. She grunted a little as she leaned on it, twisted, pried. It popped open.

Both flashlights played on the opened box. Military medals lay on top, a pair of gloves, some keys, yellowed newspaper articles. Hand shaking, Anna reached in to pull the memorabilia aside. The light glinted on something shiny and blue and a spiral roll of wire. Her heartbeat stopped short, and she heard someone gasp—her or Madeline? Then her heart pounded in her chest once, twice. She pulled out the blue notebook and crouched in the hot, stuffy closet, staring in mute fascination.

"Anna," Madeline asked, "is that it? That's it, isn't it?"

Anna flipped the notebook open, and tears sprang to her eyes. Jim's handwriting, pages full of his small, cramped hand. Names, dates, events. Everything was there. Everything. She closed the journal, pressed it to her breast and shut her eyes. She could almost hear a voice come out of the dark corner of the closet: *Thank you.* Jim's voice. Tears squeezed out from under her eyelids.

Madeline pushed the closet door open and pulled Anna's arm. "Come on. Hurry!"

In the center of the office Anna stopped and grabbed Madeline's arm. "We did it. We did it."

Madeline grinned and hugged her, then sobbed again, squeezing Anna hard, laughing and crying at the same time. "We did it," she agreed. "Oh, God, let's get out of here!"

"What's your hurry?" a voice snapped out of the darkness, and with the words the lights were switched on, blinding, glaring, bathing the office in a shocking, surrealistic glow. "Security called me, ladies," Lee Miller said, "and it looks like none too soon."

FLIGHT 847 CIRCLED the darkened valley on its final approach to the Winthrop airport. Chris stared out the window into pitch-black. The plane was on time, and he'd land in a few minutes. When he got home, he'd have to face Anna, and it wasn't going to be love and kisses this time. He'd failed her. He'd failed the flying public, too, and he'd failed in his job. The notebook, Fleisher's damn blue notebook, was gone.

He knew, somewhere deep inside that without that notebook, without the truth of Fleisher's words in black and white, without vindication or blame, whichever it was to be, Anna would never be truly free of her dead lover. It was insane, but it was true. Without the truth Anna would always be wondering, never sure, always dangling with Fleisher in a noose of guilt and anguish.

Damn, but he hated failure. Oh, he'd do his best, use Flip Akers's information, try to nail Lee Miller when the man testified at the public hearing. He'd do what he could, but it wouldn't stick the way it would with a dead pilot's firsthand testimony.

How had everything gotten all strung together like this? Lee Miller and Fleisher and Anna and that damn notebook. Could Miller really have posed as an FAA official and taken the book? The man had guts. He was ruthless enough, and as much as Chris hated to act on instinct alone, Anna had been right: Miller was the only one with a motive for stealing the book.

He wondered if a judge would issue the NTSB a search warrant for Miller's house and office. Ha! Fat chance. On a ghost's say-so. *Get real, Galloway,* he told himself.

Wearily Chris deplaned, carrying his old briefcase and one small bag, and headed toward the main door of the terminal, keeping an eye out for Todd. Where was that kid? The plane was on time. He should have been waiting right by the gate. Chris had had a trying day. He was tired and cranky and sick of the bitter taste of failure. He didn't need Todd to be late in the bargain.

Damn kid probably had an accident on the way over here. Great. With my luck that's what happened. With the rental car, too. He could hear Anna now, saying, "I told you so." *Hell.*

A lone baggage handler was standing by the conveyer belt, watching as it disgorged a few suitcases. Another employee was mopping the floor. The airport was all but shut down for the night. He went past them both, heading for the pay phone. Maybe Todd was on his way right now, but Chris was in no mood to leave it to chance.

There was no answer at home. *Give the kid an inch,* he thought, a little worried but mostly irritated. He tried Anna's number, wishing he could put off facing her until tomorrow. He couldn't, of course. But there was no answer there, either. Great.

He hefted his bag and headed to the front door. The few passengers on his flight were already gone or inside collecting their luggage. There wasn't a taxi to be had in this town. The airport was dark, empty, deserted. *Yep, things are sure looking up,* he thought sarcastically as he began to stride down the terminal road to the entrance. It was over two miles into town. When he got his hands on that kid ...

"I'LL TAKE THAT," Miller said, reaching for the notebook.

Anna shrank back from him instinctively, clutching the book. Beside her Madeline was trembling and utterly silent.

"Come on," Miller said, "just hand it over. I can take it from you, but that might get messy."

"No," Anna said, and then her throat clicked shut.

"I'll tell you what. You give it to me and I won't call the police on you. How's that for a deal?"

She shook her head, not trusting her voice. Her eyes darted to Miller, then frantically around the office. She took a step sideways toward the door, but he moved fast, edging her away from it.

"You're wasting my time. Give me the book," he said in a hard voice, closing in on her.

She backed up.

"Anna," she heard Madeline whimper. "Anna, we—"

"Hand it over," Miller said, taking another step toward her.

"You leave them alone!"

The strident young voice took them all by surprise. Miller stopped, Madeline gave a cry, Anna whirled.

"Oh, my God," she whispered, "Todd!"

Miller took the boy in, instantly dismissed him and chuckled throatily. "Get over there with your two girlfriends," he directed, gesturing.

Todd locked his jaw—just like Chris—and shook his head. "We're all leaving right now," Todd said bravely. "And you're not stopping us."

"Todd," Anna started to say, but he ignored her. His eyes were directed at Lee Miller. His whole being was concentrated on the older man, quivering with tension.

"Aw, kid, get outta my way," Miller said.

"No."

Miller moved quickly then, struck with such speed that she never saw what he did, but Todd was knocked sprawling, spun across the room to come up hard against the desk, where he lay stunned.

"Okay," Miller said as if nothing had happened, "I'll take that book now." And he moved ponderously toward Anna.

CHRIS TOOK a shortcut across the main terminal road and through the employee parking lot. It was dark and he was tired. His shoulder ached, his head was starting to throb, and he had a long walk ahead of him. He was getting madder by the minute and almost didn't notice Anna's car parked all by itself in the middle of the lot. Almost.

Later he would wonder what had caught his eye—the crescent moon shining on the windshield, the employee sticker in the window, the ski rack left on in the summer? He stopped, looked and checked the interior. Yes, it was Anna's car. Odd. Maybe she was here to pick him up. But if so, where was she? And why was she parked in the employee lot?

She couldn't be working. He'd just spoken to her that afternoon, and she hadn't mentioned being on a flight. She would have told him. Then why...?

He would always remember what made him notice his own blue Taurus. It was Todd's baseball mitt, thrown carelessly onto the back shelf, illuminated by one of the big arc lights. He noted it instantly when he looked up to see if Anna was anywhere around. Todd's mitt, the rental car parked near Anna's car in the employee parking lot... at this hour?

An alarm sounded in his head. He spun around and stared at Lee Miller's upstairs office. The place was lit up like a circus at nine o'clock at night when the rest of the airport was closed.

Swiftly he dropped his bags and headed toward the WestAir building. He prayed he was wrong, but he had a feeling he wasn't. After his phone call telling Anna that he couldn't trace the notebook, she wouldn't have been so foolish...? No, not Anna, he told himself. She was a levelheaded person. She'd never... No, she couldn't. And Todd? What in God's name was going on here?

He heard Miller's voice before he was halfway up the stairs. "I'll take that book now," the man was saying in a tone that raised the hairs on Chris's neck.

Then there was a high, wavering voice, a familiar voice, and the words sent rage coursing through Chris. "You better not touch us, mister!"

Todd!

He took the steps two at a time and burst through the door.

Four shocked faces turned toward him, familiar faces that were white and drawn with tension. Todd, Madeline, Anna. And in front of them—Lee Miller.

"Chris," Anna said tremulously.

"Dad," Todd cried at the same time.

Chris looked from one to the other, his eyes lingering on Anna's for a heartbeat. Then he saw what she was clutching. It was an ordinary blue spiral notebook. His gaze flew up to meet hers and their eyes locked. Fleisher's notebook.

"I'm glad you happened by, Mr. Galloway," Lee Miller said. "I'd like you to be a witness to these people trespassing on private property. Theft, breaking and entering."

Chris's mouth twisted in an ironic smile even as he saw an ugly red welt on his son's face.

"Dad, I didn't do anything," Todd said. "I just followed Anna and Madeline. Honest, I—"

"It's okay, Todd." His blood began to ring in his ears.

"Chris," Anna said, pleading. "We only wanted to—"

"Trespassing," Miller said furiously. "It's a good thing security saw the flashlight up here! I want my property back!"

Anna clutched the notebook, and her mouth tightened.

Chris could see that the man was bursting with rage, that his temper was barely under control. And Chris also understood why Anna, Madeline and Todd looked so damn scared. Miller was a frightening man, big and full of menace.

Chris smiled dangerously, "Well, well," he said, swiveling to face Miller. "I guess two ladies and a teenager have you nailed, don't they, Mr. Miller?"

"I don't know what you're talking about, Galloway," Miller blustered, his face darkening. He looked ready to explode.

"Fleisher's notebook. You stole it from the medical examiner's office in Seattle."

"I did not. I don't know what you're talking about," Miller repeated.

Chris tried a bluff. "The receptionist remembered the incident and identified your picture. She thought you were FAA, Miller. Theft and impersonating a government official."

"You're crazy. You're all crazy!" Miller cried.

"We're leaving now, Miller. All of us *and* the notebook. Peacefully."

"I'll have you all arrested!" he said hotly.

"Okay, try it. There's the phone. Come on, son, ladies. We're going home."

Todd moved to his side. Madeline scurried behind him. Anna sidled away from Miller toward the door, still guarding the notebook. They looked scared silly, all three of them. And for good reason.

Miller moved as if to stop them. Madeline made a muffled noise in her throat. Anna stepped back. Todd bristled beside him.

Chris stood there, weighing the possibilities. He locked eyes with Miller and realized the advantage was on Miller's side should things get physical. Chris's shoulder would give out on the first blow. Still, it would be worth it to deck Miller. He glanced at the raised welt on Todd's face. Real worth it.

"I can't let you just take that," Miller shouted, the purple veins standing out on his neck. "I *won't* let you!" And he took a step toward Chris, his fists clenched at his sides.

Softly Chris swore under his breath, then motioned for the three innocents to get out of the way. He put his full attention back on Lee Miller. "You know something," Chris said, his blood boiling now. "I think I'd enjoy laying you out flat, Miller."

It happened in a split second. Miller took another step forward and swung a fist at Chris. Chris sidestepped the blow and simultaneously caught Miller in the belly with a punch from his good arm.

Miller went down on his knees. For an instant Chris was ready to end it there, but the image of the welt on Todd's face took on a life of its own, and Chris abruptly gave Miller a last blow to the jaw that rang all the way up Chris's arm, rattling him painfully back to his senses.

"Yeah, man!" Todd shouted.

"Oh, God," Anna gasped.

They left Lee Miller lying in the center of his lit-up office, groaning, feeling his jaw.

Chris went last as they descended the outside staircase, herding his three charges before him. But as they crossed the parking lot, everyone started talking at once, Madeline crying, Anna grasping Chris by his arm, sagging against him, and Todd saying, "Like wow, man. That was cool."

They got into his rented Taurus, leaving Anna's car because she was too shaky to drive, and he drove them home through the warm summer night.

CHAPTER SEVENTEEN

THE FORMAL HEARING into the March crash of WestAir flight 629 took place on a rainy July day in a nondescript room in the federal building in Seattle. The press was there in force, as were the witnesses to be called and the legal counsels for the various federal agencies involved, for the aircraft manufacturer and for Lee Miller himself. There was a small civilian audience, as well, Jim Fleisher's parents, a few survivors from the crash, some WestAir employees and Anna Parish.

The chairman for hearings was always an NTSB board member, in this case Scott Hatcher, a fair-minded man, Chris had told Anna. And that was good, because the hearing wasn't a trial, and justice depended in good measure on the chairman's handling of it.

The windows were shut because of the rain, and the hearing room was close. Anna watched the proceedings all afternoon, and the entire time she felt just a little short of breath, keyed-up, anxious, but glad that it was all coming out.

WestAir pilots had come forward, offering to testify once Jim's notebook had been found. They corroborated Jim's stories and had more of their own. The revelations were startling.

"Captain Pendergast," Chris asked one pilot, "were you ever pressured to take off with an overloaded plane?"

Pendergast leaned toward the microphone and answered clearly, "Yes, many times. Last winter on one particular day I left some bags behind to carry extra fuel because the plane was full and the weather was bad, so I could have been forced to divert to another airport. When I arrived in Winthrop, Lee Miller called me into his office and asked why I'd left the bags, as passengers were complaining. He felt I didn't need the extra fuel, that it didn't matter if the aircraft was at maximum legal weight or not."

There was a murmur in the room. Anna looked around. All eyes were on a scowling Lee Miller, who sat with his lawyer. He looked as if he wanted to jump up, to shout down the testimony. Anna noticed that his lawyer put a restraining hand on his arm.

"Was your job threatened because of this?" Chris asked.

Pendergast looked directly at Miller and replied, "Yes, sir. He told me he'd fire me if I left bags behind again."

"Thank you, Captain Pendergast."

Flip Akers testified, too. He answered truthfully, and Chris was careful with him, because Flip had given him so much ammunition against Miller that he had no desire to destroy the man's career.

"Your pilot that day was Carl Ferraro, right?" Chris asked.

"Yes, sir," Flip said.

"There were thunderstorms approaching, so Ferraro decided to delay the flight. Can you tell us what happened then?"

"Mr. Miller radioed that we could take off because there were some holes in the storms on radar and we'd be guided through these holes. Captain Ferraro chose not to do that, and Miller threatened his job, said he was finished if he delayed flights again."

"What happened then?" Chris asked.

"We waited until the thunderstorms cleared and reached Seattle safely. Captain Ferraro was harassed constantly after that by Miller. He quit a month later," Flip said, eyeing Miller.

There was more, and Anna saw the reporters scribbling down notes. It would all be in the papers and on TV tonight. She was proud of Chris, proud of Flip, glad the truth was finally coming out. But nervous, too. Oh, yes, she was still nervous.

Chris moved on from the general to the specific: the crash of flight 629. He read excerpts from Jim Fleisher's notebook as background, instances of Miller's pressure.

January 4. Miller on radio. Wanted me to try second approach to airport after first aborted due to fog. Told Miller have enough fuel. I was going to divert to Spokane. M insisted. I turned radio off. February 20. Argument with Miller today about training manuals. M refused to order new ones. Cost. Said old ones fine. Aren't even enough copies of old ones for every pilot. Younger pilots must have proper training. Frustrating.

Anna listened, remembering the incidents. Jim had been furious about the training problems. He was supposed to be in charge of training, but it was a joke, he'd said.

Chris called the air traffic controllers one at a time to the stand. They both testified that they were aware of Lee Miller and his employees having problems, aware of complaints of Miller's handling of people. They also both testified that Jim Fleisher had been a good pilot. Chris got nothing conclusive out of either of them.

Anna knew he'd questioned all these men before; he'd talked the case over with her. He'd told her he had an airtight case against Miller, but that didn't solve the problem of what exactly had gone wrong with flight 629. She also knew Chris was hoping that some new information would surface during the hearing, something that had been hidden or overlooked previously. Jim's notebook had made the case against Miller but, of course, it contained nothing specific about the tragic flight.

Bob Johnson, one of WestAir's mechanics, got on the stand. He was nervous. His eyes kept straying to Harry Logan, his boss, as if asking him what to say.

"Mr. Johnson," Chris said, "you were on duty that March morning, correct?"

"Yes, sir. I had just come on duty. Flight 629 was supposed to go at eleven, and that's when I come on shift."

"Describe the weather, Mr. Johnson."

"It was beginning to snow."

"What were your duties that morning?"

"Well, the guys who'd been on duty left. They did all the preflight stuff. So all we had to do was deice 629."

"Describe what you did."

"Well, I, uh, was in the hangar. Ron, that's Ron Berensen, was actually deicing."

"That is, he was spraying the wings with deicing fluid. And you saw him doing this, Mr. Johnson?"

Anna wondered why Chris was pursuing this line. She'd told him that she herself had seen the deicing fluid.

"Yes, I saw him," Johnson said.

"You saw him deice both wings?"

"Of course."

"But you were in the hangar."

"Well, I..." Johnson faltered for a moment. "I *saw* him deice the plane, Mr. Galloway."

Chris walked to the table, leafed through some notes and turned back to Johnson. He put his hands in his pockets, thrust his jaw out and studied the mechanic thoughtfully for a few seconds. "At what angle was the plane to the hangar?"

"Sir?"

"How was the plane sitting? Facing the hangar? One side to the hangar?"

"I . . . ah, let's see. It was kind of tail end toward the hangar."

"Tail end?"

"Ah, yes. You know, facing out. Its left side was toward the terminal. Sure. I'm sure it was sitting that way. Yeah. Because when we refueled—"

"That will be all, thank you," Chris said, interrupting him, his brow furrowed deeply.

Johnson rose from his seat and shrugged.

When Ron Berensen was called to the stand, he was anxious, too, but then, Anna supposed, that was normal. *She'd* been nervous when she was questioned.

"Mr. Berensen, we've heard testimony that you deiced flight 629 twenty minutes after the previous crew had departed. Is that correct?" Chris asked.

"Yes. Twenty minutes. Flight 629 was delayed."

"Did Captain Fleisher ask for the deicing?"

"No, sir, he didn't need to. I was already out there."

"And your partner, Mr. Johnson, had to recheck the fuel, so the flight was further delayed?"

"Yes, sir." He paused. "I think Captain Fleisher was mad about the fuel. He wanted it rechecked because of the bad weather."

"He wanted full tanks," Chris clarified.

"Yes, in case he ran into trouble."

"So what was the problem? Couldn't he just read the fuel gauges?"

Berensen's eyes darted around the room. "Well, you see, sir, we had orders . . ." He paused and swallowed.

"Yes, Mr. Berensen?"

"There was a little problem. The plane was overgross."

"That is, it carried too much weight for takeoff? Why?" Chris asked.

Berensen cleared his throat. "Luggage. Skis and stuff. They're heavy."

"You mean the fuel tanks were low to keep the weight down?" Chris asked. A murmur spread among the audience.

"Uh, well, we were supposed to . . . uh, get all the luggage on or the passengers complained, and Mr. Miller . . ."

Miller rose from his seat. His lawyer again restrained him with a hand.

"So," Chris asked, "Captain Fleisher wanted more fuel, but the plane was overgross. What did you do?"

"Uh, they took off some bags. Mr. Logan said to, and Bob filled the tanks."

"And meanwhile you were deicing the wings?"

"Yes."

"Sounds like a busy morning. There was a quarrel going on between the pilot and your crew over excess weight and the weather was deteriorating."

"Yeah, it was snowing."

"And you sprayed the wings."

"Yes."

"Both wings, Mr. Berensen?"

"Well, sure, I . . ."

Chris looked down at some notes in his hand. "I have testimony here that indicates Bob Johnson had only an unobstructed view of the left side of the aircraft. Anna Parish, also, testified that she saw the de-icing fluid on the left wing. What about the right wing, Mr. Berensen?"

"You gotta do both," the man said quietly.

"Yes, you do, or the plane will lose lift on one wing and stall," Chris said. "And when Jim Fleisher yelled the words, 'That's not right,' he could have been referring to the aircraft's unbalanced reaction with one wing deiced and one not, couldn't he, Mr. Berensen?"

"I don't know," the man muttered.

"But you *were* in a very confusing and volatile situation that morning. The flight was late, the weather worsening, and Captain Fleisher was angry. You also knew that Lee Miller harassed everyone when flights were late and luggage was left behind. Captain Fleisher knew this, too."

"Yes."

Chris faced Ron Berensen directly. "In the confusion, Mr. Berensen, could you have neglected to deice the right wing?"

"No," the mechanic said too quickly.

"If you had, should Jim Fleisher have been paying attention? Should he have noticed?"

"Yes, sir, he should. It's his job. The pilot has to see those things. He's supposed to do a walkaround of the plane in bad weather and—" Berensen fell silent, his eyes darting around the room as if for help.

Anna drew in a breath as she felt the blood drain from her face. As clear as the room before her, she could see that left wing, the pink fluid dripping onto the snow-covered tarmac. But surely Jim had checked the right wing, too. He wouldn't have taken for granted...

The close room began to spin slightly, and she fought for control. No. It couldn't have happened that way. No!

Ron Berensen put a hand over his eyes and said something then that the microphone couldn't pick up.

"Please, Mr. Berensen, speak up," Chairman Hatcher said, "and may I remind you that you're sworn to tell the truth here."

Berensen shuddered. Anna could see it from where she sat. She held her breath as the man began to speak.

"I've tried to remember a thousand times what happened," Berensen was mumbling. "Everyday since it happened. It was a mess that morning. Mr. Miller was at home, but he kept phoning and asking if the flights were getting off. Then Captain Fleisher had a fit about the fuel, and it was getting later and later. I...I don't know. I went out there in the snow. I sprayed the left wing. Then I tried to move the hose. Well, the baggage guys came with Harry...Harry Logan... and pulled off some bags, and they were in my way. Then Bob was on the wing fueling up, and I had to help him, and then the tower cleared 629 for takeoff..." He put his face in his hands. "I must have forgotten. I don't know. It was confusing out there. And then Captain Fleisher was rolling away, and it was too late."

Silence buffeted the hearing room.

Chris started to ask a question, paused, then shook his head as if in denial. "Mr. Berensen, *did* you neglect to deice the right wing of that Convair?" he asked.

Berensen looked up, his face tortured. "I don't know," he whispered hoarsely. "I don't know, but I think...oh, God...I think I did forget."

"Thank you, Mr. Berensen," Chris said quietly, but Anna barely heard the rest. She was so stunned that her hands and feet went cold. All she could think was that Jim had fallen victim to the very pressure he'd vowed to expose.

It was unbelievable. And as Anna sat there unmoving, her face drained and pinched, she just couldn't quite fit her mind around the reality of Jim Fleisher's fatal mistake. He'd forgotten to check if *both* wings had been deiced.

In his final summation Chris described the conditions at WestAir exactly as Jim Fleisher had put them down in his notebook. Despite attempts by Miller's lawyer, it was increasingly clear that the owner of WestAir had set up a no-win situation, that even an excellent pilot like Fleisher could fall prey to psychological pressure and forget to check a wing.

For a long time Anna sat in the hearing room digesting that knowledge. It was a bitter pill to swallow. But she knew that Lee Miller had finally been exposed; in that hearing room he'd been charged, tried and found guilty. Whether or not she'd find comfort in this justice, Anna had yet to tell.

THE RAIN HAD STOPPED. The sun glared out of a white sky and waves lapped lazily at the harbor ferry as it lumbered across Puget Sound. A couple leaned together on the railing, heads close, hands clasped.

Anna shook her head. "I can't believe it. I still can't believe it. Not Jim."

"It could happen to anyone who was under constant pressure," Chris said.

She put her hand up to hold back her hair that was blown by the wind. "I guess I remembered him as perfect. I knew there had to be a reason. I just could never admit to myself that it could be Jim's fault."

"It wasn't just his fault. It was Ron Berensen's fault and the baggage handler's fault and Len Whittaker's fault. Mostly it was Lee Miller's fault. He set up the background that made all the failures possible."

She sighed and stared out across the gray water. "Yes, I know. Jim knew it, too, but it's so...so unfair."

"Yes, it is."

He put his arm around her. "Forget it now. It's over."

She held his eyes. "Is it, Chris? Is it all over?"

He shrugged. "The blue book report has to be written for the FAA. But, basically, yes, I'm through. I've done my job."

"Will they send you somewhere else now?" she asked carefully.

It was his turn to stare across the water. "I...uh...I figured I'd take some time off."

She smiled. "Really?"

"I'm overdue."

"I think I told you that a long time ago," she said.

"You were right. And now I can do it."

"Where are you going to take this vacation?" she ventured.

"Well, I thought I'd rent a little house somewhere, you know, in the mountains where Todd can fish and hike, where he can't get into trouble."

"I know just the place."

"Me, too," he said, pulling her closer.

"You know," Anna said, "I've always been one to hate admitting being wrong."

"How's that?"

"Oh, about Todd. I guess I'll just have to say it. You were right about him needing some freedom to grow up. I was wrong."

Chris laughed softly. "If you think I really knew what I was doing, you're wrong again, lady."

"Do you think...? Oh, Chris, do you think things will work out?" she asked, pressing her cheek against his.

"If we love each other enough, they will," he said firmly.

CHRIS AWOKE in his own bedroom alone, and his first thought, as usual, was of Anna. She wouldn't spend the night at his house with Todd there, and although he respected her stand, he ached for her ceaselessly.

It was dawn, the sky just lightening into mother-of-pearl, and already he knew it was going to be hot. He lay there, hands behind his head, and listened to the first birds of morning.

Things had worked out better than he could have imagined. He had Anna and Todd. A family. He and

Anna spent hours talking about the future, where they'd live, what they'd do. They touched and held hands, and Todd sometimes got embarrassed. "Geez, you're so *immature*," he'd say, blushing.

But Anna said it was good for Todd to see adults in love, and Chris said he guessed she was right. He was happy, happier than he deserved, he sometimes thought.

He remembered then why he'd woken up so early. He had things to think about, decisions to make. Yesterday he'd been offered a job with WestAir Express, now to become an employee-owned company. The courts had decided in favor of the employee acquisition corporation after the hearing, and Lee Miller was under indictment for tampering with evidence in a federal case. Yes, indeed, Jim Fleisher had led them to the truth, after all.

So he could resign from the NTSB and take this job with WestAir. He'd be in charge of pilot training. The same job he'd done for the NTSB basically, human factors, but now, instead of trying to figure out what caused an accident after the fact, he might just be able to prevent the accident in the first place. He'd told Anna right away, and he knew she'd been thrilled, but she'd only said, "It's your decision, Chris. I don't want to influence you." How many women would say that?

Oh, he loved her all right, and he felt younger than Todd sometimes, fresh and full of energy and so very grateful that he'd found her.

He could move to Winthrop. Todd wanted to enroll in Winthrop High School; the kid had made friends and seemed to be adjusting. Helen was glad and relieved and . . .

Yes, he could move here. Oh, he'd have to find a better house for the winter, for a permanent home. But there *was* Anna's house, with an empty bedroom, now that Madeline and Flip were married and in their own place. An empty bedroom for Todd and one for Anna and him. Naturally they'd have to be married first.

He'd just about decided to ask her to marry him. The thought was scary—what if he failed a second time? But he loved Anna and she loved him and Todd was happy here. Besides, you had to take a risk to get something worthwhile.

Chris lay there in the tangled sheet, his chest bare, his eyes half-closed, so relaxed that he felt himself sliding back into sleep. He was thinking, *Anna will be over soon, and then I'll tell her that I'm going to take that job. Yes, I'll phone the new director at WestAir today and accept, and then I'll call Washington and hand in my resignation. I still have two weeks of vacation pay coming. And I'll ask Anna...*

He was never sure why he opened his eyes. Later he would ponder the incident a thousand times. But at that moment Chris hadn't been thinking or questioning the occurrence. It had just happened.

He opened his eyes, and a figure was there. An apparition, merely standing there in his room, in front of the window, silhouetted against the growing light of dawn. Inside Chris there was neither fear nor wonder. He simply accepted as he stared at the figure dressed in a uniform and pilot's cap.

Chris stared. Unmoving, fascinated, he lay in his bed in that still and eerie light and stared. The apparition seemed to waver and solidify before slowly, as the light behind it strengthened, it began to fade. Legs, torso, chest. Fading. The face, too, dimmed, diffused by growing light. But the eyes. The calm eyes lingered for an instant longer, and then there was only the empty rectangle of window.

Long minutes later Chris let out a breath, feeling as if he'd run a race, as if his entire world had shifted. Yet everything was unaccountably the same. He was the same. The sun still rose in the east. Anna still loved him and he still loved her. Everything was as usual, except that he knew he'd seen Jim Fleisher. He'd seen a ghost, a phantasm, a nonexistent being, and he knew, too, that Jim had come with a message.

ANNA ARRIVED with fresh Danish pastries at seven-thirty. She walked right in the front door without knocking, calling, "Hello, anybody home?"

Todd was still asleep, but Chris was sitting at the kitchen table, drinking his fourth cup of coffee.

"Hi," she said, leaning over to kiss his cheek. "I got cheese and raspberry. I wasn't sure what Todd liked, but I know you like cheese, so I—"

"Anna, he was here."

She looked at him oddly. "Who was here?"

"Jim, Jim Fleisher."

She paled and sank slowly onto a chair, still clutching the white bakery bag. "Jim?" she breathed.

"I saw him, Anna. It was the damnedest thing." Chris got up and stalked the kitchen, hands in pockets. "It's impossible. I know that. I told you that. I can't explain it, but he was here in my bedroom."

"Oh," she whispered, her eyes huge.

"This morning, early. I was awake, and he was there, just standing there." He ran his hand through his hair. "It's crazy. I don't believe it, but it's true."

"Oh, Chris."

"I don't believe in ghosts, but I saw Jim Fleisher."
He shook his head, disbelieving. Then he stopped in
front of Anna and studied her for a minute. "I know
why he came."

"Why, Chris?"

"Don't ask *how* I know, but I do. It was kind of
farewell. A blessing. This is nuts," he whispered.

"Chris..."

"Wait," he said, interrupting. "Oh, man, this is
crazy, but I was, ah, I was really jealous of Fleisher for
a time and—"

"Chris," she said, then paused. "I was afraid. I always thought he was jealous of you, too."

"You realize how insane this is?"

Anna nodded. "Now I'm not sure, though. I
thought he kept appearing because of you. But now I
know it wasn't that—or maybe it was—but it was
more. I thought...I thought he wanted me to prove he
was innocent, but it wasn't that, either, not entirely.
Oh, God," she said, putting a hand on her forehead,
"what he really wanted was for the truth to come out.
The plain, simple truth. How such a terrible thing
could happen so it won't happen again. He made us
find his notebook. He made us."

"Yes," Chris said quietly.

"He was a good man, Chris. He only wanted the
world to know what happened."

Chris studied her for a long time, then said, "Maybe
he was a better man than I am." He raised a hand to
silence her. "I mean it. Hell, he even appeared to me
to... God, this is nutty, but I guess to tell me it was
okay now."

"He probably wanted to thank you, Chris."

"Maybe. I hope so."

"And," she added, "he was a special man, Chris. Very special. But he's gone now. Really gone. And I'm free. I'm free to love you with everything in me."

"Anna," Chris blurted out, "will you...will you marry me?" He looked at her in earnest. "Can you stand two helpless men in your life?"

She laughed lightly. "It's all I want in the world, Chris. You and Todd."

Chris couldn't say a thing. He merely leaned over and found her mouth with his, but not before he saw Todd standing in the bedroom door, yawning, hair mussed, a pair of shorts hanging around his narrow waist. The kid grinned, gave his dad a thumbs-up and then cleared his throat.

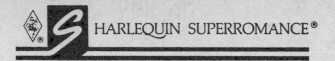

COMING NEXT MONTH

#522 JUST BETWEEN US • Debbi Bedford
When Monica Albright volunteered to be a Big Sister to troubled teen Ann Small, she never expected to fall in love with the child's father. But now that the inevitable had happened, she and Richard were running the risk of alienating Ann forever.

#523 MAKE-BELIEVE • Emma Merritt
Marcy Galvan's roots were in San Antonio. She had her business, her family and her Little Sister, Amy Calderon. Brant Holland's life was in New York—his business needed him there. Though love had brought them together, would their obligations keep them apart?

#524 STRING OF MIRACLES • Sally Garrett
A lot of slick young legal eagles had made a play for lawyer Nancy Prentice, but she was saving herself for a *real* man: Mark Bradford. The only problem was that Mark had always treated her like a sister. Well, no more. Now *she* was going to take the initiative . . . !

#525 RENEGADE • Peg Sutherland
Former country-and-western star Dell McColl lived up to his reputation as a renegade. He never backed down from anything or anyone. Then he met never-say-die Daylene Honeycutt. Daylene wanted two things from Dell. She wanted *him,* and she wanted to sing in his bar. Dell refused to give in on either count. Never again would he be responsible for a woman's destruction on the road to stardom.

WELCOME TO

The quintessential small town, where everyone knows everybody else!

Each book set in Tyler is a self-contained love story; together, the twelve novels stitch the fabric of the community.

"Scintillating romance!"
"Immensely appealing characters...wonderful intensity and humor."
Romantic Times

Join your friends in Tyler for the ninth book, MILKY WAY by Muriel Jensen, available in November.

Can Jake help solve Britt's family financial problems and win her love? Was Margaret's death really murder?

GREAT READING...GREAT SAVINGS...AND A FABULOUS FREE GIFT!

With Tyler you can receive a fabulous gift, ABSOLUTELY FREE, by collecting proofs-of-purchase found in each Tyler book. And use our special Tyler coupons to save on your next TYLER book purchase.

Take 4 bestselling love stories FREE

Plus get a FREE surprise gift!

• HARLEQUIN •
HISTORICAL
CHRISTMAS
• STORIES • 1992 •

Capture the magic and romance of Christmas in the 1800s
with HARLEQUIN HISTORICAL CHRISTMAS STORIES
1992—a collection of three stories by celebrated
historical authors. The perfect Christmas gift!

Don't miss these heartwarming stories, available in
November wherever Harlequin books are sold:

MISS MONTRACHET REQUESTS by Maura Seger
CHRISTMAS BOUNTY by Erin Yorke
A PROMISE KEPT by Bronwyn Williams

Plus, this Christmas you can also receive a FREE
keepsake Christmas ornament. Watch for details in all
November and December Harlequin books.

**DISCOVER THE ROMANCE AND MAGIC OF THE
HOLIDAY SEASON WITH HARLEQUIN HISTORICAL
CHRISTMAS STORIES!**

HARLEQUIN SUPERROMANCE®

Follow six special Superromance heroines as they discover the heartwarming joy of being a Big Sister.

Available in September—#514 NOTHING BUT TROUBLE by Sandra James
—#515 ONE TO ONE by Marisa Carroll
Available in October —#518 OUT ON A LIMB by Sally Bradford
—#519 STAR SONG by Sandra Canfield
Available in November —#522 JUST BETWEEN US by Debbi Bedford
—#523 MAKE-BELIEVE by Emma Merritt

And just for reading Harlequin Superromance books, you can receive a beautiful Victorian pewter picture frame free!

Remember, Harlequin will donate 5¢ to Big Brothers/Big Sisters every time you buy a September, October or November Harlequin Superromance.*

*Up to a maximum of $40,000

Send your name, address, zip or postal code, along with six proof-of-purchase coupons from any Harlequin Superromance novel published in September, October or November, plus $2.75 for postage and handling (check or money order—do not send cash) payable to Harlequin Books, to: **In the U.S.:** P.O. Box 9057, Buffalo, NY 14269-9057; **In Canada:** P.O. Box 622, Fort Erie, Ontario L2A 5X3.

(Please allow 4-6 weeks for delivery. Quantities are limited. Offer expires December 31, 1992.)

**Harlequin
Superromance
one proof
of purchase**

Name: _____

_____

Address: _____

_____

City: _____

State/Province: _____

Zip/Postal Code: _____

094 KAE